THE
PRINTER'S
DEVIL

A REMARKABLE STORY WRITTEN BY
PAUL BAJORIA

with ILLUSTRATIONS BY the honest
BRET BERTHOLF

LITTLE, BROWN AND COMPANY

New York → Boston

Little, Brown and Company

Hachette Book Group USA
1271 Avenue of the Americas, New York, NY 10020
Visit our Web site at www.lb-teens.com

First U.S. Paperback Edition: January 2007
First published in Great Britain by Simon and Schuster in 2004

The characters and events portrayed in this book are fictitious. Any similarity to real persons, living or dead, is coincidental and not intended by the author.

Bajoria, Paul.
    The printer's devil / by Paul Bajoria.— 1st U.S. ed.
        p. cm.
    Published in the United Kingdom in 2004 by Simon & Schuster.
    Summary: After printing the "Wanted" posters for some of London's most notorious inhabitants, a printer's boy is entangled, by a genuine convict, in a series of mistaken identities and events leading back to the boy's own mysterious past.
    (HC) ISBN 0-316-01090-1
    (PB) ISBN-10: 0-316-10678-X / (PB) ISBN-13: 978-0-316-10678-8
    [1. Printers—Fiction. 2. Robbers and outlaws—Fiction. 3. Orphans—Fiction.
4. Sex role—Fiction. 5. Dogs—Fiction. 6. London (England)—History—18th century—Fiction. 7. Great Britain—History—1789-1820—Fiction.] I. Title.
PZ7.B1683Pri 2005
[Fic]—dc22

                              2005043592

HC:10 9 8 7 6 5 4 3 2 1
PB:10 9 8 7 6 5 4 3 2 1

Q-MT
Endpaper photograph copyright © Picture Collection, The Branch Libraries, The New York Public Library, Astor, Lenox and Tilden Foundations

Printed in the United States of America

*To Mum and Dad
with infinite love and thanks*

TABLE OF CONTENTS

1

THE CONVICT

He was the ugliest, most evil-looking man I'd ever seen.

He glared up at me from the poster, his outline glistening as the ink dried, making him seem more alive and threatening. I held him out at arm's length to stop him from creasing.

COCKBURN

I scanned his name, mouthing it as I assessed the big black letters. Were they straight enough? The top part of the "R" hadn't quite come out properly. Nevertheless, the effect was striking; and, although I felt slightly afraid of the vile-eyed villain, who seemed to strain to clamber out of the picture and throttle me, I was quite proud of my handiwork. After all, I told myself, if the poster scared people they'd be all the more likely to try to help catch him.

The exclamation point, I noticed, was a bit lopsided. I'd have to go back and straighten the type before I did any more.

Being a printer's boy was hard work. I had to run

COCKBURN

ESCAPED

from our **NEW PRISON** at **CLERKENWELL**, the **14th** day of **MAY**.

The Public is ADVISED that this Man IS VERY

DANGEROUS!

errands, and do all the boring and dirty jobs, and Mr. Cramplock only paid me a couple of shillings a week, which wasn't much. But the good part of it was that our shop was the first place people came when they had any information to pass on, so Cramplock and I found out about it before anybody else. We were always making posters and handbills and books and newspapers, informing people of what was going on in the world. If there was any meeting called, or play to be performed, or auction to be held, or curious object to be displayed, or items stolen, or convicts escaped, or persons to be hanged, or corpses found drowned, or loved ones gone missing, chances were we'd know about it. It used to make me feel quietly important, walking through the streets of London and repeatedly seeing the huge inky letters of my own posters plastered across brick walls and wooden fences. They made people happy, and curious, and afraid; they made people talk. It felt as though things *happened* because of what I did.

The printer's devil, they used to call me. I had short black hair and a dirty face, usually, because of all the ink that got splashed around everywhere in the workshop; underneath the ink my skin was brown from the summer sun. I was rake-thin, in those days, and I usually worked in long breeches which didn't fit very well round my waist so I had to keep hitching them up, especially when I was running. "Here comes the printer's devil," people would say. At first I used to think it wasn't a very nice thing to call someone, but no one seemed to mean any malice by it, and I soon got used to it.

"Secure that exclamation-mark, Mog," Cramplock said, appearing at my side and surveying the poster.

"Don't he look mean, Mr. Cramplock?" I said, rather admiringly, as I held up the big poster again.

"Murderous, Mog, mmm. Mur — derous!" He repeated the word with some relish, peering over his spectacles approvingly.

"What did he do, Mr. Cramplock? *Did* he murder someone?" I asked eagerly. I was hoping fervently that he had, until it occurred to me I probably shouldn't be hoping such things.

"I don't know, Mog. Best not to take a chance, though, eh?"

"IS VERY DANGEROUS!" I read again, before laying the poster aside. As I placed it on the table, the paper bent slightly in the middle, so the convict seemed to be leaning forward deliberately to menace me with his broad, clenched face. His eyes, although quite small, like unwelcome little black blemishes on the paper, were by far the most prominent feature of his face; and they held me with a vicious stare. I'd never forget *this* face, I told myself, nor that name etched in heavy letters by chunks of black iron pushed into the coarse white paper.

"Cock," I said slowly, "Burn." And the eyes of the escaped convict flashed, as if in recognition of his name; as if there were indeed something burning behind them, a kind of sinister flame.

Almost expecting to see him creeping up on us from behind, I looked around the shop nervously. "You don't suppose he's hiding near here, do you, Mr. Cramplock?"

Cramplock laughed shortly. "If he's got any sense, he'll have fled a lot farther off than this."

He turned away, tugging at the grubby collar of his shirt to let some cool air inside. It was the hottest week of the year so far: in fact, we were having the hottest weather I could remember in my entire life, and working the presses was hard and sticky work, so that our shirts were damp and both our faces glistened with sweat as we worked. Cramplock rubbed his cheekbone just beneath the rim of his glasses with an inky finger, a habit he'd had for as long as I'd known him. He always had a smear of printer's ink on his cheek, like a bruise; and today when he rubbed his face, his finger came away wet.

"Phew . . . it's hot work again today," he said, breathing heavily. "Only May, and look at it. If it keeps this up, we're in for quite a summer. Even though we've got Winter inside. Eh?"

It was a joke. He used to make it quite frequently,

in one form or another. My name, you see, is Winter. Mog Winter. People sometimes said it was a peculiar name to have, but it's always suited me fine. Sometimes in the print shop when there was nothing else to do, I used to make up a form with just my name in, and print my name on old scraps of paper. Sometimes I used three big capitals, **M O G**, sometimes a capital and two lower-case ones, **Mog**, and sometimes I'd bring out the fancy type which made the letters look as though they were written with a quill-pen rather than printed. *Mog*. I used to stare at my name on the paper for ages. After a while, it didn't seem like my name at all: it was as though I'd never seen it before, the letters just meaningless marks which didn't spell anything. I had quite a collection of these various Mogs by now: Cramplock probably wouldn't have been very pleased if he'd found out I was using up paper like this, but I somehow couldn't bring myself to throw them away.

I wasn't going to have time for such idle pursuits tonight because I knew that before I went to bed I had to make a hundred copies of the Cockburn poster. I was about to ink up again when Cramplock came over.

"Before you do that, Mog, how about fetching us something to eat from the Doll's Head?"

I nodded, relieved, because my stomach was beginning to rumble like an old cart. It was nearly six o'clock and the shop was closed to customers, but he'd wanted to keep going until we'd finished these posters and something else he was preparing for a man in the theatre.

The theatre bills were his favorite job: he used to lavish hours of painstaking attention on their different-shaped letters and colored inks, making them seem as cramped and exciting as the theatre itself. "From Brighton, the Celebrated Mr. Symington! Flying Through the Air, Without Visible Means of Support, the Sunderclouds! And Presenting for the First Time in London, the Remarkable Mrs. Victor Reed (who Executes a Genuine Faint in the Role of Lady MacBeth!)"

I left him working the noisy press and darted towards the door before he had time to change his mind. The thought of meat and ale was making my mouth water already. I seemed to be hungry absolutely all the time at the moment. It might have been because I used to share whatever I had to eat with my dog, Lash, and most days he used to get the better of the meal. Lash was the most adorable living creature I ever met, even counting human beings. He was all sorts of dog and no sort of dog, probably five or six breeds rolled into one, with quite a lot of spaniel in him and a bit of lurcher. He was called Lash because he had great big eyelashes — and when he looked at me from underneath them, I could willingly give him every last morsel of food I possessed, however hungry I was.

As I was about to leave the shop I gave a short whistle; footsteps clattered down the wooden stairs, and there was Lash by my side, licking my inky fingers and tickling my wrists with his whiskers, and wagging his tail so hard against the panels of the wall when I said the word "Dinner" that it sounded like someone beating out a rhythm on a barrel. Lash and I went everywhere together. We were well known in Clerkenwell and, I suppose, pretty well known everywhere else. So we emerged into the evening air together, in such a hurry that I forgot my cap.

The empty windows of the house next door stared down at me as we went by. It had once been a grand town house, but it had been deserted now for many years, after being burnt out in a terrible fire. Inside, the fire damage was still there to be seen: blackened walls, the floor covered in ash and chunks of charred wood, the window-frames burnt to a crisp, the glass in the windows opaque with smuts. The humble, grey little building which was now Cramplock's shop, built right up against it, must once have seemed like an insulting excrescence bubbling out of its towering northern wall; but the printing shop had remained in use all this time, while its haughty neighbor had been left to rot. With some other children, I'd broken in once: but we hadn't stayed for long: there were too many rats, and every step caused a creak or a groan which made it seem as though the whole house was about to collapse on top of us. No one could explain why it hadn't been knocked down years ago; and its charred black facade, like a sightless face, often made me shudder as I stepped over the garbage in the lane.

I should explain that, by that summer when I was twelve, when all the things happened that I'm going to tell you about, I was very well used to looking after myself. I never had a mother and father looking after me, and I don't really know much about what happened to them, except that my Ma died in a big ship on a voyage from India, from the effort of giving birth to me, and I had to live in an orphanage for the first few years of my life. I don't know much more. Since I ran away from the orphanage I'd worked for Cramplock, and in return for a chunk of the wages he paid me he let me sleep in an upstairs room in the printing shop. It wasn't very big or very comfortable, but it had most of what I needed — a bed for me and a basket for Lash, a table and a jug of water for washing, and a little cupboard for my things — and it was the closest thing to a home I'd ever had.

If it weren't for Cramplock I don't really know what I'd have done. Become a thief, maybe, like lots of the other kids who grew up around here. A couple of streets away lay the massive prison with its high wall, behind which someone else would disappear every so often when they'd been caught stealing or doing something wicked. People would gather to watch the big iron gates swing open, admit the cart, then close. No one ever seemed to come out. They said the only way out of the jail was to be carried out in a box. They died in there. I used to be able to see the men burying them in the fields outside.

But, just occasionally, one of them found a quicker way out.

I nipped through the alleyways, with Lash getting in the way at my ankles. The late spring sky was a deep heat-soaked blue above us, but in some places it seemed like nighttime, because the houses on either side of the lanes leaned inwards at the top until they almost touched, so the sunlight could hardly get through. To get to the Doll's Head we had to go past Cow Cross, where there was always a lot of dirt lying around from the cattle which were driven through there twice a day. If the presses weren't making a noise, Cramplock and I could often hear their mooing protests in the morning and afternoon as they clomped through the streets getting in the way of the traffic. It was always smelly at Cow Cross, and if it was raining you could hardly move for the dirt, trodden into a paste a foot thick by the cows' hooves. Still, I preferred that to the smell of the Fleet, which ran between the backs of the nearby houses. People said it used to be a river, once upon a time, when you could see the green fields from the back windows of the houses there. But you wouldn't call the Fleet a river now: it was more a sort of sticky black ditch which little kids used to get scolded for going near, on account of the dirt and all the rats. Especially during the summer, when you had to breathe through your mouth if you were anywhere near it, so as not to catch the smell. The cows didn't smell half as bad as that — and since it was mainly people's filth which made the Fleet stink, the only conclusion I could come to was that people smell a good deal worse than cattle.

And here was the Doll's Head, with its big wooden pole propping up the top of the house to stop it from toppling into the street. You had to duck under the pole to get in through a little door, whereupon you found yourself in a tiny taproom, all higgledy-piggledy, as though it had been built by a man whose eyes looked in two different directions.

There was nobody in the room this evening — except Tassie, the landlady, of course. Lash gave a good-natured whimper of recognition when he spotted her plump face behind the bar.

"Tassie," I said, "Cramplock's hungry, and so's Lash, and so am I."

"Tell me when you's never *not* hungry, Maaster Mog," Tassie said, reaching over the bar to wipe a smudge of ink off my face with her fat thumb. The Doll's Head had been built a very long time ago — in Queen Elizabeth's time, someone said — and I suppose I assumed that Tassie had been there ever since then. She was usually cheerful, except on very wet days when the rainwater used to leak down through the timbers of the house and drip onto the back of her neck from a crack just above where she stood. She always called me "Maaster Mog," and when she was cross with me she elongated it even more, so it came out as "Maaaaaster Mooooooog." I used to slink about and keep out of her way on those days. But usually she made me into quite an attraction if there was anyone else in the room: she'd tell them, "Well just look who it is, it's Maaster Mog," and she might come over and blow the dust out of my hair and rub my face just like she did today, and she'd say, "He's one of my regulars, ain't you, Maaster Mog?" and she'd laugh heartily at it as though she'd just told a good joke or sung a particularly fine song.

"What can you spare us to eat, Tassie?" I asked her, "along with your middling ale?"

She put her tongue in her cheek, which made it a good deal plumper than it already was. "Well now," she said, "provided you can show me the right connidge" — she meant money — "what if I was to tell you there's a big pink ham under my larder table?"

Lash reacted before I did, with a gruff *woof* of approval.

"I'd say," I said, "that ham would do nice. And bread would do nice, too."

"What if I was to tell you," she said, "there's floury bread an' all? And what if I was to tell you there's ham and bread both, Maaster Mog?"

My eyes shone at her over the bar and she roared with laughter. "Don't that make your eyes shine, Maaster Mog?" she said; and, as if she were talking to someone else, "just look at the lad's big handsome eyes, me making his face light up like an angel's face, I declare. You've got such eyes as a woman would die for, Maaster Mog, that you has. 'Taint fair that a young man should have such eyes, when there's ladies young and old would die for eyes that big and lovely." I was quite used to hearing this, because she said it virtually every time I went to see her and, although I always made faces pretending I was bored of her compliments, I actually liked it. This piece of flattery about my eyes was nearly always followed up by another comment which she obviously thought rather clever; and, sure enough, she trotted it out again today. "Printer's devil, they calls you," she said, "but sometimes I have a hard time deciding if you're devil or angel, Maaster Mog. Devil or angel!" And she went off into the back room, chuckling, to get the food.

I sat down to wait, and Lash spread himself out under a table. I watched Tassie moving briskly about behind the two great big polished pump handles where she pulled the beer. She always kept a cloth by them so that, whenever they got too grubby from all that pulling, she could wipe them down and they'd be as shiny as ever. "The shiniest taaps in Clerkenwell," she always claimed, "and if you can show me shinier in all London, well I'd like to see 'em. See your face in 'em, you can, and it'll never be otherwise, not while I'm on this good earth." You certainly *could* see your face in them, but they were such a funny shape that when you looked in them your face appeared extraordinarily long and bendy, as if someone had taken you by the topmost hairs on your head and yanked until you were stretched out like a piece of dough.

"I've been making a poster," I told Tassie as she cut me some rich pink ham off a waxy joint, "about a Cockburn."

"Lovely," she said, "only what if I was to tell you, Maaster Mog, I ain't sure as I know what a Cockburn might be."

"Cockburn's a —" I lowered my voice in case the empty room might be harboring unwanted ears. "Cockburn's the name of a convict!" I hissed, feeling pleased with myself. "Fellow's escaped from the New Prison and he's on the loose. Horrible ugly man! Eyes like — like a rat," I said, watching a pink little nose push its way into the taproom through a hole near a chair-leg, take one look at Lash, and promptly whisk itself back into the dark again.

"I'll know 'im," said Tassie, "everyone says Tassie's the best judge of character in Clerkenwell. If he comes into this 'stablishment he'll soon know he's made a mistake." The flour from the bread she was wrapping up made her sneeze, and a cloud of flour-dust flew up and settled gradually on her polished taps, causing her to swear under her breath and reach for the cloth to wipe them. "What's he done anyway, to get himself in jail to start with?"

"I don't know," I said, "but he's Very Dangerous. It says so on the poster. It's got a picture of his face on, all ugly and mean. Mr. Cramplock reckons he's murderous."

"Well, I hope he don't murder us," Tassie said through a mouthful of ham, "or who'll keep the Doll's Head noddin' and the print shop printin'? It's more work the pair of us do, Maaster Mog, than any other body in this city, and if we was to go there'd be a fair ewe and cry." She popped another wedge of ham into her mouth.

"Here, don't eat our ham," I told her.

"'Taint your ham yet, it's mine, till you've paid for it," she countered, "and I'll do what I likes with me own ham, Maaster Mog. I ain't no thief, Maaster Mog, and you'll never catch me in the New Prison, not this year nor any other. More likely to be in there yourself afore you've growed up, barrel of mischief that you are." I didn't feel it was quite fair of her to call me a barrel. Most of the time she was going on about how I was all skin and bone, and how no one could see me when I turned sideways. "Here," she said, "seen as you're a growin' lad, you drink this here and then take some back with you for old Clamprock."

"Cramplock," I corrected her, taking the glass she passed me.

"Oh, full of argument you are tonight," she said. "Too big for your little boots, some might say, Maaster Mog. Oh, he's terrible clever, that printer's lad. Well he'd better pipe down because there's plenty cleverer than he is, and if he don't watch out —"

I stopped listening to her and lowered my head to the glass, full to the brim with cool frothy ale the color of strong tea. I took a long sip, then licked my lips and opened my eyes wide as the sour aftertaste welled forward over my tongue. I'd sometimes heard men making unkind remarks about Tassie's ale behind her back, but it always seemed all right to me; and anyone who ever tried to taste the water that came out of the pump in the square, straight from the murky depths of the Fleet, would soon agree that even the poorest ale was a better bet.

Tassie was wiping her taps vigorously, and still mumbling on, as I put my empty glass back up on the counter.

"Thank you, Tassie," I said, and I must have looked suitably humble because she stopped moaning and produced a big parcel she'd made up. "Do you good, that will," she said. "And I've put some bone in there, wrapped up separate, just for Lash. Now, that's fourpence ha'penny, and don't go getting murdered on your way back to Clamprock." I said I wouldn't, and picked up the tempting brown parcel full of fat slices of bread, good ham, and thick brown bottles of ale. I heard the chink of coins as she tipped my money into a sack under the bar. And Lash and I were out of the door.

The houses veered into my path and fell back again, as I rounded the wobbly little corners on the way back to the shop. Someone gave a low laugh as I passed by a window, and I took hold of Lash's collar nervously. The beer I'd drunk so quickly had made me feel a bit unsteady, and the lane looked narrower than usual. Flies buzzed up suddenly from a lump a dog had left on the cobbles, and I had to pull Lash hard to stop him going over to investigate it.

I was taking Tassie's advice seriously. Carrying a parcel of food through streets like these could have made me a target for any hungry villain who might be lurking on my route, and there were some who'd think nothing of murdering a child of twelve in return for a decent meal. It was reassuring to have Lash with me but, deep down, I knew there were desperate characters around who wouldn't have found Lash much of an obstacle to getting what they wanted. I ran the rest of the way to the shop and, with Lash scampering alongside, I could treat it like a game; but I was thankful when we reached the little door crouching in the shadow of the big old priory gate.

Cramplock was still there, busily working the squeaky press on which he was doing the theatre bills. He looked up as he heard me opening the door. "Ah, Mog," he said, letting go of the lever and coming towards me rubbing his cheek, "bringer of good things!" I handed him the parcel, which he placed on the table on top of my Cockburn poster. "Ham!" he said, unwrapping the brown paper, "and lots of bread!" He chuckled to himself, wedging some of the ham between two slices of bread. Lash's muzzle snuffled expectantly up over the edge of the table and Cramplock indulgently slipped him a small slice of ham. "Did you spot any murderers on your journey, eh?" He cackled, thinking he'd made a splendid joke. I didn't laugh.

"Mmm," he said, chewing the bread and ham vigorously, "this handbill's almost finished. But then . . ."

he swallowed, "I have to go and see someone." He swallowed some beer from the neck of his bottle, and blinked and coughed several times. "I'd like you to run a quick errand for me," he said, and took another large bite of bread and ham. "I've got a bill for Mister Flethick at Corporation Row," he mumbled; only it was so muffled by his mouthful of food it came out as "Mff ffrff bngg, mff-tff Flfff-Corff-ffrmmmm."

"What?" I said.

He swallowed, and coughed. Damp pieces of bread sailed out of his mouth and landed on a freshly-inked roller. He closed his eyes, swallowed again, and then opened them in relief as though he'd been afraid he might not survive the effort of swallowing. "Mr. Flethick," he said again, "at Corporation Row. But before you go —" he pointed at me with a greasy middle finger "— you can finish those." And, although he was gesturing down at the ham on the table, I knew he meant the poster which lay beneath it.

A hundred posters I had to make. After we'd finished eating, I sent Lash back to his basket and set to work. A hundred Cockburns. Every time I pulled a fresh poster out of the press I was shocked by the convict's face and the stark black legend of his name. The face seemed to get uglier and more muscly every time. The duplicate Cockburns mounted on top of one another on the table.

The Public is ADVISED that this Man IS VERY

DANGEROUS!

The exclamation marks got bigger and blacker. I wiped my brow. The mechanical grind and squeak of my press, and the rustling of the paper I was slipping in and out, were making my head ache. My arm ached too, from pulling the heavy platen down so many times. The air was heavy with ink, and my head was light with beer. I glanced at the window and saw it had grown almost dark outside.

Mr. Cramplock emerged from the back room where'd he'd been busy with something else. I saw he was reaching for his hat. Some of the printers we knew around here lived in the rooms above their shops, but Cramplock's was so small there wasn't room for anyone to live here comfortably, apart from me and Lash in our simple little room above the presses. So Cramplock rented lodgings a few minutes' walk away. I think he used to have arguments with the landlord quite often, because at around the same time each month he used to get terribly grumpy and babble on about how much profit we had or hadn't taken.

"I'm off, Mog," he said, peering over at the posters

I was piling up. "Looks like you're doing a good job. Just leave them on the bench and I'll sort them out in the morning."

"Yes," I said.

"Make sure you ink up again before long," he said, peering some more at my handiwork as he opened the door. "In fact — do it now."

"Yes," I said.

"Don't forget Flethick's bill."

"No," I said, between gritted teeth.

"And don't go out without locking the doors properly."

"Are you going, or not?," I asked him. He opened his mouth, plainly intending to tell me not to be so impertinent; but he was probably so bored of telling me not to be impertinent that on this occasion he decided it wasn't worth the effort. The door rattled shut behind him.

I carried on, nearing the hundred. The Cockburns grew higher and higher on their pile, and I was glad to cover up the awful face with a new sheet of paper — except that each new sheet also featured his awful face. Repeat after repeat!

DANGEROUS!

I was so impatient for the job to be over, so sick of seeing endless Cockburns, that I was no longer taking care to keep the paper straight. Some of the Cockburns were coming out crooked, though I was so tired I could barely tell the difference any more. On some of the sheets the word "DANGEROUS!" was slipping off the edge of the paper as I shoved them in in my haste. The posters were nearly as big as I was, and in carrying the big heavy sheets of paper over to the bench I was getting my clothes and my face covered in the fresh ink. Cockburns spun around my head, their eyes boring into my brain like woodworm eating through the cover of a book to begin devouring its contents. I started laying the newly printed posters face down so I wouldn't have to look at them.

But I'd lost count, and I had to go back to the pile and count how many I'd done, which irritated me. Cramplock would never have made that mistake; he'd always have stacked them in a rack in piles of ten so he could see at a glance how many more were still needed. Instead I had to flip through all the Cockburns, counting how many times that hideous face glared up at me.

A hundred and six. I'd done too many; but at least it meant some of the most crooked ones could be thrown out. I was so relieved as I began to dismantle the type that I completely forgot about the errand I'd been asked to run until, when I was washing my hands,

I noticed the little envelope sitting by the door, marked "Mr. Flethick" in Cramplock's appalling handwriting. It was a good job Cramplock was a printer, otherwise no one would be able to read a word he wrote. Maybe that was why he'd become one in the first place.

There was a tiny drop of ale left in the bottom of one of the bottles, and I drained it thankfully before picking up the bill, whistling for Lash, and venturing out into the darkness.

For some reason I couldn't resist another glance up at the blackened windows of the big house next door; with my head full of the eyes of convicts, there was something particularly chilling about them tonight. I clutched Lash's lead and rushed on. The streets were poorly lit, and I wasn't looking forward to walking past the prison gate, which was very close to where Flethick lived. I kept hearing low whistles in the darkness, and the sound of running feet echoing in the alleyways, and I shivered, thankful that I looked like a boy in baggy clothes and not a rich gentleman in a top hat with a watch on a chain and money to be knifed out of him.

Flethick lived in a dark court, accessible only through a narrow brick archway which looked from the street like a doorway into oblivion. Tugging at Lash's lead, I tried to drag him through, but he wouldn't come. He sat whimpering quietly, looking first at the dark archway and then up at me, refusing to budge. I had no choice: I couldn't neglect Mr. Cramplock's errand. So I tied him to a lamp-post and, taking a deep breath, I squared up to the forbidding darkness of the archway and plunged through.

I was surrounded by darkness on all sides. Somewhere close by, a baby cried, and a long way off a church clock struck the half-hour. I was suddenly gripped by panic, by the sensation of being hemmed in by walls. I was on the point of abandoning my mission completely, turning instead to flee back out through the archway; but, as my eyes grew accustomed to the murk of the courtyard, I noticed that in the far corner there was a second-story window which was glowing dully, like the moon sometimes does when it's covered by a fine cloud. It was the only sign of light and life in any of the buildings which surrounded me; and, mustering up my courage, I headed for the little doorway.

It was far too dark to read any name on the doorpost; but I pushed the door and it swung open with a dry scrape, to reveal a dim staircase rising immediately in front of me. I thought I could hear low voices from above; and as I got to the top of the stairs I could see the orangey outline of a door with a light shining behind it. Now that I stood at the stairhead, I heard the voices more clearly: deep and sporadic, a broken series of mumbles rather than a conversation.

I had approached the door, and lifted my hand to knock, when suddenly my nostrils caught an extraordinary smell. For a moment it quite disoriented me. I looked up at the ceiling, down at the stairs, and felt dizzy, as though I were in danger of falling back down the way I had come. I clutched at the banister, or at least where I thought the banister would be. It wasn't there, and I fell forward against the door, pushing it open and entering the room more suddenly and rudely than I'd intended.

I tried not to sprawl on the carpet for any longer than necessary, seeing as I'd dimly noticed several men in the room who might want an explanation for my bursting in on them. But as I got to my feet I realized I'd caused only a minor stir.

I blinked through an orange mist at a room so smoky and ill-lit I could barely see the other side. There were six men. Four of them were half-sitting, half-lying in large chairs, making almost no movement and seeming to see nothing, as though they were stuffed. The other two men were seated on the floor close to where I now stood, and were looking up at me in incomprehension.

"I've, ah — a bill for Mr. Flethick," I said, trying to sound as businesslike as possible. I coughed. The air was revolting in here.

"Er — Mr. Flethick?" I said again. There was a silence.

Then, "I'm Mr. Flethick," one of the men on the floor said, speaking curiously slowly as though his words had to fight through the murky air to reach me.

I held out the bill, and as I did so I noticed the long pipe in his hand. He didn't make any attempt to take the envelope from me. Perhaps he was crippled.

"Don't get up," I said, and crouched down beside him.

His eyes were glassy and unseeing. Was he blind?

"Who's this?" one of the other men in the room murmured — I couldn't be sure which.

"Cramplock's boy, sir," I said nervously. Mr. Flethick twisted his body around on the floor to look at me better.

"Cramplock's boy?" he queried. An expression of amusement crossed his face slowly. "The printer's devil, eh? Come to drag us down to Hell, I'll wager." His hand waved at me, uncoordinated, trying to make contact with my arm. "Siddown, Cramplock's boy," he continued in his slurred voice. "Wha'they call you, mmm?"

"Winter, sir. Mog Winter."

"Well, Mog Winter," he said, and as he turned to me I caught his breath full in my face, "you tell Cramplock . . ." He seemed to struggle for the words. He paused for a long time, and put the long pipe to his lips. The candles around the room sent the men's huge shadows shaking up to the ceiling. As I waited for him to speak, I felt dizzy again.

"You tell Cramplock," Flethick slurred at length, "I don't want his bill. Will you tell him that?"

"But Mr. Cramplock asked me to give you the bill, sir," I said.

"So he did, boy, so he did." Flethick nodded.

"If I know him aright, sir," I continued, "I don't believe he'll be best pleased if I come back with the bill undelivered."

"Well now," said Flethick, "since you put it that way. Cramplock not best pleased. That would never do." The smile that still played over his face was no longer a smile of amusement but had taken on a sinister aspect. I suddenly felt frightened of him. "Give me the bill then," he said. And, with a deliberate motion of his entire upper body, he took the unopened bill out of my outstretched hand and swung it directly into the nearest candle flame, where it took light and was eaten by fire in seconds. The thin black flakes of what had been the bill fell around the candle, as slowly as the plume of smoke rose into the air.

Everything about this room was slow. My brain felt as if it, too, was gripped in a sinking stillness, like a fly struggling in a beaker of molasses. My eyes were watering and, every time I blinked, the men seemed further away, the four in the chairs having receded so far they were almost out of sight over the horizon.

I heard an echo and realized I'd been asked a question.

"What?" I said.

"Is there anyone outside?" Flethick was asking.

"I didn't see no one," I said, rubbing my eyes.

"He won't come here tonight," another of the men said in a low voice. "It'll be the three friends for him."

"Not good enough, aren't we?" another growled from the horizon.

"He'll bide his time. The three friends ain't suspicious."

"So long as nothing's amiss." The man on the far side of the room seemed very concerned that nothing should be amiss. Flethick was sucking on his pipe and watching me, intently — rather too intently, with eyes which seemed to gaze way beyond my physical being and into some other realm. Looking at my ghost, I thought, with a sudden awful shiver.

"The Sun of Calcutta," one of the men was chanting softly. "The Sun of Calcutta! What riches!" He began to laugh, but not because of anything funny. Nobody laughed with him, and he made no noise. His body shook, as if it was in pain.

"Shut up," said Flethick, distinctly and menacingly. He turned to me. His image swam before my eyes. Without moving his lips he said, "You can get out of here, Cramplock's boy, and if you can pick up the ashes of your bill you'd better take 'em with you." Despite the slurring of his words I could detect the violence behind them. "You ain't seen this room, and you ain't met these gentlemen. You've been dreaming. You understand?"

I felt myself nodding. I half believed him. I wouldn't have been surprised to see him melt away and find myself lying in bed.

"Cos if you remember too much," Flethick continued, "there's men in London can help you forget."

"Ask the bosun nicely," giggled the laughing man, "and he'll cut your gizzard!"

"Shut up," said Flethick again, "you've said too much already." He looked back at me as though I were his worst enemy. He had told me to get out, and I was still standing there. "Off!" he hissed. "And FORGET!"

I stumbled down the stairs, almost falling into the night air, my head thick with the acrid smoke of the little room, my ears buzzing with Flethick's parting threat. The details of the interview were starting to come to me, as if for the first time. I hadn't been able to think properly in there: now my lungs filled with colder, cleaner air, and I began to take in what I'd seen. In spite of the men's lethargic manner, there'd been violence in their words, and I realized I was still trembling with fear of them. Surely they were up to no good? "Such riches!" the indiscreet one had laughed, "the Sun of Calcutta!"

I emerged from the brick archway and blinked at the high, black, damp prison wall in front of me. Still tethered to the lamppost, and scrabbling at the cobbles, Lash was straining to greet me, and when I untied him he practically knocked me over in his evident relief that I'd made it back.

"Am I pleased to see you," I murmured; and I crouched there for a few moments, letting him lick my face, and tugging affectionately at the little beard under his chin.

A bell somewhere was striking the hour. Eight . . . nine . . . ten . . . eleven. I suddenly felt immensely tired. Glancing up and down the narrow street I saw it was deserted, the only light in sight glowing faintly from the next corner, quite a long way off. The laughing man's words echoed in my head: "Ask the bosun nicely, and he'll cut your gizzard!" And I remembered with an uncomfortable crawling sensation just where I was. Despite the painted street sign designating it as Corporation Row, there was another name for this shadowy, high-walled little alley which hugged the perimeters of the prison. Almost everyone who lived around here called it Cut-throat Lane.

I stood up, gathered Lash's lead so he was tight against my legs, and pulled him after me. You didn't linger here after dark if you had any sense. As I passed a narrow entrance I heard a cautious whistle like an owl hooting, and knew it for a footpad's signal to another, the secret language of the filthy youths and children who made their living by being alert when others were tired and careless. Lash growled, and my heart began to beat faster as I thought about the cut-throats who lurked here, about the sinister men in the smoky room, about Cockburn and the prison he'd broken out of, the wall of which was towering forbiddingly to my left. I was hurrying so blindly by the time I got to the corner that I ran straight into someone coming in the other direction.

I nearly cried out, but before I could do so, the other person had melted off into the darkness. Lash was yelping, and straining at the lead in an effort to pursue the shadowy figure, whose footsteps I could hear echoing between the high brick walls as he fled. But I'd seen him, under the street lamp, and had a perfect impression of his startled face stamped on my memory. A tall figure in a heavy black overcoat, out of whose collar rose a dark head, almost bald, the big forehead shining like a dome in the gaslight; he had stark white piercing eyes, a nose curving like a crow's beak, and beneath it a black mustache which came to a fine point at either side. This was no resident of Clerkenwell! He was in a hurry to get somewhere, it was plain — a foreigner lost in London, looking for someone, or perhaps fleeing from someone. And the look in his eyes, which burned into me even now, after he'd rushed off into the night, bespoke some intrigue as dark and as menacing as the very points of his mustache.

2

INDIAN INK

Tassie came through to the taproom of the Doll's Head, accompanied by a rich tempting smell, and placed a steaming pie in front of me.

"Now, what do you say to *that?*" she asked, with a grin so broad I could count her back teeth — and there weren't very many of them.

"Ta," I said as best I could with my mouth full.

"The lad would eat all I've got if I let him," Tassie cheerfully announced to the rest of the customers, the usual slightly shabby crowd sitting round the tables enjoying a smoke and a Saturday dinner. "Though I'd say he weren't lookin' himself today. Looks like he needs some sleep, woul'ncha say, Mr. Gringle?"

The plump bald man at the bar squinted at me critically, and nodded his suet-like head. "Hollow eyes," he said meaningfully. "In fact, the lad's got no flesh on him at all."

"Wouldn't think he got more of my hot pies down

him than any other body in Clerkenwell," assented Tassie, wiping her taps.

I looked down at the table, irritated. What business was it of theirs? I was jolly glad I *didn't* have flesh on me, if it meant looking like Mr. Gringle, whose belly was at present quivering beneath his filthy and bursting waistcoat only inches from my plate. But Tassie was right to say I needed sleep. After my midnight visit to Flethick's, I'd spent the rest of the night shifting and bouncing in my lumpy bed, and my fitful bursts of sleep had been troubled by dreams of the most disturbing kind.

In my dream I was blundering around in a kind of haze, like the pungent fog of Flethick's room, in which people's faces hovered in and out of sight. Some were friendly, others menacing; but in every case, whenever I tried to speak to them, they would be pulled away from me. One shadowy figure who emerged suddenly from the mist turned out to have the face of the convict from the poster. Another turned out to be the mysterious man with the mustache I'd met in the lane: and as he floated towards me, staring with his stark white eyes, his head had seemed to change into that of a crow, his prominent nose becoming a huge black beak before my very eyes.

To tell the truth, I'd had this dream, or something like it, quite regularly since I was tiny. It was so familiar now that, when it started, I always knew what was going to happen, and I dreaded it so much I often tried to wake myself up so I wouldn't have to have the dream. The part I always hated the most was when Lash's barking face appeared, and I reached out to try and hug him, and he drifted away, and I tried to grab his lead to pull him back, but I couldn't get hold of it, and he barked and barked without making a sound, and he was gone.

The final time, just before I woke up, the dream had been especially vivid. A delicate, shining human figure drifted towards me and I found myself gazing into the beautiful face of my mother, whom I had never seen but whose face I always knew instantly in these dreams, encircled by a headscarf of what seemed to be green and gold silk. She was mouthing silent words in the most earnest, imploring way, as though trying to make me understand something terribly important; but, try as I might, I couldn't make it out. "Ma!" I called to her, "I can't hear you! Talk to me! Tell me again!" Her lips continued to move but she was receding now, her eyes alive with urgency, calling out to me silently. Real tears welled in my eyes, from frustration and the pain of parting, as I watched her getting further and further away, still calling . . .

I shuddered. I didn't dare say a word to the crowd in the Doll's Head about last night's expedition: I knew

I'd be laughed at, and besides, it didn't seem quite so serious now, in the light of the next day, with the spring sun overhead and the street outside full of fruit barrows and shouting boys and animals. And I harbored a nagging fear that, the moment I did say anything, dark forces would be lurking and waiting to grab me.

But my mother's apparition haunted me. I was certain that what she had been trying to tell me was in some way connected with last night's events. My mind worked feverishly all morning, trying to make sense of what I'd seen and heard. Flethick's friend had been told to shut up when he talked too freely about something called the Sun of Calcutta. "Such riches!" he had chuckled. They had also seemed especially anxious about someone they thought might have been waiting outside. I was convinced that the stranger I'd met in Cut-Throat Lane must be the person they'd been talking about — the one with three friends — and that he had something to do with the Sun of Calcutta, whatever that was.

Gringle took a sip of his beer, and went over to sit down with some cronies, coughing loudly as he went. I thought it might now be safe to ask Tassie something.

"Tassie," I said, in a low voice, "where's Calcutta?"

"Where's Calcutta?" she echoed loudly, and I winced as her voice pierced the hubbub of the tap-room. "Well, er — it's a foreign place, Maaster Mog."

"I *know* it's a foreign place," I said, "but where is it?"

Her mouth worked for a couple of seconds with no sound coming out. "Well, er — it's — a long way off," she said, and it was obvious she hadn't a clue. "It's in, er — the South Pole." And she seemed satisfied with this sudden piece of inspiration — triumphant, even.

"What are people like there?" I asked her, through a mouthful of pie.

"What are they like?" She echoed again. "Why, they're — different," she blustered.

"How, different?"

"Well, they, er. They." She wiped her taps furiously, as though they were crystal balls and might supply her with the answer. "They probably look like sheep, with curly horns. But I ain't never seen anyone from there, so I can only say what I've heard."

I decided Tassie was no use at all when it came to geography. But things started to look up almost immediately with the arrival in the inn of Bob Smitchin, a cheerful youth well known in these parts of town. There wasn't much that went on that *he* didn't know about. He always had a winning word for everyone, and usually something extraordinary to sell — which people were better disposed to buy after he'd been nice to them.

"Hello, Mr. Gringle! Mr. Ratchet! Another warm

one, eh? Hello, Tom, get the bricks all right? Mornin',
Mr. Fettle. Dot, my love, how was that bacon?Mornin',
Charlie, still on top?" Indeed, wherever he went there
were so many people he knew that it was a wonder he
ever got anything done at all: he could have spent his
entire life greeting people. Once he'd worked his way
through the taproom, exchanging handshakes and
pleasantries, he came to lean against the bar close to
where I was sitting.

"Mog!" he said, noticing me. "The printer's devil,
large as life!" He knelt down to make a fuss of Lash, who
sniffed and licked at his fingers happily. "You look like
you've got something worryin' you," said Bob, standing
up again. "Nothing amiss, is there? Nobody ill?"

"No, Bob," I said, "just a bit tired. I was working on
posters till late last night."

"Posters! Not that escaped convict?" he said, giving
money to Tassie in return for a full pot of frothy beer
she'd just plonked on the counter. "That's a great job
you done on them posters. I seen them up on doors
and walls in I don't know how many places today.
What a villain! Murderous! Eh?" He gave a whistle,
and then a bright smile.

"I was sick enough of seeing his face after I'd done
a hundred of 'em, I can tell you," I said.

"I'll bet you was," he replied, putting the beer to his
lips. "Aaah!" he said, after taking a sip. "Tassie's finest,

just the thing to lay the dust." A slight wince creased his face as the aftertaste hit him. He'd acquired a white mustache from the foam on the beer, and he wiped it away with a stained shirt cuff. "Yeh, that convict poster," he continued, "what fine big letters, Mog, big bold ones. Not that I knows what they say, but I can tell sure enough they're big bold words fit to make any citizen watch their step where convicts is concerned. And what a face! What a fine murderous convict's face to stick up around town. Eh? Only thing is —"

He took another draught of beer, and acquired another frothy mustache in the process. "Only thing is, Mog," he said again, "I seen that face before."

"What do you mean, seen it before?" I asked, intrigued. Was he about to tell me he knew where the escaped convict was?

"On another poster. I mean, it's a fine face, for a villain that is, a fine murderous convict's face to frighten anyone what lays eyes on it. But it's the same face what was on another poster for an escaped convict a month or two back."

I stared at him. "What, exactly the same?" I said.

"No two ways about it, my son," Bob said cheerily. "Never forgets a fiz, doesn't Bob, and that one I seen before. Same eyes, same crooked stare. Same big square chin."

"Well, maybe he's escaped twice," I said, "maybe

they caught him the first time and locked him up again, and he's just escaped again."

Bob shrugged. "Maybe he has," he said. "Except I feel sure it ain't more than a fortnight since he did a bit of dancin' on thin air. The old Paddington frisk? Eh?" He made a strange jerky movement with his body and stuck his tongue out.

I was looking at him blankly.

"They hanged him," he explained.

"What?" I said, worried now.

"I could have sworn I heard tell," he said, "that the convict on the other poster was caught and hanged. I could have sworn old Tommy Cacklecross the prison gatekeeper told me that. And if he was hanged, well, they wouldn't be putting out posters of him saying he's on the loose, would they? Before you go back and face Cramplock," he said, leaning closer as if to impart a confidence, "it might be worth you going and having a word with old Tommy, see if he knows the face. He'll put you right." And he stood up again, beaming, looking around for someone else to talk to.

"Well, thanks for the advice," I said crossly. Who was Bob to come criticizing my handiwork, telling me I'd put the wrong face on the poster? If there was anything wrong with Bob it was his habit of putting his oar in where it wasn't wanted, reckoning he knew more about other people's jobs than they did themselves. But an uncomfortable dread nagged at me: might I have used the wrong picture? One big ink-covered engraving could look remarkably like another as we fitted them into the blocks in the shop. And Bob's memory for faces *was* usually impeccable. What on earth would Cramplock do if it turned out I'd misprinted the poster a hundred times over?

As I ate the rest of my pie I tried to work out where I'd live and what I'd do if I lost my job, and how I'd find enough food to give Lash — and I'd soon constructed an entirely plausible future which saw me sleeping on the cobbles beside the Priory gatehouse covered up in waste-paper I'd stolen from Cramplock's garbage cans — until suddenly the word "Calcutta" woke me up.

"Yes, Maaster Mog's quite the mysterious one this morning, ain't you Maaster Mog?" Tassie was leaning over her bar, chatting to the effusive Bob. "Asking me all sorts of questions about Calcutta and the South Pole, you'd think I was a schoolmaster to be inquired of!"

"Questions about Calcutta?" queried Bob. "Why, that's a funny thing, Mog, because that's exactly where this came from." And he produced from his inside pocket a very large silk handkerchief in an exotic pink and orange pattern, with gold thread running in an ornate trace around the edge. "Thought I might find a likely buyer for this," he said. "Keep me in beer for the evenin'. Eh?"

"That came from Calcutta?" I asked, intrigued.

"Off an East Indiaman who came home last night," Bob replied, "straight from the Orient, full of riches to dazzle the worldliest of us! And I can offer this little square of the mystic East —" he was getting into his stride and waving the handkerchief around at the amused crowd, "— silk of a quality you never seen, for a song, to the highest bidder. Direct from the hold of the *Sun of Calcutta,* and unloaded not two hours since. Picture this fine silk softly stroking the neck of a Maharaja's beautiful daughter." He put it to his nostrils. "Mmmm! Still richly scented with her heavenly perfume!" There was a ripple of interest among the other customers. He was good at this. "And now, here it is," he continued, "available to anyone with the wherewithal, to adorn themselves like a true princess!"

But I wasn't listening to Bob's eloquent salesmanship. I'd latched onto one specific part of his patter, and I wanted to know more. "The Sun of Calcutta," I said, "it's a ship, then, is it?"

"She certainly is, and a finer one you won't find in the whole port of London," Bob enthused. "Laden with the gifts of the Orient!"

"Where is it? Where can I find it?"

"Where can you *find* it?" he repeated. "Where can

you *find* it?" He turned to the little crowd and waved a hand towards me, inviting them to share the joke. "He wants to know where he can find the *Sun of Calcutta!*" he said, and laughed aloud. "Where d'you find any new-returned East Indiaman, young Mog? In the dock, that's where — and I don't mean the kind of dock your escaped convict makes it his habit to stand in!"

Clattering and screeching like the noise of hell itself, the wheels of a hundred carts and carriages mingling with shouting voices and the screaming of wheeling seagulls filled the hot air above the London docks. I fought my way along the riverside, holding tight to Lash's lead; dodging horses' hooves, avoiding persistent costermongers trying to get me to buy fruit from their untidily laden barrows; and pushing with difficulty between the heavy coats of gentlemen and tradesmen who thronged the dirty streets. The heat was almost unbearable, the horses whinnying in frustration at the crush. Everyone was sweating. The further I went, the more like a foreign country it seemed, with sailors from overseas laughing and gathering in the doorways of inns and shops, Jewish men in black coats and hats, men carrying things and shouting at the crowd to part and let them through, everyone babbling in foreign languages, arguing and fighting with one another. Every now and again I stopped to ask someone if they knew where I might find the *Sun of Calcutta;* and every time, if they knew at all, they'd point me further east, towards Wapping and Shadwell.

What Bob had said about Maharajas had made me more sure than ever of the connection between the agitated fellow with the crow's beak nose, and the *Sun of Calcutta*. A stranger in London, I told myself, a foreigner lost in the maze of streets the same night as the *Sun of Calcutta* arrived, must surely have come ashore from that very ship. But the more people I saw as I wandered between the hot, dirty brick buildings, the less convinced I became. How many ships might there be in London just now? And how many countries might they all come from? I realized too that I was venturing into what many people said was the thickest nest of thieves in the world. Most people said so quite importantly, as though it were a matter of national pride that London's docks should be so notorious. Nevertheless, my curiosity had been aroused, and my progress eastward never halted.

My feet were beginning to ache, though; and I persuaded a passing drayman to let us sit up on his cart next to a few beer barrels. I climbed up first, using the hub of the wheel as a step; Lash bounded up after me in a single leap, with a little yelp of excitement, and sat there with his tongue lolling out, surveying the passing crowds with a superior air from his new vantage point.

After a while the drayman pulled up his horse and gestured with a wordless nod of his head down a dark narrow alley leading to the river. We'd arrived. We jumped down and I fished in my pocket for a penny to give him.

The masts of ships jostled for position in the foul-smelling dock, stretching as far as the eye could see. Time and again people shouted at me to get out of the way as they pushed and pulled great cartloads of goods over the cobbles. Dockers and sailors milled in the narrow yards, stripped to the waist, with skins like alligators as a result of years of exposure to salt and rain and scorching foreign sun. We passed huddled little inns: the Galleon, the Sun, the Ship's Cat, the Crow's Nest, all playing host to hordes of seagoing men who'd come ashore eager for drink and food and female company. As we got nearer the water, the smell rose and the masts grew higher and higher; loose ropes flapped in the spring breeze, timbers were ranged along the bank for miles, making a noise like the groaning of a thousand wild animals as they bobbed on the water and scraped against one another's flanks.

Far below, in the dock, I saw a man helping people down into a little wooden boat. Every now and again he shouted up to the crowd on the dockside, "See London by water! Ride on the great Thames! See the City! Room for two more!" The boat was rocking as though it could have done with two fewer, rather than two more, to carry; but the faces grinning up from the cramped little vessel seemed happy enough at the prospect of their trip. The angular man in charge, with a sharp little face like a water rat, looked so untrustworthy I was quite sure the grinning foreigners would soon find themselves robbed once they got out of sight.

I pushed onward, every now and again yanking at Lash's lead to stop him going after seagulls or some other fascinating distraction. Someone had just pointed out the *Sun of Calcutta* when I spotted a pair of strange-looking men standing by themselves, eyeing the crowd and whispering to each other. Something about them made me stop and watch. One was tall and very untidy, sturdily built, with a raggy shirt open to reveal a hairy chest and stomach. He had a bandage around his head as though he'd recently been in a fight or an accident. His companion was shorter and skinny; older, it seemed, with a slight stoop. His eyes were grey and lifeless, and his face seemed fixed in an expression of utter weariness, his mouth hanging slightly open, his skin drooping as though it was all being pulled by gravity towards the ground.

I was convinced they were up to no good, from the nervous way they kept looking around. They were making their way towards the mooring where I'd been told the *Sun of Calcutta* stood; and, keeping my distance, I followed them.

But I didn't get very far. I found my way blocked by a broad-chested man in a dark coat. "Where do *you* think you're going?" he asked. Lash growled, sensing sudden hostility — something he didn't do very often — and I felt for his collar, both to reassure him and hold him back. I wondered if I should point out the two suspicious types, and turned to look for them — but they'd gone. In that single second I'd let them get out of sight.

"Erm — I'm looking for the *Sun of Calcutta*," I said, rather awkwardly.

"Oh yes? And what would you be wanting with her?"

"I've, er — come to collect something," I mumbled, and then wished I hadn't, because he immediately asked me what. I looked up at him. I couldn't possibly slip past him, and the determined look on his face didn't give me much cause for hope that he would let me through. I thought quickly. What on earth might a kid like me want with a ship like that?

"Ink," I said suddenly. "Indian ink. I'm Mog Winter and I work for Cramplock the printer at Clerkenwell. I was asked to collect Indian ink off the East Indiaman."

The man bent down and hissed his reply into my face.

"Ink, eh?" he said. "Mog Winter, eh? Winter the Printer." He showed his teeth.

"Yes," I said as brightly as I could. "Where can I pick it up?"

"Nowhere," he hissed. "You show me proof you's who you says you is. There's a thousand horrible kids might pretend to work for a printer just so's they can get on board a ship and snoop around and thieve and do."

I didn't have any proof, and I had to tell him so. Lash was still growling softly, and I could feel him tensing beneath my grip. The customs man eyed me suspiciously.

"How *much* ink?" he wanted to know.

"Twenty-four bottles," I said confidently. "Big bottles," I added.

"How you going to carry 'em to Clerkenwell then?"

"Er —" Again I had to think quickly. "I've left my cart back there," I said, gesturing vaguely behind me.

"Really? Then chances are it'll be gorn when you gets back to it!" The man was rapidly making me feel like a fool. "And I might tell you, for your *hinformation*, that you can only get your ink on presentation of the necessary monies at the Customs Warehouse, in the City," he added, stabbing his finger shortly in the direction from which I'd come. "But if you was to let me have something for my trouble, I might just see that nobody else makes off with your master's ink."

"Have you seen a man in a bandage?" I asked him,

"because there was one over there, and his thin friend, and they looked like they were up to no good."

It didn't work. "Could be," he said, "my brother has a bandage, and a thin friend. Could be a full three-quarters of sailors have a bandage, and a thin friend. And if you don't want a bandage, to cover up the kick I'm going to give you," he said in a low voice, "you'd better hook it, Mog Winter."

This was persuasive enough, and I turned back reluctantly, pulling Lash after me and casting an occasional glance over my shoulder to see if the mysterious pair had resurfaced in the crowd. The more I thought about it, the more certain I became that they were mixed up in the affair Flethick and his sinister friends had been talking about last night. Why else would they be snooping around the *Sun of Calcutta,* looking so shifty?

Suddenly, there they were again. I edged behind a nearby pile of empty barrels so I could hide and watch them. They were carrying a large decorative chest between them, and were still looking around as if checking to see who was watching them. Then I noticed the Customs man — the same man who'd just turned me away — striding purposefully over to them. The game was up! I was far too far away to hear what was being said — but I was sure they would be in trouble now.

Yet, as the customs man began to talk to them, he didn't seem at all angry. I could see his face quite clearly, and it was a picture of calm and good humor. He even began to laugh. He was sharing a joke with them! They were making off with a precious chest full of all kinds of exotic treasure, and he was laughing as if it was all a huge joke! But I suddenly understood why when I saw the bandaged one take some large banknotes out of his pocket and pass them quickly to the official. They'd hoped no one had seen the transaction, but they hadn't reckoned on me watching from behind these smelly, leaky tar barrels.

Only then did I look down at myself, and realize that my hands and clothes were black and sticky from being pressed up against the barrels. Lash, sniffing round them, had acquired jet-black tips to his grey whiskers, and was leaving rings of dark shiny paw-prints as he scampered around me, impatient to be off.

I didn't have time to worry about my ruined clothes. Right now the most important thing was to follow the two suspicious-looking men. I caught up with them again by the corner of a warehouse, where I saw them talking to a man with a horse and cart. Was he an accomplice, or just a carter they were hiring to carry the load? Dismayed, I watched them all sweating as they lifted the heavy chest up onto the cart. It was going to be much harder to keep up with them now.

I wondered if I should tell someone else. But who could I trust? The customs man, who was meant to prevent this kind of thing, was obviously up to his neck in it. I had a feeling that shouting "Stop, thief!" in a place like this would only make all the thieves laugh.

So, dodging between the people and hiding behind them as I went, I tried to keep up with the ugly pair and their carter companion as they trundled away from the dockside and up the road towards the Galleon Inn, one of the most packed and notorious of the local taverns. Every now and again, I could see them moving ahead of me as the crowd parted. I noticed that the chest had been covered up with a big dark canvas sheet. It could have been anything under there: a chest of drawers, or a couple of ordinary wooden boxes. Nobody even noticed them as they jolted on up the hill.

As the cart reached the Galleon I lost sight of them again. I was running, trying to catch up, when someone pulled my arm.

"Nick!" said a gruff voice, and I turned to see a stocky sailor with a filthy flat cap on his head, his neck blue with tattoos.

"Sorry," I said, "I'm in a hurry, could you —"

"Not so fast," he growled, grasping my arm more tightly. "Your Pa's after your hide. Watcha done?"

I didn't know what to say. The sailor obviously

thought I was someone else. His breath smelled strongly of drink and he was speaking so fast it was all but impossible to understand what he was saying. "I — I think you've —" I began; but he wasn't listening.

"Your Pa's up to his neck. He's three sheets gone and he's roaring," he was saying. "Picture of palsy, the man is. Your hide'll not be worth tanning when he's roped you in. What's his rag for, eh?"

"Let me go," I said, "you've got the wrong person."

"Hang fire then," he said, grasping me even tighter. "You tell old Samson what your Pa's rag's about, and mebbe I let you go. Or mebbe I beef on you, lad. Seems he's missing summink, and missing it sore."

"Look, I've *got* to go," I said, twisting and wriggling in a vain attempt to slip out of his grip.

The man pulled me close to him, violently now, and I caught a powerful hot scent of rum full in the face. Lash barked, but the sailor showed the dog his teeth in a sudden grimace and Lash fell silent, astonished.

"Now you listen," he said to me, gruffly and quietly. "Your Pa's in a fine chafe over you, young snaffer, and if I wasn't so soft I'd run you into that tailshop and let him hang you by your kegs for all to glory over. Now you be warned, chimp, and get yourself out while your molly's still in one piece, and don't say I letcha. Hook it!"

I stumbled away, with Lash at my heels, tripping on

the cobbles, not daring to look back at the tattooed sailor. What on earth had he been talking about? Furious, I looked up and down the street, but of course the pair of thieves were now nowhere to be seen. Maybe the sailor had stopped me on purpose, to slow me down and let the villains escape?

My eyes stung with sudden tears. Thrusting my hands deep into my pockets, letting Lash follow at his own pace now, I trudged in the direction of home, getting more and more furious about the thieves and the chest I'd watched them taking. As I walked along I realized how strongly I smelt of tar — but when I tried to rub the sticky stuff from my clothes it just made a worse mess than before. I'd have to change when I got back to Clerkenwell.

Suddenly, as I walked past the low doorway of a courtyard, I caught a glimpse of something which made me stop in my tracks. Was it . . . ? I took a step backward and looked through the passageway again; and sure enough, standing against a wall, apparently abandoned, was the cart with the chest on it. I could hardly believe my eyes. They'd just left it here! I whistled for Lash and bent to take hold of his lead again. Keeping him close, I tiptoed up the passageway towards the cart. The nearer I got, the more certain I was it was the same one: I recognized the dark tarpaulin and the shape of the chest beneath it. But surely the villains couldn't be far away! I had no time to lose. I rushed up to the cart and looked around quickly to make sure no one was watching — then took hold of the cover, and lifted it.

The disappointment was like a hammer blow. An old sideboard! A rotting old piece of useless furniture, with grimy green paint flaking off all over it. This was the villains' cart all right — but wherever they'd gone, they'd taken the chest with them, and had probably left this here deliberately to throw people off their scent.

It was only then that I noticed a group of children, a bit younger than I was, watching me from a corner of the yard. They had a battered-looking dog with them, which started to yelp when it saw us, and Lash snarled back. The dog looked ill, with milky eyes and a mouth that hung open as though its jaw didn't work properly. I didn't want Lash to go near it.

"Did you see the three men who brought this cart?" I asked the children.

None of them said anything. They all just watched me.

"I need to know where they've gone," I said, "the men who brought this. Did you see them? One of them had a bandage on."

Still they stood, looking dumbstruck. Why weren't they talking to me? One of them whispered something into the ear of another; and I suddenly realized they weren't really looking at *me,* but at something above my head.

I turned too late. Above me there was a scraping sound and, as I looked up, I saw another boy poised on the top of the wall in a crouching position. Just as I noticed the brick he was holding in his hands, he sent it tumbling down towards my upturned face; I remember hearing Lash barking; and the boy's wild, satisfied little smile was the last thing I saw before the sky seemed to fill with brick, then blood, then darkness.

3

THE SWORD

I woke up to find a pair of eyes about an inch from mine, and the stench of warm breath in my nostrils.

I came to with a jolt, and realized it was the skinny half of the villainous pair, peering down his snout-like nose at me.

"Ere, Coben," he said suddenly, "ere, 'e's comin' to."

"Who are you?" I asked indistinctly. As I moved, a sudden smarting in my forehead reminded me in a flash of the child on the wall, and the brick which must have hit me.

I groaned, and let my head fall back onto the pile of old rags on which I was lying. I was in a very dim corner of some damp little room, lit only by a candle flickering on a table nearby. Both of the villains I'd followed were here: the bandage-headed one appeared now, beside the other, and they both looked down at me as I lay there.

"Andsome creeter," murmured one, ironically.

"Soft-lookin'," said the other, with a note of scorn. "Pelt like a wench."

I tensed. Since I'd lived in the orphanage, several years ago now, I'd never forgotten one of the older children once saying that when I was asleep, I looked like a girl. It didn't matter much, because nobody usually saw me while I was asleep; but these two hideous characters had caught me at my most vulnerable, and their sneering tone was making my skin crawl. I heaved myself up onto my elbows to put myself at greater advantage.

"Lash," I said suddenly, looking around me. There was no sign of him. "My dog — where's my dog?"

"No 'arm will come to your dog," said the bandaged one, "long as you do as you're told."

"*Where is he?*" I insisted, beginning to panic.

"That's for us to know," he said sharply. "What was you doin' stalkin' us?"

"I don't understand," I lied, wincing from the pain in my forehead.

"You followed us with a dog," the other, skinny one piped up. "What was you followin' us for?"

"I wasn't," I lied again.

The man with the bandage pushed his way forward, bent over me, and took me just a little too firmly by the shoulders. "Now then," he said, squeezing with his huge grimy hands, "we knows your Pa put you up to this, but he'll regret it, we'll make sure o' that. You tell us what the bosun's done with that camel."

I stared at them blankly. *They* thought they knew my father too, just as the sailor outside the Galleon had! What on earth was going on? I was too astonished to say a word.

"Come on, Master bosun's lad," said the skinny one, "stow makin' it rough."

"You'll only mak' it painful for yerself," growled the bandaged man. "See if we can't make you squeal. What's the bosun about, and where's the camel?"

The pain in my forehead was making my head buzz and I couldn't be sure I was hearing properly. For a while I thought these two must have the same strange condition, whatever it was, that had made some of Flethick's friends talk gibberish last night. But it was starting to be obvious that people were mistaking me for someone else entirely. "Ask the bosun nicely," a voice intoned somewhere inside my head, "and he'll cut your gizzard." A churning feeling in my stomach told me I was in deep trouble. If only Lash was here.

"I don't know what you're talking about," I told them, "I don't know no bosun."

The bandaged one laughed shortly. "There's plenty wish they didn't," he said, "his own brat among 'em, I warrant." His face turned dark. "You squeal," he said, taking hold of my throat. "You been aboard that ship from London to Calcutta and back again, and you seen every move that camel's made, an it's your own Pa's what's nailed it, an' we knows it!"

I couldn't begin to understand what bandage-head was on about. Did he really say *camel?*

"What camel?"

"Coben," said the skinny one, "'e might've forgot. That brick might've knocked the sense out of 'im."

"Don't feel sorry for 'im, Jiggs," said the one called Coben, "if you believe a word 'e says you're an even bigger fool than you look." Jiggs opened his gormless mouth, but obviously thought better of arguing. Coben placed his massive, filthy hand around my chin and asked me again, more threateningly this time, *"Where's the camel?"*

His clenched fingers were genuinely hurting my face, and out of instinct I brought both my hands up to try and wrench his arm free. Fortunately I hadn't cut my fingernails for about a fortnight and I managed to dig them into his oily skin and produce about six deep satisfying crescent-shaped welts in which blood appeared as he stared down at me.

Slowly, he bared his filthy brown teeth in a snarl. "You've really asked for it now, you little ship's rat," he growled. "'Elp me, Jiggs."

And as I kicked and struggled, the hideous twosome took my legs and arms and carried me across the room where, for the first time, I noticed the ornate chest they'd brought from the *Sun of Calcutta*. The golden decoration on its lid sparkled in the candlelight: patterns like peacocks with their tails fanned out, liquid shapes like falling teardrops of gold. But I didn't have much time to appreciate it — at least, not from the outside. Before I knew what was happening Coben had opened the lid and I was being bundled inside! I shouted, enraged, letting out all the foul words I knew, which probably weren't half as many as I'd have known if I really *had* been a bosun's boy. Kicking wildly, I managed to land a resonant blow with my heel to the one called Jiggs, at a point on the front of his trousers which made him let go of me abruptly and turn away, clutching himself in alarm. But Coben was quite strong enough for two; and I might just as well have been a baby, wailing and feebly kicking, as he stuffed me into the chest and banged the lid down on me.

It was a couple of minutes before I could think straight. The low voices of Coben and Jiggs filtered through into the darkness of the chest as I lay cramped up inside. I strained to make out what they were saying, but their words were muffled by the solid wood, and they were speaking to one another in a strange slang I couldn't really understand.

"You better sound out the three friends," I heard Coben say.

There were some indistinct murmurs from Jiggs, some of which sounded like, "That chavy wants drowning." His tone of voice suggested he was still in pain.

"Not yet," said Coben, "we can get more out of 'im." Another indistinct murmur from Jiggs, then Coben said: "We ain't got long. My name's out."

Again Jiggs said something I couldn't make out. How irritating he was! "The man from Calcutta knows," came Coben's voice again. "But there's something I don't like. It's a trick, Jiggs. Fact is, I need a boat."

There was a clattering. It sounded as though they might be preparing to leave. I listened as their footsteps creaked up the hollow stairs. Somewhere above, a door was slammed, and a key turned.

Silence. They'd gone.

I began to feel around the inside of the chest to see if there was any way of opening it. But no amount of pushing at the lid would make it yield. I was locked in, bent almost double, with my knees in my face and several hard lumpy objects underneath me. Fumbling with my fingers around the floor of my prison, I scraped them against a sharp edge, like a large knife. But it was wedged tightly under my weight, and try as I might I couldn't move it.

I could see absolutely nothing. I just hoped there was some crack in the chest somewhere where air could get in, or else I'd suffocate. As the reality of the situation sank in I began to panic, and started shouting and kicking at the sides of the chest; but there was so little room to move that I could make no appreciable sound at all. I was just exhausting myself. I gave up, my eyes filling with tears of frustration. Where was Lash? What had they done with him? In the darkness I could clearly picture the nasty boy's face, and I wondered how much Coben and Jiggs had paid him to throw the brick at me.

Faces spun around my head: the man with the mustache and the wily crow's face he had taken on in my dream; the sneering Coben and Jiggs, the customs official laughing as they handed him money. The air in this chest was making me dizzy. It was heavy with an alien smell which reminded me of the foul air in Flethick's sluggish den. A strange music seemed to be reaching my ears, fading in and out: music which sounded like nothing I'd ever heard before, rising and falling and seeming to avoid all the familiar notes. The events of the last two days mingled in my head, out of sequence, running riot. I was printing posters with the face of a dog on them. Bob Smitchin was talking about camels, with three other people gathered around him. "Mog," he said, "how rude of me not to introduce you. These are the three friends." They turned to look at me, and I realized in horror that they all had the face of the escaped convict. Looking down at myself, I noticed my clothes rapidly blackening with tar, which was seeping all over my body. "Ink!" I shouted at the three convicts, "Indian ink from Calcutta!" They glared at me, their heads getting bigger and bigger on their shoulders, until suddenly one of them picked up a brick and it came spinning towards me, revolving in the air, infinitely slowly.

❖

I woke to thuds and crashes from outside the chest.

How long had I been asleep? It was still pitch dark: I tried opening and closing my eyes but it made absolutely no difference to what I could see. Someone was clattering around in the room, knocking things over. Had Coben and Jiggs come back? If so, it sounded as though they were drunk.

My head ached as if it had been battered for hours with spoons. Doing my best to move in the cramped chest, I felt a sharp pain in my thumb, and remembered the knife, or whatever it was, wedged underneath me. With difficulty I lifted my thumb to my mouth, and found my tongue immediately covered with warm welling blood.

Right next to my ear, something clicked.

The chest was being unlocked! Suddenly light flooded in, making me squint and gasp after such a long time in total darkness: and I found myself blinking up into the astonished face, not of Coben or Jiggs — but of the mysterious man with the mustache!

I cried out instinctively, in sudden terror — and so did he. Above his beak-like nose his eyes were, if anything, wider and whiter than they'd been when I met him under the street light last night.

For the first few seconds I was too shocked to know what to do; but then, scrambling to my knees, I reached down to grab the knife from the bottom of the chest. Only when I'd raised it above my head did I notice it was actually a huge curved scimitar with a golden handle, a weapon formidable enough to drive back a herd of elephants. The man with the brown face was no match for this — a tar-stained child springing like a jack-in-the-box out of the chest and waving a giant sword which flashed in the candlelight! He was off up the stairs, leaving the old wooden door swinging crazily behind him.

I sat back on the rim of the chest. I was trembling. For the first time I took a proper look at the weapon I held in my hands. It was at least half my own height. Its polished blade was smeared with some of my own blood, and I wiped it on my shirt tail, adding a patch of bright red to the black tar stains.

My thoughts were coming thick and fast now, a new one with every thumping heartbeat and every droplet of blood which squeezed its way out of my gashed thumb. This stranger, who'd just found me in the chest and who'd bumped into me as I ran from Cut-Throat Lane last night, was looking for something. What was he after? Was he looking for the same thing Coben and Jiggs wanted, including the mysterious "camel"? Did this chest in fact belong to him, and had he come around here to try and get it back? "The man from Calcutta knows," I'd heard Coben say. This man *was* the man from Calcutta, wasn't he? I was absolutely sure of it. And Coben and Jiggs were scared of him.

I shuddered. If he struck terror even into that violent pair, what kind of evil must he be capable of?

I looked up at the open door. I mustn't stay here for long. Coben and Jiggs might be back at any moment. And I *had* to find Lash. Gazing at the big sword, I was tempted to take it with me, as much for self-defense as anything else. But I'd have caused a bit of a stir carrying it through the streets, and I could hardly hide it up my sleeve or under my shirt. Reluctantly, I laid it back in the chest; but as I did so, my eye was caught by some inlaid carvings on the handle which made me pick it up again. I ran my good thumb across the design, to clean it. Glistening snakelike strands threaded around one another in complex knots. There was something very familiar about them.

On the table, a stubby old stump of candle was still flickering. I could hear my heart beating in my chest and I knew I had to get out. But beside the candle, under an empty rum bottle, there was an untidy bundle of papers, which I couldn't resist quickly surveying. The top one was an untidy note scrawled on ragged parchment.

gentlmen .

   yul hev to be qiuker nex time .
   if i gets my way yu wont be geting
   anuther chanc. this is my lay now
   and my lot ar on yur tale.
   the law is watching the 3 frends
        & 👁 am wachin yu.
           Yur frend the BOSUN.

I gathered this and all the other papers up, and stuffed them into my shirt. Before I left, I closed the lid of the chest and locked it, so it wouldn't be so obvious I'd escaped; and took care to close the cellar door behind me too as I ran up the stairs and out into the air.

I found myself in an overgrown backyard, with a crippled little apple tree, its roots half-submerged in bricks and broken glass, doing its best to claw its way out of the rubble and spread its branches up over the low roof of the dirty, decrepit house. I was debating which way to turn in order to hunt for Lash, when I heard an unmistakable *woof* — and there he was, near my feet, cooped up in a low kennel shaped like a pyramid, made of splintery old wood with bars nailed across it like a cage. There was barely enough room in there to keep a rabbit, let alone a dog like Lash, I thought furiously as I wrenched it open; but Lash evidently forgot the discomfort of his prison almost instantly, as he leapt at me and rested his paws on my chest and licked my face, even more overjoyed than I was at our reunion.

I had no idea where we were as I crept out into the lane, but the buildings around me didn't look like the place where the child had thrown the brick at me. The villains must have carried me here. A tingle of fear ran through me as I thought of the charcoaly little eye on the boson's note, and I wondered what eyes might be watching the pair of us as we ran, as fast as we could, in what I thought was the direction of the city. It was evening, and the glow of sunset was sending shafts of orange light through the smoky air between the buildings. Attracted by the noise of voices and horses' hooves, I turned a corner into a wide street and, as the buildings fell away like a clearing in the forest of brick and plaster, I could see the shadowy bulk of St. Paul's belled out like a floating monster against the sunset. Keeping it to my left, I soon found myself in Cheapside, its bustle dwindling as the light faded; and I hoped, as I scuttled home, that I'd be able to remember the way to Coben and Jiggs's lair, should I ever need to go back there.

When I reached Cramplock's it was almost dark. I let myself in, and unhooked a lantern from the back of the door. I was extremely tired, and my head hurt, and part of me just wanted to sink into bed; but I was also dying for something to eat, and I was sure, after being locked up in that nasty little kennel for several hours, Lash must be too. I went to look in Cramplock's little larder, where I was thrilled to find the remains of the ham I'd bought from Tassie last night, along with some of the bread and a couple of pieces of rather hard cheese which had probably been there some-what longer. I gathered the food scraps together and scampered upstairs, with Lash close behind, to the little room where we slept, and laid out our feast on the bed.

Munching, and feeding morsels to Lash little by little, I took down my treasure box from the cupboard. It was really an old biscuit tin, but to me it was a store of the things which were most precious to me in the whole world — apart from Lash, of course. I didn't really have many things I could call my own. I couldn't afford to buy much with my wages, except just enough to eat, and even if I had been able to afford any possessions I had nowhere to keep them. But I often took down my treasure box, and admired the things in it, before I went to sleep. A little peg figure with matted woollen strands of hair which I'd brought with me from the orphanage and which I was far too old for, but which I couldn't quite bring myself to get rid of. A fat and rather tatty bound book of blank pages, which Cramplock had let me make, bearing a title page proclaiming "Mog's Book," and into which I used to write or paste things I found particularly interesting or important. A quill pen; a few coins; and a heavy and ornate key I'd found once, for which I had no earthly use but which I kept because it seemed grand.

Tonight, though, I had a particular reason for getting out my treasure box. When I'd been looking at the handle of the big sword I'd found in the chest at the thieves' den, I'd thought the markings on it looked familiar. And here, in my box, was the reason why.

My bangle. The only object I own which came from my mother. A small, bright, silver bangle, far too big for my skinny wrist but still delicate and beautiful; an elegantly stretched and twisted band of pure silver as wide as a couple of fingers. And all around its outer surface, it was decorated with finely etched patterns: gracefully curving, snakelike lines twining themselves around one another in a complicated lattice, a pattern which must have taken painstaking hours, days, even weeks to create. It was certainly the only *really* valuable thing in my treasure box, and I made sure I always kept it hidden away, for fear of its being stolen. Now, as I turned it over and over, I was gripped by a weird feeling of something momentous which I couldn't possibly explain. This bangle had belonged to my mother — who had traveled to India and given birth to me on the voyage home, but had died before she got here. I had arrived in London very much alive, and hungry, and a couple of weeks old, and in need of looking after. That's how I came to be sent to the orphanage, when I was still a tiny child. It had provided me with the companionship of other children, and walls and roofs for shelter, and just enough to eat; but no love. I was lucky to have found work as a painter's devil at Cramplock's and left the orphanage behind; and this bangle had come with me, the only thing I still possessed from those harsh years. Its beautiful patterns had been a source of fascination and comfort to me when nearly everything else in my life was cruel and ugly. Nowadays I barely gave them a second thought — until now, when I'd suddenly seen almost exactly the same patterns on another beautiful object which had come, I had no doubt at all, from India.

I can't describe how it made me feel, sitting there in my little room with my dog resting his head on his paws in the basket by my bed, except that I felt more curious than I ever had in my life. The sword; the ornate chest; the man from Calcutta; the villains' impenetrable questions, and the sailor who'd stopped me on the dockside as though he knew exactly who I was. . . . Something was happening, and I was a part of it, without my having known it. For all I knew I might have been a part of it for months, or even years, and never had a clue. What I had to find out now was — just what was going on?

I reached for the bits of paper I'd stuffed into my shirt at the thieves' cellar, and laid them out across the bed. In some small way, they might be able to give me some clues. One or both of the ugly villains who'd locked me up today was obviously able to read quite well, since some of the papers were densely covered with tiny writing. I wondered if they'd returned to the cellar yet to find me gone. Instinctively I looked up at the dark window, and felt so uncomfortable I got up to pull the curtain across.

As well as the scrappy note from the bosun, I found a list of names covering two sides of a sheet of paper, scrawled almost illegibly in brownish ink. Holding it near the candle, I saw one or two names I could decipher. "Blandarm" seemed to be one, "Fetchwood" another, "Jacob Tenderloin" a third. There must have been forty or fifty names altogether. Were these people involved in the plot? It was rather foolish, I felt, to keep written lists of them, if they were. I laid the list aside and unfolded the next piece of paper. It was a letter, in quite a refined hand. It had obviously been folded up for rather a long time, and the words closest to the creases had more or less faded away. I had to strain my eyes to read any of it, but a few phrases emerged. "I charge you with this solemn duty," I read. Then, farther down, "whatever the imminent fate of the soul." Was it a sermon?

And, farther down still, a line which appeared to read: "I fear it will not be possible to reach Damyata now."

This didn't make any sense to me. If it was the name of a place, it was nowhere I had ever heard of. The writing was faded and it was hard to be sure of the exact letters: it might possibly have said "Oomyata," or, in a pinch, "Damyalu." But whatever combination of letters I tried, I couldn't make it mean anything. I folded it up again with a shrug.

Beneath it was a tatty strip torn from a newspaper, with a tiny notice in one corner which someone had ringed in blurry pencil.

The EAST INDIA COMPANY vessel the *SUN OF CALCUTTA* under Capt. Geo. Shakeshere will put in at London at the end of her voyage this coming SUNDAY the 16th day of MAY. Traveling with her, Company employees returning from duty in Calcutta, also Sgt. CORNCRAKE of the Third Welsh, reported severely ill, and Dr. Hamish LOTHIAN of Edinburgh. Cargo principally of SPICES to be released before TUESDAY. Unloading under GUARD.

There was also a square of rather tatty parchment with a grubby little hole in one end, as though it had been nailed to something. On it was the oddest writing I'd ever seen, if it was writing at all. No matter which way up I held it, I couldn't make head or tail of the funny little shapes.

इम्यता

I sat staring at it for a while, trying to fix the characters in my mind. Eventually I put it aside and picked up the last piece of paper, which was a handwritten document seeming to have something to do with customs duty. The lamplight, glowing through the translucent parchment, picked out a strange watermark with a symbol like a dog curled up asleep. Its head was facing its tail and the tail seemed to stretch forward right into the dog's mouth, as though it were beginning the slow process of eating itself. I was so intrigued by the watermark it was a while before I read the words. I didn't fully understand it, but I gathered it was a customs document certifying that someone had paid four pounds for the receipt of certain goods from overseas. It was dated the 17th of May, which was yesterday's date; and at the very end there was a signature like a firework exploding, and then the name "W. Jiggs" in another, childish hand, like the crude scrawls some of the children in the orphanage used to make when practicing writing their names. Was this the piece of paper Coben and Jiggs had received from the customs man, while I'd been spying on them? The document might be perfectly genuine: it certainly *looked* official enough, with an ornate seal, and a signature for His Majesty's Customs: a spidery scrawl which seemed to say "L. W. Ferryfather" or possibly "L. N. Follyfeather," or some such name.

I yawned, and made a mental note to show the papers to Cramplock, who with his knowledge of paper and printing might be able to tell me more about them: where the paper had been made, for example, and what the watermarks meant. For the moment, I decided, for safekeeping, I'd put them in my treasure box. I gathered them up and closed the lid, and was about to stand up and put the tin back up on the cupboard shelf when I heard a sudden muffled clatter.

I started, and Lash sat straight up in his basket with his ears cocked, and gave a short but anxious *woof.* It sounded as though it had come from inside the cupboard. Perhaps something had slipped off a shelf inside. I opened the door and peered inside, but everything seemed to be in its place.

Was there someone downstairs? Had I locked the door behind me? I couldn't remember. I stood still, listening, but could hear no footsteps or voices from below.

But now there it was again! A bump, like something being knocked over; and now, with the cupboard door open, it sounded even more as though it came from the other side of the wall. And yet, it couldn't have — because behind this wall there was only the big empty burnt-out house next door, where nobody had lived for years.

Lash was whimpering now, and looking up at me quizzically; he definitely thought something was amiss. I was going to have to go down and investigate. I grasped Lash's collar and, holding up the lantern, I pulled the door open and let the light fall down the steep short stairwell.

There was no sound. I took a deep breath.

"Who's there?" I called out, as sternly as I could manage. My words disappeared into the dark space below.

I ventured down, holding the lantern out beneath me to light up the printing shop. There was nobody to be seen. I had a walk around downstairs, even a rummage through the cupboards where Cramplock kept his paper and other supplies, but it was quite clear that Lash and I were alone after all.

The noises had stopped too. I climbed the stairs again to prepare for bed, half believing I'd imagined them, and that my exhaustion, and the pain in my head, and the strange adventures I'd been having, were making me hear things which weren't really there.

In spite of my tiredness I couldn't rest before I'd spilled some of my turbulent thoughts out onto paper. Written down in black and white, they might make more sense, might be tamed, be less frightening. It was what I always did when things were crowding in on me like this. Lash came and curled up on my feet at the bottom of the bed. I pulled the scratchy old blanket up to my armpits, dug my feet under Lash's grudging weight to keep them warm, and reached for the treasure box. Taking a pencil, and opening Mog's Book at the first blank page, I thought for a few seconds and began to write.

Strange things have begun to happen, I wrote.

I stuck the pencil in my mouth and fondled Lash's ears while I contemplated whether this was quite adequate. On second thought, I decided to add a word at the beginning. There was just room, between the edge of the page and the first word, to squeeze it in.

VERY Strange things have begun to happen, it now read.

It is Tuesday, I continued. *This weather is the hottest in my whole life, and things have become a little unreal. A ship, the* Sun of Calcutta, *has brought great excitement to the worst thieves of London. It has only been in port for two days and already I cannot escape from the talk of its treasures. A strange man has come with it, and I have now met him twice. His presence here seems to have caused a great stir among the thieves, like birds who have caught the scent of a tomcat.*

I was in my stride now.

I can't say what's happening, but I feel I am caught up in an adventure that seems more important and more interesting than anything that has ever happened. I have seen patterns on a stolen sword which are exactly like the ones on my bangle. Last night I dreamed about my mother, and she was more real than I have ever known her, and I felt —

I paused, chewing the end of the pencil. What *had* I felt?

— that she was trying to tell me this all matters to her somehow.

Also, people I meet keep thinking I am someone else. First a sailor, and then Coben the thief, asked me about my Pa. Why do they think they know my father? It makes me feel very peculiar inside.

I reread what I'd written, and shivered. I was exhausted. I placed the papers I'd brought from the thieves' hideout between the pages, and closed the book.

Suddenly something occurred to me, and I took out the pieces of paper again to look through them. Quickly I found what I was looking for. The note with the mysterious writing on it. I laid it on the blanket in front of me and copied the strange shapes, a little shakily, into Mog's Book beneath this evening's entry.

इम्पता

I looked at the marks I'd made. They made even less sense in my handwriting, if that were possible. I yawned, enormously.

"Can't stay awake a moment longer," I said to Lash.

A guttural, rhythmic snore floated up from my feet. Lash was already asleep. I just hope, for his sake, he had nicer dreams that night than I did.

4

THE *SUN OF CALCUTTA*

I awoke very early with a headache and, after fixing a fresh piece of cloth across my tender forehead to act as a bandage, I slipped quietly out of the house. Lash was surprised but pleased to be up and about so early, and trotted in a kind of zigzag from one side of the street to the other, his muzzle close to the ground, as though the smells of the city were intriguingly different at this time of the day when there were no people milling about to obscure them. A grey light was beginning to spread sluggishly from the marshes to the east, and morning fog was lying in the streets so that buildings seemed suddenly to emerge from thin air as we approached them. Smithfield was still deserted, and the four-pointed tower of St. Sepulchre's gulped a sombre chime for five o'clock as we ran past the giant cliff-like wall of Newgate Prison. But the fish market was already pungent and alive, and I looked about for someone who might be able to give me a ride out to the dock. I was determined to have another try at getting aboard the *Sun of Calcutta:* or at least to hang around and see what I might find out.

On the misty water the pale lights of small boats, patrolling up and down like water-spiders, glided and swung in drifting constellations. Just as the streets had their scavengers, people looking among the rubbish for things they might use, so the river had its little boatmen who hauled out flotsam from the sewage and piled it in their stained prows. And there were thieves too, using their lights to signal to one another, sliding between the merchant ships and reaching above their heads to take the weight of goods handed down to them by accomplices onboard.

In the mist, I became one of them. A little rowing boat moored by the steps near the fish market gave me my chance: after a swift glance around to make sure the owner wasn't watching, I stepped in, and tried to steady it as Lash leaped in excitedly after me. I fumbled to untie the thin black rope, greasy from years of trailing in the river; then I was off, my heart pounding as I pulled at the unwieldy oars, sticking close to the bank and the sides of ships which were ranged alongside in increasing numbers as I rowed downstream. I wasn't managing very well: I'd only ever rowed once before, and I hadn't been very good at it then. Lash was thrilled, and I had to keep growling at him to sit down, because in his eagerness to peer first over one side of the boat, then the other, he was making it rock about rather alarmingly. But, after swinging around in circles a few times, and bumping into one or two hulls, I found a tolerable rhythm; and no one seemed to be taking much notice of me as I pulled my way down past the wharves and warehouses.

But London looked very different from the water, and I had no idea of how far I'd have to go to find the *Sun of Calcutta*. It had seemed quite a long way in the drayman's cart yesterday. There were few clues to be had from the endless forest of masts either side of me: I felt much the same as a spider might feel in a corn-field, trying to remember where she'd tied up her latest fly. Aside from all this, I was starting to feel a bit sick: a combination of the foul smell of the river and the fact that I'd had no breakfast.

As the sun was beginning to cast a weak glow through the mist, and long after I'd begun to wish I'd stayed in bed, I drifted through a gap between two tarry, groaning hulls and spotted a lance-like prow with the letters "LCUTTA" emerging from behind the nearest ship, bobbing high above my head. The boats were creaking in a deep-throated medley as though in the throes of waking yawns. Propelling myself toward an iron ladder set in the dockside, I found my little boat wedged between the dock and the planks of the *Sun of Calcutta*. I'd never be able to get Lash up onto the dockside from here: I'd have to leave him in the boat until I came back. He seemed to understand; and, praying he wouldn't decide to take a dip in the filthy river while I was gone, I was soon letting myself over the side onto the deserted quarter-deck of the ship.

My feet landed dead in the center of a coil of rope, laid like a sleeping snake guarding an Oriental treasure house. I looked around. The deck was damp and slippery, and a shiny green color in places, especially at the edges. There wasn't a person to be seen. To my right a huge mast rose, taller than any tree, with its grubby sails tied in clumps along the beams and piles of nets which surrounded it. To my left was the fore-castle, where ladders and doorways led into the cabins and spaces in the foremost part of the ship. Ropes sat everywhere, some secured, some trailing over the deck; and as my eyes followed them back along the rails I suddenly noticed a sailor's boot poking out from a corner near the mast behind me. I was about to dive back over the side when I realized with relief it was nothing more than an empty boot, without a sailor attached.

I was terrified in case I met anyone onboard, and I winced at every creak my weight squeezed from the timbers, despite their being lost amid the orchestra of groans and bumps the massed boats were uttering. As I pushed open the door into the forecastle, my heart was thumping so loudly it seemed to echo around the damp little chamber I was entering. There was a sudden hot stench of sweat and sewage from deep within the ship, so strong it made me instantly dizzy, and I had to grab the doorframe to stop myself swaying and falling into the dark hole below my feet. As the light fell across the boards, the tails of brown rats slithered like rapid worms into ragged little holes in the woodwork. It was a long time before I could pluck up the courage to set foot on the ladder which led down to the ship's interior.

The first little door I opened revealed a small, dimly lit cabin, with the tiniest of windows covered by a canvas curtain. Now the smell which met my nostrils was a mixture of oak and tobacco. In a dark corner, another curtain hid a narrow bunk in which, I suddenly realized, someone might be sleeping. I listened carefully. I could hear the water beneath the ship and a hollow banging from the timbers; but the only breathing I could detect in the little cabin was my own, bated and apprehensive. I reached over and pulled aside the curtain to let the light in.

Immediately something began to twinkle in the opposite corner. As the room lit up I saw for the first time a large golden lantern hanging there, on a level with my head. It was the most beautiful object I'd ever laid eyes on. Its flame extinguished, it was revolving slowly with the motion of the ship, firing sparkles of golden light back at me as the daylight struck its intricate surface. I couldn't imagine how any goldsmith could have made this: surely it must have been created, like the sun, by something or someone beyond the scope of our knowledge. It was breathtaking, magnificent, a dense basket of fine, glinting, crisscrossed lacework, made entirely of gold, sending its bright reflections over the furniture and walls of the little cabin. For a moment I stood spellbound, hypnotized by its beauty. A jeweled globe; a ball of bright tears.

So this was the kind of object Coben and Jiggs had been trying to steal! If they'd escaped with anything half as precious as this, they'd be rich men. It was also clear that, with something like this just hanging here for the taking, the place wasn't going to remain unguarded for long. I'd better not linger.

I glanced around me. There were a few pieces of furniture in here: a couple of ancient chairs covered in worn red leather, and in the center of the room a map table with several charts laid out upon it. Their lines and figures meant little to me as I lifted their corners. But there were also two drawers beneath the table, and, pulling them open, I found a pistol, a small jeweled snuffbox, and a number of documents. With trembling hands I picked up the sheaf of papers and began to shuffle through them. Many of them were very grand-looking, with big elaborate seals in blood-red wax; but as far as I could see they weren't very interesting. I was about to put them back when a word boldly written near the bottom of one of the sheets caught my eye.

DAMYATA.

Something about it made the hairs stand up on the back of my neck. Here it was again. The word which wasn't a word. Was it somebody's name? One of the other documents held a long list of names, and was headed "Licensed Traders under His Majesty's United Company of Merchants of England Trading to the East Indies." Beside each name was a date, and a sum of money mentioned. The writing was florid and difficult to decipher; but as far as I could make out, none of the names meant anything to me. I wondered whether I ought to take this list with me; but something about their official appearance and their grand seals persuaded me that, if I got caught with papers stolen from here, I might find myself in real trouble. As I slid them back into the drawer I caught sight of an inscription in gold leaf on the lid of the snuffbox, in the same strange characters I'd seen in the note among Coben and Jiggs's papers. It looked like writing, except that the letters seemed to hang down from the line instead of sitting above it.

I didn't have time to take it in properly though, because I suddenly heard a sound from above my head. A regular *thud . . . thud . . . thud . . .* Someone was walking across the deck, and the footsteps were moving with some determination towards the forecastle and the ladder I'd just come down.

Panic welled up through me. The forecastle door swung open and the footsteps began clomping down the steps towards me. My innards felt like a column of hot lead, from my groin up to my throat. I was going to be discovered! Diving for the bunk, I rolled behind the curtain just as the cabin door clicked open and the heavy footsteps came in.

I could hear a man breathing heavily, almost grunting. I didn't dare to move, or breathe myself, simply hoping that whoever it was would go away. He was standing just a couple of feet away from my head, his boots creaking on the floor. My lungs began to crave air as I held my breath, terrified, trapped. I was going to die.

Long seconds went by. They might have been hours. I was frozen, my eyes closed, my brain intoning "Go away! Oh, go away!" as the heavy breathing continued on the other side of the curtain. Still he stood there, listening.

And then suddenly his boots creaked again and I almost breathed a sigh of relief as I supposed he was leaving the cabin. But he wasn't. In a flash the curtain of my hiding place was pulled aside and I was staring up at a giant sailor with a face like a beam-end. I was too shocked to scream: I simply looked at him, as though if I said nothing he might close the curtain and go away and I might wake up and find all this had been the most hideous nightmare of my vivid young life. For what seemed like ages, nothing happened.

Then, a frenzy of movement. With a convulsion like a man in a fit, he launched his meaty arms forward and yanked me with practiced violence out of the bunk and onto the wooden floor. Then, equally roughly, he yanked me to my feet, so that I thought he'd bring my arms clean out of their sockets. I looked up at him. A smile spread across his flat, weathered face and all the way down his powerful arms, tightening the grip of his hands on my fragile shoulders. He showed me a long, ragged skyline of widely spaced yellow teeth.

"Caught in the hact," he said, savoring every word and grinning horribly into my terrified face. "A thief about to make off with the Sun o' Calcutta — and I caughtim! I caughtim in the hact and strangled 'im dead before 'e could say a word! Well done sailor! Extra rations for you, sailor!" His grip tightened still further. I had gone completely numb with terror: it was as though the rigor of death had seized me in anticipation, before I was even killed.

"I'm not a thief," I heard my voice saying, weakly.

"Oh no? Caught in the hact in the captain's cabin and not a thief?" With every noun his grip came closer and closer to throttling me and before long all I could see was the blood crawling in blotches across my eyes, and all I could hear was the gurgling of my own breath.

But he must have changed his mind at the last moment because I was suddenly drawing gasping breaths again, realizing he'd released his grip on me.

"Hexplain yerself," he was saying, as the cotton wool cloud around my head seemed gradually to disperse. "What was you doin' in 'ere?"

I coughed a couple of times, gathering myself, trying

desperately to think of an answer. As I looked into his big flat face he was still grimacing, but I thought I detected a flicker of alarm behind his eyes, as though he'd found himself suddenly unable to cope with the act of killing me.

"I wants to see the captain," I said, putting on my best urchin-boy voice. "I come lookin' for 'im."

"You come lookin' for *somethin'* all right," the sailor replied, grimly. "I seen you sneakin' onboard. Up in the riggin', I was, watchin'. Never thought to look up, didja? Never thought you was bein' watched from above!" He was grinning triumphantly and I suddenly panicked again, convinced he was still going to kill me.

"I told you, it's the captain I wants," I said. I'd seen his name on his documents: what was it, oh what was it? "The captain, captain . . . Captain Shakeshere," I said, in sudden relief. The sailor was still looking suspicious; but I could see his hostility abating as his brain worked to fathom how I knew the captain's name.

"Oo sentcha?" he asked.

I had a sudden flash of inspiration. Yesterday I'd been mistaken, in my tarry clothes, for a bosun's boy. Well, in that case, I might have a perfect reason to be onboard. "The bosun," I said. "I've a message for Captain Shakeshere from his bosun." Something in the giant face told me I was onto a lifesaver. "I was told 'e might be aboard. Important message, I got." My nerve was starting to come back. "And the cap'n might not like it," I continued, "if his bosun's lad got strangled before 'e delivered his message. And my Pa might not like it," I said, "if I was brought back to 'im dead." I knew enough about life at sea to be sure that the average sailor preferred to stay on the right side of the bosun; and the consequences of harming the bosun's lad were clearly starting to filter through even to this dim-witted brain. I saw him swallow. "And 'Is Majesty's Company of Merchants Trading to the East Indies might not like it," I said grandly, rather enjoying myself now, "if their business was to get neglected 'cos of a strangled messenger."

He was obviously flustered. "Well," he said, crestfallen, "I ain't to know that when I sees you sneakin' onboard, am I? You might've bin any old common panneyboy come to see what you could get yer 'ands on. Anyway," he continued, "the cap'n ain't 'ere. 'e's at the three friends."

I opened my eyes wide. *"Where?"*

"At the three friends. The Three Friends Inn." He pointed vaguely toward the dockside buildings, and before he had time to say another word I'd ducked past him and was scrambling back down the ladder to the welcoming bark of my dog, still sitting up in the bobbing rowing boat as the morning sunshine glinted on the water.

◈

We found the Three Friends without much difficulty, on a steep little lane opposite a cracked old church with a high, blackened spire. It was a tall, narrow house with a pointed roof, embedded in the grime of the city, the glass in its windows opaque with scratches, the stone discolored by long streaks of filth and damp. It proclaimed its function with an inn sign the shape of a gravestone, which hung from an old iron frame as a man hangs from a gallows, swinging gently every now and then and giving a faint creak. Nevertheless most sailors laughed when they clapped eyes on it, because of the cracked painting of three naked women which adorned it. Not only this, they laughed because they knew it meant a chance to drink as much beer, rum, and other intoxicants as their paltry pay would afford them.

I tied Lash's lead to an iron post outside and ventured in. It wasn't long after breakfast time, but I found the taproom heavy with yellow smoke and several figures discernible through it, sitting eating or drinking ale or puffing at pipes, silent, or else engaged in low conversation which was temporarily halted as they turned to look at me. Instantly reminded, by the thick air, of Flethick's strange little smoking den,

I tried to greet the staring sailors as cheerfully as I could. But my heart sank in dismay with the realization that the captain I wanted to speak to was probably one of these tight-lipped, wary gentlemen.

Still the object of the customers' collective stare, and beginning to feel very uncomfortable, I made my way across to the shadowy little hatch where I could dimly see a face peering at me behind the beer taps. As I got closer I saw it was an old woman with a noticeable mustache. Her face looked as if it had been taken off, screwed up like an old piece of paper, then unfolded and stuck back on again. She was so ugly that, if it had been me, I'd probably have thrown the piece of paper in the nearest fire instead of sticking it back.

"Fine mornin'," she croaked at me suddenly. At first I thought she'd burped.

"Oh — er — yes," I said. "I'm looking for Captain Shakeshere. Is he here?"

"Can you see him?" came the cracked reply.

"Well — I don't know him," I said in a low voice, "but I want to talk to him if he's here. Please."

"Might be here," the old woman said; and I stood waiting for her to call him. But she just stood there. Was that all she was going to say?

"Well, er — how can I find him?" I asked.

The woman was still just standing there motionless,

behind the bar. Was she thinking? Or had she perhaps died, without falling over? Suddenly I noticed a tear trickling down her cheek, slowly following the channel of her deepest wrinkles.

"What's the matter?" I asked her.

Her reply, like the creaking of an old door, came slowly. "Such a lovely boy," she said, and the drops continued to well in her wrinkly eyes and dribble down her crumpled face. "Such a lovely boy."

"Thank you," I said uncomfortably, and edged away, realizing she was going to be no help at all. I wondered if I should ask one of the sailors. I'd ceased, at least, to be the center of attention, most of the clientele having gone back to their beer or their furtive conversations.

"'Scuse me," I said to the nearest sailor, and he turned to look at me. "What's the matter with her? With the lady there?"

"Meg?" he said gruffly, looking across at her. "She's old. And she wishes she was young. That's all."

"Does she often cry?" I asked.

"Depends," he said. "See, I don't s'pose she often sees young folks like you in 'ere. You've reminded her how old she is. That's all."

"How old *is* she?" I ventured to ask.

"Oh, I don't know. Least a hundred years, I s'pose, that's all."

I felt like going up to the woman again and apologizing for being only twelve, and vowing that I'd be a hundred too if only it lay in my power to be. "Do you know Cap'n Shakeshere?" I asked the man.

"In the corner," he told me: and as I looked towards the corner of the room by the window I could make out a thin man in a frock coat sitting alone: a man so thin, indeed, that he looked like a set of pipe cleaners wrapped in specially tailored clothes.

"Not that corner," said the sailor, "the other. Over there." And he moved his head to indicate the group of four men on the other side of the window nook, who were arguing in low voices and seemed quite agitated. The one with his back to me was the tallest of the four, and there was something masterly in his demeanor.

"The nearest man? The tall one?" I asked.

The sailor I'd been talking to was getting to his feet. "That's him," he said. "Now, I've got to be going, that's all." I thanked him and watched him stride, a little unsteadily, out of the smoky room and into the daylight. Suddenly I wished I was going with him.

Instead I stood debating what I should say to the captain. Should I tell him I'd seen men making off with goods from his ship the other day? Should I ask him if he knew anyone called Damyata? Should I ask him if he knew Coben and Jiggs?

The foursome suddenly erupted. One of the men had attacked another. As they leapt to their feet and beer spilled everywhere, I saw that they'd been playing cards. Perhaps one had been cheating, and that was why he was currently being throttled by another, while the other two tried to pull them apart. I'd chosen a bad time to approach the captain, I decided. The brawl was quickly over though, everyone sat down, and the combatants were soon glaring at one another with cards in their hands again. None of them seemed to notice me as I stood nervously by the table.

"Cap'n Shakeshere?" I asked, trying to sound offhand.

The tall man turned in his chair and I found myself looking up his nose. He had a high narrow nose which seemed to stretch up far between his eyebrows before it finally stopped, and a long face, made even longer by his high collar and straight back. He was so upright he might have been hewn from his own mast. He didn't seem impressed as he looked me up and down.

"What is it, boy?" he asked, rather impatiently, turning back to the card game.

"Have you got a moment, sir?" I said, speaking

rather fast, "only I've found out a couple of things I thought you should know, sir, about people — taking precious things off the *Sun of Calcutta*. Thieves, sir, I s'pose I mean. Yesterday I —"

He had turned to look at me again, with a rather haughty face which seemed to resent my interrupting his game.

"Who sent you?" he asked. "How do you know me, boy?"

"Please, sir, I've been asking after you," I said, nervously taking my hands in and out of my pockets; "I saw thieves, sir, making off with a precious chest from the ship, sir. I followed them, and —"

"Really, boy," he said, "I've no time for your pestering. Go and see the Customs men, or go and worry my bosun about it. What do I care about thieves, here in London where they're on every street corner?" He turned back to the game, and for the first time I noticed that the cards the men were playing with weren't ordinary cards, but were strangely marked with shapes and symbols, like the foreign letters on the snuffbox and in the note I'd taken from Coben and Jiggs.

"Where can I find the bosun, sir?" I asked, feeling that even if he told me I'd really rather not find him.

"What?" the captain bellowed.

"Where can I find —"

"Yes I heard you! I don't keep tabs on my crewmen so as to know where they choose to live in this pigsty of a city. Be off and let me concentrate!"

And that was the last I got out of him. I could always try the Galleon, I told myself, remembering how I'd been accosted there by the sailor who claimed the bosun was after my hide. But then I noticed the man in the frock coat with the pipe-cleaner limbs in the opposite corner, watching me intently, and smiling, as though he knew who I was. Another idiot, or drunkard, I thought as I watched his eyebrows rising and falling. But I decided to have a word with him.

"Do you happen to know," I said, "where I can find the bosun of the *Sun of Calcutta*?"

The pipecleaner man spoke very quietly and very hesitantly, his lower jaw quivering slightly as he tried to get the words out. All the time his eyebrows were moving animatedly, as though trying to supply by a kind of semaphore the information his voice couldn't put across. I waited patiently through the long silent gaps in his sentences.

"B-bosun often . . . Galleon," he said breathily. "Mm-mm . . . but he lives . . . ss-sign of . . . Lion's Mane."

"Thank you," I said, and was about to get up to

leave when he grasped my arm.

"B-be c-c-careful," he gasped, with a little visible explosion of spittle droplets which shone in the sunlight and died as they fell, like shooting stars. "D-don't mm-meddle . . . bosun's affairs. He's d-dangerous. "G-g-got d-dangerous ff-friends." There was a furrow of earnestness above his jolting eyebrows which convinced me he was serious. "Want m-my advice, k-k-keep out of it!"

"Have you ever heard of —" I began, but he was putting his finger to his lips and his eyebrows were bouncing up and down alarmingly. I turned and saw one of the Captain's companions staring darkly across at us.

As I left, nodding my thanks to the stuttering man, I passed the cardplayers again and noticed one of the strange cards poking out from under the captain's backside, at the edge of his chair.

"Excuse me," I said, "excuse me, sir, but I think you've mislaid a card. It's here, on your seat."

The captain was staring at me as if he couldn't believe his eyes. The other cardplayers were stiffening with anger and staring at him. His long face began to redden and a gap opened to display a clenched set of teeth, including a couple of gold ones. Realizing what I'd done, as his eyes bulged further and further outward, I was off through the door, leaving the foursome staring at a couple of overturned tables and a roomful of heavy smoke, before any of them had a chance to rise from their chairs.

5

THE BOSUN'S BOY

I had never heard of the Lion's Mane Inn before, and as I walked home I stopped a few people to ask if they could tell me where it was. I felt somehow drawn to this mysterious bosun; but at the same time I was afraid of him. I couldn't help remembering the words of the laughing man at Flethick's, about gizzards — and then there was the earnest advice of the pipe-cleaner man, warning me to keep out of it. But as I thought about it, I realized I couldn't be sure whether he'd said that out of genuine concern for me, or because he was an accomplice of the bosun's and didn't want me poking my nose in.

It had turned into another roasting hot day and some boys were playing round a pump, splashing one another and jumping in and out of the spurting water. I was tired after my morning's adventures, and the cold water looked very tempting. As I watched the boys my throat felt drier and drier. One of them saw me watching and shouted.

"Come and get wet."

Shyly, I joined them and stood under the pump while the boy who'd shouted leaned on the handle and made it belch a great cascade of water over my head. It was cool, and a bit smelly, and I shook the water out of my eyes, delighted. Lash ran round the pump, trying to get wet, veering in and out of the splashing water and barking with enjoyment.

There was a big tub underneath the pump, brim-full of water, where people used to take their horses to drink. One of the boys suddenly pulled off all his clothes and jumped into the tub, sending water welling up over the sides and all over the ground. The other boys laughed raucously and ran around him, their feet getting black as the ground around the pump turned to mud. Caught up in the game, I ran too, dodging the squirting of the water pump. The boy was still sitting in the tub and another of the boys was trying to push his head under the water. There were squeals. Two of the other boys pulled off their clothes and tried to haul the first boy out so they could have a turn at sitting in the tub. As I ran round and round the pump, with Lash barking and jumping beside me, I became aware that I was the only one still wearing my clothes.

"Come on," said one of them, "you come in too."

I stopped, and watched them grappling and

laughing on the edge, skinny and naked, their bodies slippery with the water.

"No," I said, suddenly, "I'd better go."

"Aw, come on," he said, and began tugging at my sleeve. "Not scared of getting wet, are you?"

"No, I —" I couldn't explain myself. One of the other boys stood up, dripping, and I was suddenly really scared that they were going to grab me and tear my clothes off for a prank. "No. Let me go," I said, pulling away.

The first boy stared at me, hostile all of a sudden. "Suit yourself," he said.

I wrapped Lash's lead tightly round my wrist. "I've got to find the Lion's Mane Inn," I said uncomfortably. "Do you know where it is?"

The boy pointed; and gave me a lingering and suspicious stare as I thanked him and walked off, my wet clothes clinging to me, and Lash licking at my wet fingers as we went.

Even after this it took me a while to find the place. The inn nestled in the warren of streets around Christ's Hospital, between a workhouse and a rather shabby group of broken stables, whose smell convinced me they were still home to living creatures. Peering in, I saw two rather shabby and broken horses, one of whom was coughing alarmingly; and after a few seconds I noticed, with a slight shock, that there was a person in the stable too, sitting on an old box in the corner. It was a grey-haired, filthy old man, slumped in an apparent sleep, looking like a disembodied head on top of a shapeless pile of grey clothing — in fact, he was wrapped in a horse's blanket. I didn't dare investigate in case he turned out to be dead.

There seemed to be no one about in the little courtyard of brick buildings adjoining the inn. I could hear a drain trickling, and as I crept round a corner I saw a filthy stream of water dribbling from a pipe in the wall, leaving a spreading patch of brown slime over the brickwork all the way to the ground. A flight of stone steps led up to a door halfway up the house side. This irregular, badly whitewashed yard must be where the fearsome bosun lived.

I decided I'd rather not knock on any doors. Holding tight to Lash's lead, I peered through the nearest grimy window and could see nothing. The place looked deserted; except that there was a washing-line stretched over an upper balcony, with a gentleman's breeches and two huge pairs of bloomers hanging on it.

There was a grille in the ground nearby, and as I squatted down to squint through it I could see another grimy little window beneath it, as opaque and unhelpful as the other. I was about to give up, and make my way home, when I thought I saw a face peeping out behind the grille at my feet.

I crouched on all fours now, like a beetle, and peered down. The window creaked noisily open, and Lash started backward, making the snuffling noise he often did when he was surprised by something.

A boy's face appeared, with short untidy hair a bit like a bird's nest on his head.

"Who you looking for?" he said.

"Oh — er — no one," I replied, rather stupidly.

"Why get on your knees to look down the cellar then?" he asked suspiciously. "Lost something?"

I cast a wary glance into the yard behind me. "Do you know a bosun?" I asked.

"My Pa," said the boy. "He ain't here. Who wants him?"

"It's not that I *want* him," I said. How much ought I to tell this boy?

"You off the *Sun of Calcutta?*" he asked, evidently believing like everyone else that I was some sort of sailor boy. "What you come here for?" He was starting to be hostile. "What's your name?"

"Mog," I told him. "Where is your Pa?"

"Search me. Don't know how long he'll be, neither. All day and all night. Three months. Five minutes. Probably getting drunk at some tavern. And you're lucky Ma Muggerage ain't here neither, or she'd have your hide for a wash-leather by now, crawling round here." It was only now that he noticed Lash, who came nosing forward to try and stick his nose in between the bars of the grating. The boy grinned, and I suddenly saw something in his big eyes I thought I recognized.

"Can you come out?" I asked him.

His eyes lit up. "No — but you can *help* me out. See that pink door there? There's no lock on it. You'll find a big heavy barrel in the scullery there. Shift that, and there's a trapdoor I can get out of."

I got up off my knees and led Lash over to the scullery door. It opened easily, shedding flakes of old pink paint as it swung open. A bare little room with a stone floor met my eye, cobwebs dangling like flags from the ceiling. There was no furniture except for a large empty washtub and a big keg standing against one wall.

With difficulty, I pushed the keg aside, an inch at a time, until a small square wooden trapdoor was completely uncovered. As I bent to knock on it, it opened upward towards me, making Lash sneeze again with gruff surprise.

"Someone keeping you prisoner in here?" I asked the boy, panting from the effort of moving the barrel.

"Not far off," the boy grumbled, climbing out. He was dressed in clothes very much like mine. Indeed, as he stood up in the little scullery I suddenly saw that he was similar to me in several ways, and some of the events of the past couple of days started to make more sense. "Good thing you came by," the bosun's boy said, grinning with gratitude. "Sorry, what did you say your name was?"

"Mog," I said, "and this is Lash." The boy reached out a hand and Lash's damp nose met it, pulling back in disappointment when he found there was nothing to eat in it. The boy laughed. For the first time he looked at me properly.

"Your clothes are all wet," he said.

"Sorry," I said, "I, er — was playing in a pump."

"Sounds fun," the boy said, "it's so hot. It's been awful down in that cellar these last few days. But my Pa, and Ma Muggerage, reckon I should be kept out of mischief. I reckon the pair of *them* ought to be locked up in there. They cause more mischief than anyone else in London."

"They didn't mean you to get out easily," I said. And then: "What *sort* of mischief?"

"Not sure I know, exactly," the boy said, "they don't tell me nothing. But they're both in it. People come to see 'em in the middle of the night. They go off at all hours, chasing people, carrying things, bringing money home. People leave notes. I see bits and pieces, but never the full story. Know what Pa brought home the other day? A camel."

I stared at him.

"I think," I said, "there's a story I ought to tell you."

His name was Nick ("Dominic, by rights, they say, but no one ever called me that before"), and he was the bosun's son. His mother had died when he was very young, and he had been placed in the care of a formidable woman called Mrs. Muggerage, whom he hated, and who quite evidently hated him back. He'd seen his father rarely, since he was most often away at sea, coming home between voyages to pay Mrs. Muggerage for looking after his house. At one time Mrs. Muggerage used to pretend she treated Nick like a king; but when it became clear the bosun didn't care how she treated him, she dropped the pretense.

"She's always knocked me about," he said, "treats me like a dog. Worse," he added, scratching Lash under the chin. "It's twice as bad just now, 'cos my Pa's home, and they both hit me as hard as the other. At least when Pa's away there's only her to look out for." He'd been forced, for most of his life, to live by his wits, and he freely admitted he'd become a habitual thief. His father had taken him to sea a few times, and in foreign cities he'd seen people with fabulous wealth, animals he'd never heard of before or since, and women more beautiful than he'd ever imagined. But the violence and harshness of the sailor's life frightened him, and he hated the storms and the poor food; and his father's embarrassment at his son's lack of aptitude for life at sea had quickly turned to contempt. "He says I'm soft," he grumbled, "he's always saying I'm soft, whatever I do. He hates me for it, Mog, really hates me. But onboard ship, they do things — well, they do things you'd never believe if I was to tell you." He was supposed to accompany his father on the voyage from which the *Sun of Calcutta* had just returned: but less than an hour before she set sail he'd sneaked ashore and hidden until he was quite sure she'd gone. Now that his father had returned he was paying the price. "Most sailors would get flogged and left for dead for that kind of thing," he said, "so I s'pose I'm lucky to get away with being locked up in a cellar."

"You've *got* a Pa, at least," I said to him. "I've got no parents or family at all, that I know of."

"Reckon I might be better off without, sometimes," he said in a low voice.

In practice, it turned out he was able to slip away from the bosun and from Ma Muggerage regularly, and for long periods, without their worrying too much about where he was. He knew the streets of London as if they were part of his body; and it wasn't just their layout he knew, but their different characters, which were dangerous and which were safe, who lived in them, whose favor to court and whom to avoid, how to get from one place to another in the quickest possible time, and how to disappear completely. His best friend was a dwarf in Aldgate who'd taught him to read. "I didn't used to see much point in it," he said, "I used to think, if you want to know something, why not just ask someone who knows? Whatever someone can write down, they might as well tell you out loud. But I changed my mind. Believe it, Mog, I learn more things off books and papers now than ever anybody tells me," he said. "Folks think I can't read, see? So they leave things lying about. It's my best secret."

"I can't remember learning to read," I said, "I just — always could, I suppose. I must have learned while I was in the orphanage. But I can't say I know who taught me."

"You too!" he enthused. "Well, you know what it's like then. Easier to find things out, easier to fool people and lead 'em astray. Know what I do? Sometimes I write notes for my Pa to find, making out they come from someone else! I can find out gentlemen's business just by picking their pockets. Oh, I know things I'd never know in a million years if I couldn't read." When I told him I worked in a printer's shop, his eyes grew wide with envy. "Imagine!" he said, "posters and newspapers and announcements! You must know more of what's going on than any kid in London!"

His eagerness to listen spurred me on. I told him

about the men at Flethick's, and about the man with the mustache, and about Coben and Jiggs and how I'd come by the wound on my head, and about the chest and the great knife and the *Sun of Calcutta* and the golden lantern and the man with the stammer . . . and all the time Nick's eyes grew bigger and bigger until they'd almost pushed everything else off his face.

"What a detective you are!" he said admiringly. I laughed. "But listen," he said, urgently, "the camel all those people are after is still here. In this house!"

"Where?" I asked, "in the stable?"

Nick pretended to laugh. "Very funny," he said. Then he saw I hadn't got the point. "It's not a *real* camel," he explained. "Look, come with me. I'll show it to you."

There was a door from the scullery, leading up a flight of stairs into the house. "Who's that man in the stable?" it suddenly occurred to me to ask, as Nick led me through the untidy rooms.

"What man?"

"There's an old creature asleep under a horse blanket in there."

"Can't say. 'S not our stable, that. Might be a drunk," Nick said. "Now then — this is the room he's got it hidden in, I bet." We were standing among a pile of odds and ends so extraordinary it made a rag and bone shop look tidy. Old clocks, bits of cloth, pieces of wood, ropes, brass trinkets, pewter mugs, odd shoes, rolled-up rugs, tins, candles, a wooden leg, hats, bird-cages, and meat forks were just some of the things I could see stuffed into tea chests and spilling out over the floor and the window seat. Lash went nosing and clattering among it all, his tail flapping with absorption.

"All looks pretty useless to me," I said, surveying the piled-up junk.

"Probably," Nick said, "but that's what folks are *meant* to think — know what I mean? It's a good place to hide real valuable stuff, under all this junk." He began pulling blankets out of a nearby chest. "For instance," he said, "look what's here."

He'd found it. An ornament in the shape of a camel — a foot high, no more — with a single hump and a long neck arching outwards at the front, and a rather dazed expression on its face, as though it had just been clouted over the head with a frying pan. It was made of brass, and was designed so that it could stand on its four legs. Bits of it had turned a crusty green.

"*That's* the camel?" I said, disappointed.

"Yes, but there must be something valuable about it 'cos he was pleased as punch when he brought it home," Nick replied. "I heard him talking to Ma

Muggerage and he was laughing fit to burst, as though he'd got the Crown Jewels."

"I think," I said, "Coben and Jiggs expected this to be in the chest they stole. They kept saying the bosun had it, and asking me where it was." I turned it over in my hands. "Are you *sure* this is the right one? This couldn't be a false one, to throw people off the scent?"

"That's the one he was gloating over," Nick said, "I saw it with my own eyes. And shall I tell you something else? He's got customers who are interested in this. He told Ma Muggerage he was meeting some men at the Three Friends to arrange a little deal."

"When?" I asked eagerly.

"Dunno. Maybe now. But more likely at night. That's when all their shady stuff goes on, far as I can —" He stopped, and his brow furrowed. "I'm not so sure I should be telling you all this," he said. "How come you're so interested anyway?"

I shrugged. "I don't know," I said, truthfully.

"You seem to know plenty about thieves, for an honest lad. You're quite excited about it all, aren't you?"

I had to confess I was.

"Well, you shouldn't be," he said. "If you take my advice you'll stay out of it, and then you'll still be an honest lad when all these characters are locked up or dead. Look at this." He reached into his pocket for something — a crumpled piece of paper. He handed it to me, and I unfolded it curiously.

Dont think You Can tred on ur patch.
You migt hav less frends than you think. Eys ar watchin you evry niht.

Eys ar watchin you now.

"This came last night," Nick said, "pinned to the window frame, it was. There's men after his blood for taking this." He lifted the camel, and it stared stupidly at me.

"He wrote a note to Coben and Jiggs," I remembered, "and drew a big eye on it to warn them. Seems everybody's watching everybody else."

Suddenly there was a clatter from downstairs.

"Oh no! Someone's come back!" Nick flung the camel into the chest and grabbed my arm. "Run," he said, "get lost, or we'll both be killed."

"Lash!" I hissed, and his startled head popped up from behind a chair. "Come here boy!"

But feet were already stomping up the stairs. "NICK!" came a bellowing woman's voice.

"It's too late," I said, looking around in a panic, "We'll have to hide."

"NICK!" As the door burst open I dived behind it out of sight, and Lash skidded to a halt by my side, leaving poor Nick standing in the middle of the room with his hands in his pockets.

"Who let you out?" the woman screamed, and as she advanced into the room I saw that she was huge, her bulk wobbling like a badly stacked haycart. Her arms were bare, and as she moved them angrily they reminded me of hams swinging in a butcher's window. In one of her fists, I suddenly saw, she was holding a big square meat cleaver. Anyone who got in the way of that wouldn't stand a polecat's chance. I saw Nick glance towards me, and he moved his head slightly to tell me to be gone.

"What are you twitching at?" the woman bawled at him. She moved forward with her arm flexed as though to clout him, and Lash responded with a sudden growl which made her stop in her tracks.

"What was that?" she screeched. "Is there a dog in 'ere?"

I wasn't going to let Lash anywhere near the meat cleaver, with which the fearsome woman could have split his head in two with a single stroke. The only thing for it was to run; and, dragging Lash by the lead, I slipped between the door and Mrs. Muggerage's back and launched us both headlong down the stairs. Too late, she wheeled around and saw us half-running, half-falling towards the scullery.

"OY!" she roared, so loudly that the whole house seemed to vibrate. Tripping over one another in a tangle of arms and legs at the bottom of the stairs, Lash and I struggled to run as Mrs. Muggerage's footsteps began clomping down the steps after us. Lash's lead was caught around my ankle and I yanked it in a panic, making Lash yelp as the rope snagged and bit into his neck as he tried to right himself. After what seemed like a lifetime, we finally scrambled onto our six feet and ran; and as we did so, the meat cleaver whizzed past my ear, missing me by no more than an inch.

❖

Cramplock was busy in the printing shop when we came in, but that didn't stop him eyeing me severely over his half-moon glasses. Guiltily, as though it were all his fault, Lash slunk up the stairs to his basket — leaving me to face the music.

"*Now* you crawl in, Mog Winter," Cramplock said reproachfully, "where do you suppose you've been for the best part of the day?"

"Sorry, Mr. Cramplock," I said, "I had meant to come back sooner, only —" What was the use of explaining where I'd been? "I was feeling a bit ill," I mumbled, making a show of holding my bandaged head, but knowing it was a poor and transparent excuse.

"Not too ill to gallivant round the city with your dog," he responded sharply. "If you weren't feeling well you could have stayed upstairs and got some rest. I might have been able to spare you, if you'd asked." He was speaking quietly, but it was obvious he was furious. "I just expect to be told if you can't work, Mog," he pointed out. "It's not unreasonable." I didn't say anything. He was quite right, and my cheeks burned with embarrassment at his scolding. I went over to the bench where some blocks of type were waiting to be dismantled. I'd become good at reading the type before it was printed, even though it was back to front and all the letters were the wrong way round. I could see the blocks had been used for an advertisement.

"Been doing advertisements?" I asked. I was trying to sound bright, but there was a lump of shame in my throat as big as a plum.

"Yes, Mog, seeing as you weren't here to do them,"

Cramplock replied sourly. "Fifty for the chemist."

I picked up a sheet of paper to lay over the inky type, and lifted it off. It had printed a little square advertisement with a picture of a medicine bottle, and the proud announcement:

We'd printed this advertisement many times before. I'd always wondered what "recalcitrance" meant: I had a suspicion it was just a long word for wind.

"Stop wasting time, now that you're here, and

take those forms apart," Cramplock was telling me, "I've an important job coming in this afternoon and I'll need the type." I set to work quietly, knowing I'd be in real trouble today if I stretched his patience any further. I began the slow, messy job of taking each tiny little metal letter and throwing it back into the right compartment of the type case. It was sometimes difficult to tell the letters apart, and if I got them mixed up I used to get shouted at, or worse. Capitals weren't so bad — but with the lowercase letters, because you had to remember that they were back to front, it was often hard to get "d" and "b" and "p" and "q" in the right boxes if you weren't concentrating. I once printed a whole five hundred playbills in which the name of a celebrated actor called Mr. Thomas Tibble came out as "Mr. Thomas Tiddle," and I hadn't noticed until they were all done. Cramplock wasn't normally a violent man, but I thought he was going to knock my brains out of my ears that day.

"When you've done that," Cramplock said, "you can pull a hundred of these."

He'd set up the type for another elaborate poster; and after he'd disappeared into the back room to do some accounts I went over to have a look. Even without taking a copy I could make out what it said. It had type of several different sizes, and an engraving which seemed to be of some sort of animal.

The engraving was of an absurd-looking creature with two large ears, and a person standing next to it holding up his hands in what was meant to be astonishment.

Laughing, I reached for some scrap sheets of paper to make a couple of test copies, to make sure the poster was properly laid out.

"Do you suppose this ass really *can* tell fortunes, Mr. Cramplock?" I ventured to ask, pulling out one of the tests and examining it.

Cramplock grunted. "Not if Hardwicke's got anything to do with it," he said. "Biggest swindler in London. The poor fools who flock to see it will probably find it's an ass standing in front of a curtain, with his wife hiding behind the curtain shouting out."

I printed off five or six more and looked them up and down with admiration.

"Did you give my bill to Flethick?" Cramplock suddenly asked.

I froze.

"Ah, Yes," I said.

"Good. That's all right then. He owes me plenty, and it's high time he settled his account. The number of things —"

"But," I butted in, "he didn't give much impression that he'd pay."

Cramplock looked at me intently and rubbed his cheekbone. "Why? What did he say?"

"He, er — he told me to tell you he wanted no bill, Mr. Cramplock," I said, my face going bright red with embarrassment again, "and he, ah — burnt it up."

The little man's eyes nearly fell out of his head, and would have done if his glasses hadn't stopped them. "He *what?*"

"Erm — burnt it up," I said, starting to wish I'd never told him. He still showed no sign of understanding. "Burnt it," I repeated helpfully, trying to smile. "Up."

Cramplock made a noise like a chicken. "But — but — but — why did you let him?"

"I didn't have much choice," I said. "He's not a nice man, Mr. Cramplock. There were lots of his friends there. He was behaving very strangely."

"He'll behave more strangely when I get my hands on him," squawked Cramplock. "Burning my bills! Who does he think he is?" He wasn't just cross now, he was enraged. He pushed me out of the way of the press and started printing the rest of the posters himself, working the machinery furiously and almost throwing the ink at the roller. For the next ten minutes he carried on muttering to himself, occasionally slamming things down on the table. I sat picking at the type in the cases, not daring to say any more.

After a while he addressed me again. "By the way," he said, "that poster you did." He still sounded annoyed.

"The convict?" I said, wondering what was wrong.

"Yes, the convict. A man from the jail came to see me yesterday. It seems you made a bit of a mistake with the picture."

A horrible dread crept over me. "What mistake?" I asked, quietly.

"You printed the wrong face," Cramplock said, irritably. "The wrong engraving. That wasn't the fellow at all. That was some other convict from months back."

So Bob Smitchin had been right. But I felt sure that was the engraving Cramplock himself had given me to print — so it was his mistake, not mine, though I couldn't possibly say that to him in his present mood.

"Made me feel quite a fool, the fellow did," Cramplock was continuing. "How can you expect to catch a criminal when you put out a poster with somebody else's face on? He must be laughing like a jackass, wherever he is." He flung an inky old rag at me. "And more to the point, the jail won't pay!" he shouted, getting more and more angry. "Because we got it wrong! Call yourself a prentice? Well, if I get no money for the posters you get no wages this week, and that's that."

"But —" I said.

"Don't give me any sob stories, Mog Winter. First you disappear for nearly a whole working day without any explanation. Then I trust you to run a simple errand and you come back from Flethick's with nothing but a pathetic tale about how he burnt his bill — fact is you probably lost the bill before you even got there. Don't argue, Mog! And then to cap it all you print a hundred pictures which are meant to be a man called Coben only the face ain't a man called Coben, it's some other fellow who was hanged months ago. It's no good you looking like that, Mog; whether you've been sick or not you won't get any sympathy today."

I must have gone as white as a sheet. I felt as though a knife had hit me in the back.

"Did you say C-Coben?" I stuttered. "What on earth makes you say Coben?"

"Because that was the name of the escaped convict, as you well know," Cramplock said.

"His name was *Cockburn*," I protested.

Cramplock wheeled. "Don't you know *any*thing, Mog Winter? It's pronounced Coben. It might look like Cockburn, but you pronounce it Coben, as a rule. So now you know. And you can get that sick look off your face, because I'm not changing my mind about your wages!"

6

CAMEL-HUNTING

The dirty sky was full of pigeons as I left the shop and ran through the streets and lanes. I just *had* to talk to Nick. The afternoon had passed interminably, with Cramplock in a foul mood and my head so full of my recent adventures I couldn't concentrate on the job in hand. Because I'd been late, he'd made me stay behind for hours. But how was I supposed to concentrate at a time like this?

At last he'd let me go, with very little daylight left, and within minutes I was tiptoeing into the forlorn little yard at Lion's Mane Court, keeping a beady eye open for observers. I had deliberately left Lash behind tonight. Mrs. Muggerage now knew what he looked like, and following our near-miss with the cleaver the other day she was on the lookout for a boy with a dog. This way, I thought, I'd be less conspicuous. I really didn't fancy running into her, or the bosun for that matter; and I pressed myself against the stable wall pretty rapidly when I heard both their voices floating down from above. Well — floating is the wrong word, really, their voices being more the plummeting sort. When Mrs. Muggerage spoke it was like a man playing a concerto on an anvil.

I peered round the corner and could see them both up there on the balcony. I think the bosun was drunk, because he was laughing uncontrollably and he had nothing on over his vest. For the first time, I sized him up.

He was huge. His skin was grimy, and there was almost no hair on his bulky great head. He was badly shaven, the lower part of his face almost black with short bristles; and black hairs spilled out of the holes in his string vest, as though he were really a gorilla posing as a bosun, and I'd caught him out of costume. I had little doubt, either, that with his great broad arms and unshakable bulk he could have taken on most gorillas in a hand-to-hand fight, and won. With both of them up on the little wooden balcony, I wondered how it remained attached to the house.

"Ha ha ha ha," the bosun was bellowing, "Mrs. Muggerage you'll be the death o' me, ha ha ha ha!"

"With a bit of luck," I murmured to myself, pulling my head back round the corner. Nick had said the gruesome pair usually went out at night — how long might I have to wait before the coast was clear?

"There's hot puddin' 'ere waitin' for ya," came Mrs. Muggerage's voice, "you naughty boy! Come and sink yer teeth into this, it'll keep yer out o' mischief!" And there was more laughing from both of them. I couldn't resist another peep round the corner, and there they were on the balcony, the bosun and Mrs. Muggerage, clasping one another as best they could in an amorous embrace, like a pair of prize bulls with their horns locked.

I shuddered, and decided to lie low in the stable until it grew dark. The horses shifted uneasily as I pushed open the wooden half-door and slipped inside. Usually, when someone came in, I suppose they knew it meant they were about to be ill-treated or put through some punishing job of work.

"Shh . . . it's only me," I whispered, patting their flanks, and the sick one coughed violently in reply. There was no one over in the corner today, just an upturned wooden box where the old tramp had been slumped last time, against an especially damp patch in the stable wall. As I sat down there, I noticed a little knothole in one of the planks of the wall. When I pressed my eye to it, I found I had a perfect view of the door of the house and the balcony, and of the bosun and Mrs. Muggerage still sitting up there, their voices echoing round the yard. Inspecting the wooden plank more closely, I could see that it wasn't a knot in the wood at all, but a hole crudely and quite deliberately cut. So someone *had* been watching! Evidently this was what Coben and Jiggs had meant in their note, when they'd written

Eys ar watchin you now.

Still, it was ideal for me, I reflected. I could keep track of the bulky twosome's every move, without anyone having a clue I was here — so long as whoever was more accustomed to sitting here didn't come back and find me.

I hunted about for any other clues I might find: anything dropped in the hay, or scratched on the planks of the wall. There seemed to be nothing of any significance — until I lifted up the box, beneath which I found a little book lying among the dirty straw. Whoever had sat here had been reading, perhaps to relieve the boredom of keeping watch for hours on end. It was a flimsy little volume, badly sewn together, with about twenty-four pages; the edges of the paper were ragged, and the sheets seemed to be of slightly different sizes, so they didn't quite fit snugly together when the book was closed. If I'd produced such a thing for Mr. Cramplock he'd have given me a thick ear. Holding it up to the light I noticed, every few pages, the same watermark cropping up that I'd seen on the customs document the other evening — a sleeping dog, with its tail curled around to touch its own nose.

It was a poem. Now, I'd come across a fair amount of poetry, because we were quite often printing poems and ballads in the shop; but I'd never seen a poem quite like this one before. It seemed to be a kind of riddle, but try as I might I couldn't make much sense of it.

> *Gilded, like a tigress in the light*
> *Of evening on the Brahmaputra plain,*
> *Whose sudden motion puts the foes to flight*
> *That trespass on the heart of her domain,*
> *I prowl, with an inimical delight*
> *In ruin, and in chaos, and in pain;*
> *I slink, and shift my shape before the night*
> *Makes black and gold and white all once again.*
> *The moment I am seen, I disappear,*
> *And smile at the confusion I can spread;*
> *My power will outlast eternity.*
> *I lift my subtle nose to smell the fear,*
> *And settle down, inhabiting your head,*
> *Confounding your attempts to fathom me.*

This was as much as I'd read before I felt my eyelids

growing heavy and my mind sinking eagerly into a beckoning sleep.

But I had to be on my guard in case the bosun came by, or in case the old tramp came back. I tried to wake myself up, by putting down the book, taking another glance through the peephole, taking a few deep breaths. But try as I might, I still couldn't rid myself of the urge just to close my eyes and drop off, leaning against this stable wall.

And then suddenly a noise from outside made me sit up. Through the peephole I could see the bosun coming down the front steps. The daylight was fading fast and he was just a grey collection of moving patches in the dusk, but it was unmistakeably him; and he was off out somewhere. I saw him stop in the middle of the yard and look purposefully about him, as though trying to detect any unwanted eyes. I half-feared that mine, peeping from the split plank in the stable side, might radiate some sort of visible glow and give me away. But after a few moments' pause, he walked off. I think he'd heard the coughing of the horse, and had stood listening just to make sure it wasn't the coughing of a person.

Although, as far as I knew, Mrs. Muggerage was still in the house, the yard was so still and dark that I decided to take my chance. Perhaps I could attract Nick's attention without disturbing her. But as I tiptoed over to the scullery, where the trapdoor led into the cellar, I could hear a distinct sound of snoring from behind the pink door: a deep, throaty grunting noise, more like a pig than a person. There was no point in trying to get in this way.

I ran across the yard to the grille above the cellar window; but I could neither hear nor see anything down there.

"Nick!" I hissed softly.

Nothing.

"Nick!" I whispered again. "Are you there?"

I didn't dare call any louder. I lifted my head and took a quick look around, in case the bosun should be coming back; but there was no sound.

I took hold of the grille and, almost in desperation, gave it a tug. To my alarm, there was a loud scraping sound as plaster fell from the wall, a brick sprang out, and the whole grille came away in my hands. I closed my eyes in despair. If this hadn't woken Mrs. Mugger-age it would be a miracle! I crouched there, not daring to let go of the grille or lift it further, in case it made more noise.

There was a scratching sound from the cellar and I heard the window creak open beneath me. I froze.

"Who's that?" came a bold voice. It was so positive in the fragile silence I almost ran for my life, until I realized it was Nick.

"Ssshh!" I whispered, "it's me — Mog!"

"Mog! What are you doing here? If Ma Muggerage finds you . . ."

"I've got something to tell you."

"Well you can't get in. You better go."

"Can you get out?"

There was a pause. "Hang on," he said.

Nick was an old hand at slithering through gaps, and the hole I'd made by pulling the old grille loose was just big enough. Within a minute or so he was standing next to me in the darkness, brushing himself off.

"Wait," he whispered. Holding one hand against my ribcage to signal me to stay back, he moved through the dark courtyard, his eyes far more alert to unusual noises or movements than I could have been. Furtively, peering round each dark corner before venturing round it, he led me out through a low passage towards the more lively yard of the Lion's Mane Inn, where there were lights, and people leading horses by the reins, and calling out to one another. He pulled me back suddenly against a damp wall as a small group of men walked past.

"Not your Pa," I said, fearful.

"No — but men who know him well enough. And know me."

I could see Nick now, in the light coming from the inn. He was wearing the same clothes as yesterday; but with a shock I noticed that tonight he had an enormous bruise on his forehead which hadn't been there before.

"Nick!" I exclaimed. "Where did you get *that?*"

He grinned tiredly. "Look good and shiny, does it? It feels pretty big I must say. Ma Muggerage gave it me this morning while you were running off. I think she got a decent look at you, you know. If she finds you round here again she'll kill you."

"Does it hurt?"

"It did before. Can't feel much now." He looked at me. "It's in the same place as yours."

I reached up to make sure my bandage was still stuck on. Cautiously, he pulled me back into the shadows against the wall again. "Listen," I said, deciding not to waste time, "Coben's a murderer. He's just escaped from prison. I found out today."

"How do you know?"

I told him the story of the Cockburn poster.

"Lots of 'em about," said Nick, sounding grimly grown-up all of a sudden. "Murderers, I mean. My Pa knows plenty of them, and I wouldn't wager against his having a few murders to his own name down the years."

There was silence while I contemplated this. I could easily imagine the powerful bosun murdering someone . . . crushing the life out of them, or strangling them with a length of rope. . . . The images which came to mind were so vivid my knees began to knock together.

"Has he still got the camel?" I asked.

"Far as I know."

"Well, I think we should shift it," I said.

"Shift it where?"

"Anywhere. You know that tramp I said was in the stable this morning? He must have been spying for Coben and Jiggs. There's a little stool there and a peep hole where somebody's been watching this house pretty often, I reckon. They know that camel's here, Nick, and they'll try and get it, I know they will."

"Well, that's why Pa left Ma Muggerage on guard," said Nick, in a tone of voice that suggested I was being stupid not to have realized that myself. "Pa's getting scared. I heard them talking this afternoon. He won't have the place left empty. It was that note put the wind up him, the one about the eyes."

"Well, there *are* eyes," I said. "Somebody's going to kill somebody to get that camel."

Suddenly there was the clatter of a footstep, and a bright lamp swung deliberately around the corner and exposed us as we stood in the passage. For the first time I heard Nick swear, in the language he'd picked up from sailors. We couldn't see who was carrying the light because its sudden glare dazzled us — but whoever it was evidently wasn't interested in us, because after inspecting us briefly, they moved on and we were left in shadow again.

"This isn't very safe, is it?" I said.

"Come back in the tunnel a bit further," Nick whispered.

Now the darkness was virtually complete. Nick was nothing but a low voice and a hint of warm breath on my face. He spoke quickly.

"What are we going to do then? How do we get the camel down, and where do we take it? Anyone watching the place will see us making off with it, and murder *us*."

"I thought *you'd* have a suggestion," I said. "You're the thief, after all." I could tell he was losing interest in this adventure. His father's violence had seen to that.

"Look," he said, "I know what my Pa's like. This isn't the first time people have been out to get him and it won't be the last. I was minding my own business till you suddenly popped up, and within five minutes of meeting you I was getting a beating. Now it looks like you want to get me in even *more* trouble."

But I was too excited to think about what he was saying. "Nick, I can't just leave them to it," I said. "I can't really explain it, but — I feel sure all of this *means* something."

Nick said nothing. He didn't understand, and I

didn't blame him. But my mind was racing. I'd remembered something he'd told me earlier.

"You said today," I whispered, "you often write your Pa false notes, pretending they're from other people."

"Sometimes," he said, a bit sullenly.

"Well! You can make it look like someone else took the camel, by writing him a note from someone else!"

"Mog," he said, "you don't get it, do you? This isn't a game. The sort of people my Pa's mixed up with don't play games. They harbor grudges while they're at sea, and then when they come ashore, people they don't like just — disappear. They settle scores, Mog, years later if need be. People who cross my Pa might think they're safe the moment he sails out of the river mouth, and so they might be till he comes home again. But one day they go missing and end up being fished out of the river, all green, half-eaten up by worms. If they're ever found at all."

He'd finally made me listen to him. We stood in the dark, saying nothing. I was terrified: even now my heart was pounding; but something inside me was still desperate to work out what on earth was going on.

"You don't need to get mixed up in this, then," I said eventually. "Just go back and get the camel from upstairs, and I'll hide it. You needn't get in trouble.

Just let me take it, Nick. I'll do it myself. I'll write the note. I can't just give up now."

I heard him draw in his breath, and there was another long silence before he said anything.

"You know something?" he finally said. "I think you might be the stubbornest boy I've ever met."

❖

It was the dead of night when Nick went camel-hunting.

I stood watch in the pitch-dark yard while he moved like a cat over the walls and low roofs of Lion's Mane Court, seeking a way in to burgle his own house. A quick listen at the scullery door was enough to assure us that Mrs. Muggerage was still snoring: all Nick had to do was find an upstairs window he could creep in through. As the formidable woman snored purposefully downstairs, dreaming no doubt of winning a famous victory in the All-England Cleaver-Throwing Championships and being congratulated by a whole navy of amorous bosuns, Nick's light feet moved on the floorboards above her head, and his fingers felt softly for the neck of the brass camel in the darkness.

I revolved, slowly, trying to keep an eye on all angles at once. I was paying particular attention to the corner of the stable, where I knew it was only too easy for an observer to lurk, completely unseen, behind the flimsy wall. Were murderer's eyes even now fixed firmly on me? Was someone waiting to pounce? Was there a —

A hand closed over my mouth. I almost died of shock.

Nick's voice hissed into my ear. "What kind of lookout *are* you? I could've been *anybody.*" He'd been so stealthy I hadn't realized he'd emerged from the house.

"Have you got it?" I asked.

"Sh! Keep your voice down! Yes, here it is — and I brought you a cloth to wrap it in."

With trembling hands I took the shapeless bundle he passed me, feeling the awkward contours of the camel inside the cloth.

"The note," I whispered.

"I'll leave it under the scullery door," Nick said. "Just get lost before Pa comes back."

"Or anybody else," I said. I squinted at his face in the dark, trying to make out his expression, thrilled that he'd decided to give me so much help after all.

"Well?" he said, after a pause. "What you waiting for?"

"Thank you, Nick," I said.

"Don't thank me! Just buzz off!"

Clutching the bundle close to my chest, I tiptoed the length of the stable wall and scuttled through the passageway into the inn yard. After casting a careful eye in either direction, I began to run through the dark, whispering streets towards Clerkenwell.

There was no sound at Cramplock's as I let myself in, except for the hum of the gas lamps in the square outside, and the familiar snuffle of Lash greeting me as I slipped through the heavy door. Once I was inside, his muzzle filled my palm, and I went to fetch a pitcher of milk from the cupboard to give him something to drink. I'd been gone a long time, and he was whimpering.

"Hang on," I said, "it's coming, it's coming!"

Then, before going upstairs to bed, I turned up the lamp on the table, the better to inspect the bundle in which the camel was wrapped. Lash's nose appeared at the table edge, sniffing inquisitively at the old cloth as I unwrapped it.

I held the camel in my hands. It really was most unimpressive: tarnished and scaly, about the size of a hen. Why on Earth was half the criminal population of London running around after this?

Lash was jumping up and scrabbling with his front paws at my shirt in his curiosity, and I held the camel out for him to sniff. "What's up, boy?" I asked him. "It's a camel. Seen a camel before? Mmm? It's a funny old thing, isn't it?"

He seemed to be trying to gnaw its head off.

"Stop it," I said impatiently, pulling it from him, "get down, you silly dog."

He'd left its head smeared with his saliva. I dried it off with the old cloth I'd wrapped it in, and then folded the cloth back over it.

Lash was still looking up, alert and expectant, his eyes following every movement of my hands. I bent down and hugged his shaggy head close.

"Well, what a day," I said to him. "Quite a lot's happened, hasn't it, boy?"

As I held his head tight against mine, he was trying to stick his tongue out of the side of his mouth to lick my face. I took hold of his muzzle and looked at him square on.

"Did you like Nick? You did, didn't you? Do you think he'll be our — friend?"

I hesitated a little before I uttered the word; and when I did, it sounded strange on my lips. Since I'd left the orphanage, I'd learned to look after myself, really. There hadn't been many people my own age whom I trusted enough to call "friends." It was me and Lash — and it had been, for almost as long as I could remember. But something about Nick had made me feel different: I had the unfamiliar sense that I'd discovered somebody I really wanted to spend time with. And it was more than this, too: as I'd tried to say to Nick, this adventure we were now both involved in somehow felt important, for a reason I couldn't begin to explain.

I thought about the note we'd forged for the bosun; and I couldn't help grinning in satisfaction as I imagined him finding it, and barging up the stairs to find his precious camel missing.

DEAR 👁

DIDNT WATCH CLOSE ENOHG DID YOU.

I was rather proud of our imitation of the villains' dreadful spelling. What made me smile especially broadly was the thought of Mrs. Muggerage trying to explain to a furious bosun how the thief had managed to remove the treasure from under her nose while she'd been on guard downstairs. What kicks might she sustain to her vast rump? I pictured him chasing her around Lion's Mane Court, making the buildings shake, like a couple of trumpeting elephants.

I got up to climb the stairs to bed, picking up the lamp and the camel from the table. I expected Lash to scamper up after me; but when I was nearly at the top of the stairs I realized he was still sitting at the bottom.

"Come on," I said, impatiently.

But he just stayed there, his head on one side, and gave another small pathetic whimper.

"Come on!" I said again, more encouragingly this time. But he wouldn't budge. Something was wrong. For some reason he was refusing to come upstairs. Had he hurt himself? Had something frightened him while I was out?

I suddenly felt uneasy. Pushing open the door of the upstairs room, I stood for a moment peering inside. Was there something up here that was frightening him? I lifted the lamp to light up the room in front of me, but everything seemed to be in its place, just as I'd left it this morning. Lash was just being silly. Yawning, I put the camel down on the bed and pulled my grubby clothes off, briefly splashing some chilly water onto my face and forearms from the bowl on the low bedside table. I realized I was utterly exhausted. Shivering slightly, shaking my hands to dry them off, I reached for my nightshirt; and before sinking into bed I picked up the camel again and opened the cupboard to put it away.

Suddenly I leapt back in alarm. There in the cupboard, something was moving. Crawling about among the old ink bottles in the bottom, making them chink against one another unmusically. Was it a rat?

I couldn't see the inside of the cupboard properly and I reached over for the lamp. My shadow loomed huge on the wall beside me. Now I could see right to the back of the cupboard, and when I saw what had

been making the noise I thought at first I was halluci-
nating and had to rub my eyes.

Curled up on the shelf, at my eye level, was a snake.

Its scales shone like polished metal in the lamplight.
It lifted its tiny head, as though it were suspended from
an invisible cord fixed to the ceiling. In a flash, a tongue
appeared and disappeared, like another snake, blacker
and more slender, trapped inside the body of this one.

I was dimly aware of Lash still whimpering down
below. I simply couldn't believe what I was seeing,
and I stood transfixed, watching the coiled creature
wavering in the light of the lamp, reflecting deep
golden light back at me. Slowly, it moved over the shelf,
crossing its coils over itself, creating intricate knots
and sliding powerfully out of them. All of a sudden the
head seemed to swell, big flaps like a black hood bristling outward at either side as the head rose, silently, up
into the air, the lithe body dangling beneath it like the
string of a kite. It seemed to have brought a mysterious
scent into the room, like incense, making my brain
swim and my own towering shadow on the far wall
grow and diminish with every beat of my heart.

I realized I was still holding the camel. With all my
force I hurled it at the shelf, into the mass of sliding
snake, wanting it smashed in all directions.

The camel crashed among the boxes and bottles,
scattering the contents of the cupboard and sending

things cascading off the shelves and onto the floor-boards with a clatter loud enough to wake everyone in the square. The camel lay in the bottom, on its side, its head facing me, its glazed expression illuminated by the lamp. There was no sign of the snake.

I hadn't seen it move: one second it was there, the next it wasn't. I wheeled around to try and work out where in the room it had gone. The room swam before my tired eyes. There was no snake to be seen, anywhere. I even put the lamp on the floor and got nervously down on my hands and knees to peer under the bed; but I could see no sign of it. There was virtually nowhere else for it to hide.

Could it have gone down the stairs? Looking down, I was greeted with the sight of Lash sitting exactly where I'd left him, gazing anxiously up at me from under his eyebrows. He gave a little bark. No snake had come slithering past him, that much was clear — or he certainly wouldn't still have been sitting there. Might it have disappeared into a crack in the rotten skirting board? I was trembling. Maybe it really *had* been a hallucination. I went over to the little window and grasped the splintered wooden sash. It was shut tight: the snake couldn't possibly have come in or out that way.

I was about to move away from the window when I noticed someone outside. Down below, moving in and out of the light cast by the street lamp, was a man: tall, his head covered by a black hat, casting frequent glances up and down the street, wary of being seen. And as he turned to look upwards, the sudden sight of a familiar face made goose bumps stand up all over me. I knew this night-watcher, this tall and alert figure, all too well.

It was the man from Calcutta.

7

FLOUR AND ASHES

The night was full of strange dreams.

The faces in the fog had returned. Cramplock was one of them, roaring at me in rage, hurtling away from me as he shouted, but coming back several times to remind me of my negligence. Some of the figures who ballooned up out of the mist held up lanterns, as though to peer into my face, and I had to squint and screw up my eyes to stop the light from dazzling me as they drifted off. Mrs. Muggerage had appeared, cleaver in hand, roaring silently into the murk, and the image of Nick's anxious little face with his shock of black hair swam around her, dodging the cleaver as she swung it mercilessly from side to side.

And I'd dreamed of the man from Calcutta, too, though he hadn't been one of the faces in the mist. This time not just his head but his whole body had become that of a crow, sleek and shining, his eyes glinting jewels which darted and pierced; and he was sitting on the edge of my bed, in the dream, watching me. But instead of feeling frightened of him, I felt as though he were guarding me. Perched on my bedpost, alert but protective, his presence seemed somehow important and comforting, like the ravens at the Tower.

I woke in a sweat, with Lash licking the salt from my temples. Light was flooding in through the window and I could hear the sounds of morning activity outside. The first thing I did was sit up and check that the camel was still there — and, sure enough, it was still in its raggy bundle in the bottom of the cupboard.

Cramplock was already at work. His hands and face were black and smeared with ink.

"Strange letter arrived this morning," was the first thing he said to me.

"Who from?"

"Can't say." He reached for a stiff piece of paper. "Make any sense to you, Mog?"

I scanned it quickly. "Where was it?" I asked him, uncomfortably.

"Nailed," he said, dramatically, "to the door."

I swallowed.

CLEAVER BOY,
SO CLEAVER FIND HIS CAMEL.
I SHOW HIM DEATH SOON.

And beneath this extraordinary message, the strange
letters again:

इम्यता

It had obviously been left last night by the man from
Calcutta, and there wasn't much doubt about what it
was getting at. The way he'd misspelled "clever" was
rather unsettling, I thought, under the circumstances.

"I can't make head or tail of it," Cramplock said,
"some sort of joke I suppose — from a friend of yours,
is it?"

"Mm," I said.

I SHOW HIM DEATH SOON.

Not an especially funny joke, I was thinking — and my
face must have made it clear I wasn't amused. The
man from Calcutta had had a good try at "showing me
death" the night before. It was clearer than ever that,
after he'd failed to find the camel that evening at
Coben's hideout, when I threatened him with the
sword, he had become convinced I was working for
Coben and Jiggs, and was hiding the camel for them.
He must have seen me bringing home a bundle last
night, and guessed straightaway what it was.

It was absolutely vital to find another hiding place

for the camel — and I had to do it today. I was beginning to wish I'd taken Nick's advice and left it where it was in the first place.

"Mr. Cramplock," I said, "has, er — has somebody come to live next door?"

He stared at me. "Not as far as I know," he said. "Nobody's lived there for ages. It caught fire years ago — and it's been empty ever since, I think."

"Only — I thought I could hear someone moving about in there," I said cautiously.

Cramplock shrugged. "Probably some poor old soul who's broken in, using it as a place to sleep. But it's not safe. As far as I know there are no floors in there."

I said nothing.

"Is something wrong, Mog?" Cramplock asked. "You've been acting a bit strange lately, as if there's something on your mind."

"Nothing much," I said vaguely, not wanting him involved.

But for the whole of the day I was miles away, pondering over the man from Calcutta and the house next door and the whole camel affair. The more I thought about it, the surer I was that someone *had* been moving about next door the other night, and that it had probably been the man from Calcutta. He was hiding in the house next door, to spy on me. I was so preoccupied I couldn't concentrate on my work, and

Cramplock had to tell me several times to stop day-dreaming. At one point when I'd been told to pull out a long length from a roll of paper, I was particularly careless and managed to tear a huge gash right up it; and this time he shouted at me.

"Wake up, can't you?" he barked. "Did you knock your brain out when you hit your head the other day? Just pay attention to what you're doing or you'll get another knock you won't forget."

He took me by the arm and dragged me through into the filthy little storeroom where he kept most of his paper and old woodblocks. "You can scrub the floor and the cupboards in here," he said, "seeing as you don't seem to be able to do anything more complicated. This has needed doing for months."

More like years, I thought grumpily, as I began the job. I had to move all the heavy boxes out of the way first; and, crouching on my knees, I discovered astonishing amounts of dust and rubbish, rags and inky old fluff, which had accumulated behind the boxes and cupboards over a long period of time. It made me cough so hard I thought my lungs were going to turn inside out. After half an hour I looked as though I'd been scraped out of a forgotten corner myself. As I was picking up the final few scraps of discarded paper before moving the boxes back against the wall, I noticed one with some rather surprising words on it.

It was a short handwritten letter in a rust-colored ink. It wasn't addressed to anyone by name, and it wasn't signed. It just said:

I don't appreciate the deceit, and neither do some of my friends. You can hide nothing, and you could save yourself a great deal of trouble by remembering it.
I thought I had made myself quite clear: but it seems you require a further reminder.
This is most certainly your final warning.

I read it through several times. The handwriting and spelling suggested someone well-educated: it was certainly a far cry from the garbled notes of the man from Calcutta, or those with little drawings of eyes which the villains had been exchanging. How had it got here, among the scraps of Cramplock's storeroom? I don't think I was supposed to see this: but I felt sure it must have been sent to Mr. Cramplock, and it suddenly seemed as though he must know something he was keeping quiet about.

A sudden thought occurred to me, and I lifted the paper up to the light from the little storeroom window.

I wasn't entirely surprised when I found the strange watermark of the dog yet again, curled around so its nose was touching its tail.

I jumped as the storeroom door swung open suddenly, and made a poor fist of hiding the note as Cramplock popped his head in. I was convinced he must have noticed it in my hand; but he didn't ask me about it. Instead he said:

"Are you nearly finished, Mog? Only I want you to go out with some bills for me."

I beamed at him. "I've, er — just got a couple of boxes to put back," I said, going red.

"It looks much better," said Cramplock, surveying the flags of the floor and probably remembering for the first time in years what color they were supposed to be. "But these must be delivered — now." He waved a fat handful of envelopes. I clambered to my feet, and lumps of clinging dust floated into the air like thistle seeds.

Lash was excited at the chance to get out of the dusty shop and was sitting patiently by the door even before I emerged from the storeroom. As I picked up the envelopes, Cramplock grunted. "Just make sure you don't lose them, and bring me back some cock-and-bull story about people burning them up. Or about . . . about them being eaten by goats, or trampled by giants." He seemed very pleased with his own sarcasm.

"I won't lose them, Mr. Cramplock," I said, "I promise."

"You'd better not," he said, "or the last printing job you ever do will be an advertisement saying W. H. Cramplock seeks a diligent boy to be a printer's devil."

I looked at him to try and decide if he was joking or not, but as he turned his back I decided he wasn't. Scanning the various addresses on the bills, I had a sudden idea. I'd have to be out of the shop for a good hour, delivering all these. And at least one of the bills had to be delivered fairly close to where the bosun lived. I might as well try and get a message to Nick while I was at it.

Jamming the bills into my pocket and knotting Lash's lead hastily around his collar, I dove out into the sunshine. I couldn't resist a glance up at the blackened face of the house next door. Nothing appeared to stir; but my imagination conjured up eyes watching me from every one of the dark windows, and I ran past with a shudder of fear.

But when I got to Lion's Mane Court I found Mrs. Muggerage was very much in evidence. From the narrow passageway I could see her hanging up her laundry in the yard, moving between the dangling, dripping garments like a big ape in a forest of linen. I couldn't possibly sneak in unnoticed. I ducked back out of the passageway and tied Lash to the nearest post.

As I was doing so I became aware of a familiar chant from down the street. An old cart was clattering along, driven by a toothless old gypsy in a brown cap. He was a rag and bone man. Suddenly getting an idea, I rushed up to him and flagged him down.

Mrs. Muggerage was no doubt surprised to see a rag and bone cart jolting its way into the yard, its wheels bumping over the pitted ground.

"Any rags or bones," the old man moaned, looking at her. Setting her face in a grimace, she marched over to him.

"What do you mean by draggin' yer flea-ridden old cart in 'ere?" she screamed. "There's no rags and no bones, now get lost!"

"Rags or bones," the man wailed again. I wasn't sure whether he was an idiot, or just pretending to be; but I was very grateful for it. While Mrs. Muggerage blared at him, I crept down from the back of the cart, where I'd been hiding among the smelly rags. Ducking between the big sheets which hung around the yard, I scuttled for the cellar grating.

I didn't dare call, or make a sound of any sort. There was a light wind, and every now and again a dangling sheet blew aside to afford me a view of Mrs. Muggerage, just a few feet away, arguing with the blank-faced old carter. In the back of the cart I'd scribbled a tatty note with a stub of a pencil I had in my pocket.

Nick TROUBLE!
DOLLS HEAD 6
M

A scream went up as the ragman's horse began eating Mrs. Muggerage's washing. Fishing down through the grating, I slipped the note in through a crack in the dirty little window, and started to tiptoe back to the cart.

But Mrs. Muggerage had begun clouting the feeble old carter over his flat-capped head and, finding the onslaught too terrible to bear, he'd geed up his horse and rattled off out of Lion's Mane Court before I had a chance to leap back among the rags. The big woman was just turning away, wiping her hands on her bulging sides, when she spotted me lurking behind a sheet.

A big smile of satisfaction spread across her beefy face and, without warning, she advanced. It was like trying to dodge a collapsing house. She barged through the yard, saying nothing, merely grinning as I tried to avoid her swiping arms. If one of them had hit me I'd have been out cold.

Mrs. Muggerage may have been big and strong but fortunately she wasn't especially agile; and her grin began to look rather strained as I led her like a matador through the maze of wet linen. Waiting behind an enormous pair of bloomers, hanging from the line like a ship's mainsail, I watched her calculating her next move. When she was almost close enough to reach out and grab me by the throat, she lurched; and I ducked, and was gone. Looking back as I sped out of the yard I saw her bulky frame tangled up in her own bloomers, fighting for air amongst the billowing material, wrapping it around herself in her thrashing confusion until she'd twisted the entire washing-line up and pulled it onto the filthy flagstones.

❖

"What you been doin' to your head then, Maaster Mog?" asked Tassie as I walked into the Doll's Head that evening.

"A kid threw a brick at it," I told her, truthfully.

"In a fight, was you?"

"Not as such," I said meekly.

"Well if you don't mind me saying," Tassie said, polishing her taps, "you don't smell so fresh this evenin', Maaster Mog, neither."

There were four other people in the taproom, all of whom I knew. No spies in here, then, it seemed — but no Nick either.

"Is it six yet, Tassie?" I asked her.

"You take a look over there, Maaster Mog," Tassie replied, "at that sizable clock what's been here since the first day you set foot in here, and what's more since long

161

before you was ever born. And you tell *me* if it's six yet."

Sheepishly, I glanced over at the longcase clock against the wall, with its slightly tarnished brass face which was at least twice the size of my own head. Five minutes past six. Tassie was obviously in no mood to be trifled with this evening.

Lash's nose appeared beside me at the bar, sniffing and dribbling slightly at the scent wafting from the little back room. "Do we smell stock, Tassie?" I laughed.

"Maybe it's more than stock you smells, Maaster Mog," she said, "maybe it's a big pot o' my best knuckle soup!"

My eyes lit up, and Lash whimpered in anticipation as Tassie disappeared, still laughing, into the back.

Trying to appear casual, I tightened my grip on the handles of the big canvas bag I'd brought with me, and heaved it under the table. To any observer, I hoped, it looked like a bag full of rolls of poster paper. What nobody else knew was that hidden among them was a brass camel which was apparently the most coveted object in the city's criminal underworld. Although I was trying not to draw attention to myself, I was terribly nervous and I didn't dare let go of the bag for a single second. I yanked at Lash's collar to make him sit down quietly next to it.

Looking up, I noticed one of the drinkers looking at me, a disheveled old soul called Harry Fuller who drove a stagecoach between here and Cambridge.

"Hello, Mr. Fuller," I said, "it's been a nice day again."

"Noith for thumb, maybe," he replied. He spoke rather strangely as a result of his having no front teeth — they'd been missing for as long as I'd known him. When he drove his coach he used to hold the reins with both hands and keep his horsewhip clamped in the gap between his remaining teeth, poking out of his mouth like a kind of long floppy pipe as the coach lurched by. "Noith for mouth folk, I don't wonder." I could tell he was in a bad mood, and there was still no sign of Nick, so I asked him what was the matter.

I immediately wished I hadn't. In his gruff lisp, he began to rant, about how much trouble he went to to ensure that his passengers were comfortable, and how much of a sacrifice it was, driving a coach back and forth in all weathers and never being at home with Mrs. Fuller and the five or six little Fullers — he didn't seem to be able to remember quite how many children he had. But just as I was looking around the room to try to think of an excuse to talk to someone else, he said something which made my ears prick up, about his coach being stopped and searched by soldiers on his way out of London.

"Soldiers?" I asked.

"Thowdjerth," he affirmed, flinging a fine spray

from his mouth with every syllable in the evening sun-light. "Convict looth, they thed."

So there was a search on for Coben. Oh, where was Nick? My mind raced again through the things I had to tell him, as Mr. Fuller grumbled on about how he was convinced the soldiers were just using the search for the convict as an excuse to rifle through passengers' luggage, and how they were no better than uniformed robbers and highwaymen. "Crawled out o' pigth-tithe and gut-terth, mouth of em, Mathter Mog," he was saying.

It was Tassie who finally cut short his grumbling, by returning with two deep bowls of soup. One she placed on the table in front of me, the other on the floor in front of Lash's glistening whiskers. The sound of slobbering filled the room as he dug his nose delightedly into the soup.

"Might there be more?" I asked her.

She looked at me with mock disapproval. "You spoils that dog rotten," she said.

"I didn't really mean for him," I said, reaching down to ruffle his ears. "I meant, for a friend of mine."

"I dare say there might," she said, amused. "What friend are you expecting?"

"Oh, just a lad I know," I said airily. "If he comes. I asked him to."

But the longer I waited, the more certain I became that something had gone wrong. Maybe my note had got stuck in the grille and he hadn't found it. Or worse — what if the bosun or Mrs. Muggerage had found it first? Even now they might be marching over here. Every time the door opened I almost jumped out of my skin, half expecting one of the enormous couple to come stamping in.

To my relief, at just after twenty past, a small face peered round the taproom door, saw me, and hurried in.

"I've got a bone to pick with you," he said in a low voice, as he sat down.

"What sort of bone?" I asked, putting the last spoonful of knuckle soup into my mouth.

"I've just had a good clouting off my Pa for something I never did. Nothing new that, I suppose. But —" Suddenly he stopped, looked down at me, and wrinkled his nose. "Where've *you* been?" he asked; "you smell like a drain."

"Thanks very much," I said, "I had to hide in a rag and bone cart to get that note to you. But never mind that — what happened to you?"

"Pa came home this afternoon," continued Nick, "saying he'd been to the ship. To the *Sun of Calcutta*, you know. And someone there told him I'd been snooping round asking for the captain. I never, I said. Don't you lie to me, he says." He did a passable imitation of his father's throaty voice. "Wasn't you described to me in perfect detail? Some sailor apparently told him there was a kid aboard wearing tarry breeches and a white shirt, skinny with a sprout of dark hair and a big cut on his forehead. That's you, innit, says my Pa. Yes it is, I thought, and I know who *else* it is."

"You didn't —" I began.

"No, course I didn't tell him," Nick said. "But I got a bruise or two more to boast of, out of that little conversation."

"I'm sorry, Nick," I said.

"Course, he was in a foul mood," Nick said, looking around nervously, "you-know-what being gone."

"When did he find out?"

"Just this afternoon when he came in. He'd been out all night. He found the note, came down to bawl at me, threw me at the wall, and left again straight away. I don't fancy being Coben or Jiggs when he gets his hands on them."

Tassie came over with some soup for Nick. Lash jumped up when he saw it, but seemed quite crestfallen as he realized it wasn't for him, and lay down again with what sounded very much like a sigh. As Tassie walked back to the kitchen I heard her telling someone, "Look at them two. Spitting image of each other, like a pair o' magpies, they are, and twice as mischievous I'll wager." And she couldn't resist a quick vigorous wipe at her taps as she went past them.

"Listen," I said in a low voice, "I've got a story and a half to tell you."

"Trouble," quoted Nick.

"Yes," I said. I looked around, just to make sure no one new had entered the room, and I told him all about the snake in the cupboard and the man from Calcutta lurking outside.

"Are you sure you didn't dream it?" Nick asked.

"It did cross my mind," I said. "But look at this." Under the table I unfolded the note I'd received that morning, and leaned back to let Nick read it. He gave a grim smile.

"What does SO CLEAVER FIND HIS CAMEL mean?" he asked. "Does he mean Ma Muggerage's cleaver?"

"I think he means 'clever,' doesn't he," I said. "He probably doesn't speak English very well. I suppose he's trying to say, 'You think you're so clever to find the camel,' or something like that. But the point is, he knew I'd got it, didn't he? I think it was the camel he came looking for at Coben and Jiggs's as well, when he found me in the chest. And I reckon he's watching us from the house next door to Cramplock's. I bet he's seen me coming and going all the time."

"I *told* you it was stupid," Nick said. "You've only had the camel a few hours and already you've had people coming after you with real live snakes and death threats."

I was beginning to think he was right, but I said nothing. Nick continued to stare at the note in my lap. "What's this?" He was pointing at the strange lettering.

"It's writing of some sort," I said. "I've seen it before. In the captain's cabin, on a snuffbox lid. And it was on another piece of paper I got from Coben and Jiggs."

"Keep your voice down," Nick muttered. I stopped talking. I'd been getting too excited, and had forgotten. There was silence for a while as Nick began attacking his soup.

"What did you tell the sailor on the *Sun of Calcutta?*" he asked, after a while.

"Mmm? I told him, er — that — that I was the bosun's boy," I said, going red, "and that I was on an errand for my Pa — your Pa, that is. And that it had something to do with the East India Company. It sounded grand, I read it on a document."

"So you told him you were me," said Nick, drily.

"Sort of. Except I didn't know you then. I didn't even know the bosun *had* a boy. I — I guessed, because that's who everyone seemed to think I was."

Nick took another mouthful of soup, saying nothing.

"Anyway," I said, anxious to change the subject again, "we've got to move the camel again. The man from Calcutta won't leave the place alone till he's got it."

"Well, maybe it *belongs* to him," Nick said. "Have you thought about that? Maybe he'd only trying to get it back because it's his. Where is it now?"

"Here," I said, "under the table. Don't look! Someone might be watching." Now it was Nick's turn to look around nervously. I reached over and ate a spoonful of his soup. "I've got another note to show you," I said, licking my lips. "I found it in the storeroom at the printing shop." I fumbled in my pocket but couldn't find the note, and I didn't want to draw attention to it. "I'll show you it later," I said, "but I think it must have been sent to Mr. Cramplock. It's like a — threat." I tried to remember how the note had begun. "Something like, *I don't appreciate the deceit, and neither do my friends,*" I quoted.

Nick grimaced to himself. "So let me get this straight," he muttered. "You're being watched by the man from Calcutta, who's got a deadly snake as a pet, and who lives next door. Someone's been sending you notes threatening to show you death. And Cramplock's mixed up in it too, for good measure. This is too close for comfort, Mog. Seems to me you'd be better off staying away from there altogether."

I shifted uncomfortably. "Oh, and something else," I said. "Soldiers are searching for Coben. They're turning out carriages leaving the town. A coachman's just been grumbling at me about it."

Nick scraped the last of his soup from his bowl, and sucked his spoon clean.

"I don't know," he said, "who Coben needs to hide from most. Those soldiers, or my Pa." He looked at me significantly. There was silence. I could hear Tassie laughing. I couldn't resist a quick glance down at the bundle at my feet.

"What are we going to do with this, then?" I asked at length.

❖

Our shadows were long, stretching in front of us like stick puppets wherever the clustering of the houses gave way to the reddening sunlight. Every time some-one rounded a corner unexpectedly, I jumped halfway out of my skin.

"Calm down, can't you?" Nick murmured. "You'll give us away."

"How much further?" I asked. I was convinced it must be obvious to passersby what we were doing. That boy with the dog looks nervous, they'd be saying — ah, yes, of course, he's taking a stolen camel to a hiding place in Aldgate.

"Not far," said Nick. He'd already told me he was deliberately going to take me by a very indirect route, so as to lead any possible spies off the scent, and con-sequently it was taking us twice as long to get to our destination.

"Excuse me, now," said a high-pitched voice from a dark corner. I was about to take to my heels and run for it, when Nick grabbed me by the shoulder. There was a dusty old man sitting up against a broken wall. Lash went over to sniff him and I called him back nervously.

"Did ye hear it, now?" the man was rambling, tunefully. "A most remarkable thing, it was, to be sure." He spoke in a lilting voice like a pennywhistle. "A mooo — ost remarkable thing." His face suddenly disappeared into itself like a sponge, and flopped back out again. It took a while for us to realize that this was meant to be a smile. "Music!" he added, portentously. "The most remarkable music that ever was."

"Er — yes," I said, pulling Nick away.

"Music," the tramp was continuing, "like I never heard before. Like a bagpipe . . . like a flute . . . like a violin . . . like nothing I ever heard before in me life. What music is it," he lilted, "that sounds like all the snakes of the world rippling over one another? Why should music like that be heard, now? Music from far away."

Nick nudged me, to urge me on, and we left the tramp sitting there, laughing and softly singing to himself.

"Isn't that strange," Nick said, "what he was saying about music like snakes?"

"I suppose people like him imagine all kinds of music," I said, "just like they imagine all kinds of sights. A drunk once told me he'd seen a woman with a horse's mane and hooves going into a house. He swore all kinds of oaths he'd seen it."

"It must be quite fun in a way," Nick said, "to imagine you see and hear things. No difference between things that are real and things that are a dream."

"Sounds like my life just now," I muttered.

We turned a corner into a wide street, still busy with coaches and barrows; and Nick stopped by a little shop-front, so shabby it almost looked uninhabited. Just above our heads, over a low front window, I could dimly make out the words

SPINTWICE
JEWELER & SILVERSMITH

painted in smut-caked letters. I called Lash and took hold of his lead, and Nick knocked on the little door, which barely seemed high enough for us to get through, let alone a grown-up customer. After a few moments it opened and a child's face peeped around it. When it saw Nick, the child pulled the door further open and disappeared inside. We followed him in.

"This is Mog," Nick said when the door was closed. "Mog, this is Mr. Spintwice, my good friend."

The person I had taken for a child was Mr. Spintwice himself. He was shorter than either of us, and his face, now that I could take in his appearance properly, was a strange mixture of infant and adult. He had rosy cheeks and a permanent broad grin, like a mischievous child of about five or six; but his eyes were quick and dark and, I suddenly thought, sadder than the rest of his face. He really looked most peculiar, and I took my cues nervously from Nick, watching his responses to the little man before deciding what I thought of him or how to behave.

"Mog," he said, in a piping voice. "How do you do, Mog?" He reached up for my hand, all the time smiling in his unchanging way, and I shook hands with him slightly stiffly. "And this is?"

"Lash," I said, hoping the tiny man wouldn't be intimidated by a dog almost as tall as himself. But he had immediately recognized Lash's trusting nature and was already reaching out the palms of his hands for exploratory licks. "Lash," he said, "you are welcome."

We followed him through the carpeted hallway into a tiny sitting room. "Nick and I have known one another many years," he said in his precise little voice; and it was perfectly plain that Nick was entirely comfortable in his presence and didn't think he was peculiar at all, so I said nothing. "Please sit in here. I can see you can't quite believe your eyes. Well! Nick was just as surprised as you, the first time he came here years ago. If you make yourselves comfortable, I'll fetch some tea."

I looked around in wonder. There were armchairs, a mantelpiece, pictures hanging from a picture-rail, tables with plants in pots, a cabinet with glass doors revealing rows of books, and a warm welcoming fire blazing in the grate with neat fire tools and a coal scuttle beside it; but all of it was built to around half the normal size. This, and the presence of numerous clocks of various kinds ranged around the room, ticking and tinkling at several different pitches, made me feel as though we had stepped inside some extraordinary toy. Some of the clocks were so tiny, I marveled at how anyone could make a mechanism small enough to fit inside them. Others were quite big enough for Mr. Spintwice himself to climb in, next to the pendulum, and be hidden completely. When Nick and I sat down in the armchairs we filled them, finding them if anything a little tight. Even Lash looked around slightly bemused, as though afraid to wag his tail in case he knocked something off a shelf.

"I love this place, don't you?" Nick said. "Listen to all those clocks." He had barely sat down before he'd slipped out of his chair again and gone to kneel by the bookshelves. Soon he was opening one of the cabinets and taking out a big crimson book almost the size of a flagstone. "This is one of my favorites." He dragged it back to his chair.

Something in my face must have betrayed my misgivings because, without my saying anything, he leaned close to whisper in my ear.

"Don't worry," he said. "Spintwice is all right. I think we should tell him the whole story, and see what he says. He's a jeweler, so he might be able to tell us a bit more about the camel. And he'll hide it for us, I'm sure."

The longer I listened to the mechanical music of the clocks, the more it seemed to overwhelm us, lapping round us, spinning us into a web of sound.

"Why don't you stay here?" Nick whispered suddenly. "Don't go back to Cramplock's. The man from Calcutta's too close."

I was unsure. I was genuinely afraid we might have been followed; and if I stayed here, there was every chance I'd just be putting the dwarf in unnecessary danger too. There was something about the familiarity of Cramplock's that made me feel instinctively safer there; and, despite having Nick's word for it, I still didn't know Spintwice well enough to feel I could fully trust him.

"I'm still not —" I began; but Nick was immersed in the book again, oblivious now to sights and sounds around him, completely and instantly relaxed. His eyes were wide as he took in the rich decoration which spread across both pages: figures in red and purple, woven patterns in gold leaf along the pages' edge, and a Moorish landscape with two figures clinging to a brightly colored flying carpet. He seemed a different person altogether from the watchful, edgy, suspicious boy I'd met at Lion's Mane Court. I suddenly realized how little I still knew about Nick. I wondered how he had ever encountered this strange little man, whose tiny house and wonderful bookshelves seemed such a world away from his violent home life. "He's about the only grown-up who's ever really been kind to me," Nick had told me on the way here. My eyes wandered around the shelves of books, fascinated, enticed by the patterns and lettering on their spines. They looked impossibly rich and full of promise: no book ever printed at Cramplock's had been as splendid as these, I felt sure. What on earth would Nick's father say if he could see him sitting here, leafing through them?

"Does your Pa know you come here?" I asked him.

"There's a lot my Pa don't know," he murmured, unconcerned.

Mr. Spintwice came back with a tray of teacups, again miniaturized to match his size; and he had also brought a dish of water and bread for Lash, which he put down in front of the fire. It was at this point that I decided I liked him.

"It's a very nice surprise to have visitors, I must say," he said, after taking a sip or two. "And at such an unexpected hour!"

"I'm sorry if we —" I began, but he cut me off.

"Not at all! A pleasure, a sheer pleasure, Mog," he said, "an unexpected hour is the very best hour for visitors! It would be boring always to have guests turn up when you expect them."

Lash had made himself completely at home, curling up in front of the fire as though he'd lived there all his life. My suspicions were beginning to melt away, and I found myself thinking about what Nick had said and being very tempted to stay here, cocooned in this warm music-filled little sitting room, reading book after book. I was flooded with a strange sense of safety and well-being, a feeling so unfamiliar it gave me goose bumps.

"We really called to ask a favor," said Nick, rather apprehensively, putting down the book.

"Of course! Anything I can do for two such hand-some fellows."

Nick looked at me. "It's quite a long story," he said. "Maybe you'd better tell it, Mog, since it's really yours."

I put down my teacup. "I'm not really sure where to start," I said.

I told him the whole thing, more or less. As I told it, I began to feel a lot better, and Mr. Spintwice listened with complete attention. When I got to the bit about the camel, I pulled it out of its wrapping and passed it across to him. He spent the rest of the story examining it, turning it over and over in his hands, with a mystified expression on his little old face.

"It sounds," he said, "as if you two are getting into deep waters. And over what? Over *this?*" He held up the camel by one of its legs. Lash, looking up from his cozy spot by the fire, got to his feet and trotted over to the dwarf's chair, where he began sniffing at the camel much as he had done the night before.

"We wondered," said Nick, "if you might tell us anything about it."

"It's brass," Mr. Spintwice said simply. "Cheap. Tarnished. Made in a mold which must have made hundreds like it. The sort of trinket that comes from the Indies every time a ship puts in. As far as I can see it's worth nothing at all: it doesn't even have jewels for eyes, or anything like that. It's a complete mystery why anyone would want it." He began lifting it up and down, holding Lash's head away with his other hand. "The only thing is," he said, "its weight is all wrong."

"What do you mean?" I asked, intrigued.

"Well," he said, "it's obviously not solid brass because it's not heavy enough. So it must be hollow. But somehow . . ." he lifted it up and down a few more times, just to be sure, "it's not light enough to be hollow, either."

Nick stared at him, and then at me. "Of course!" he exclaimed. "It's hollow!" He took the camel from the dwarf, and waved it. "What a pair of idiots we are!"

"What are you talking about?" I asked, still mystified.

"Don't you understand? Look, we've been wondering

for days why anyone would want to steal it, let alone threaten to *kill* for it. But it isn't *this* they want. It's something hidden *inside* it." He shook it, but it didn't rattle. "There must be something valuable inside," he said, "and that's why it feels too heavy to be hollow."

The little jeweler began laughing and his eyes twinkled. "What a clever lad," he chuckled, "he's right, he's quite right."

Nick was turning the camel over and over furiously, looking for a way to get at whatever was inside. He pulled at the legs, scratched at it, tried twisting it around its hump. Suddenly he gave a cry. "The head comes off! Look!"

Grasping the drowsy-looking head in his grubby fist, he twisted it and it began to unscrew, squeaking, and sending little grains of powder trickling to the floor out of the grooves. Lash gave an excited bark.

"Well, I never," said the dwarf, intrigued.

"*You* knew, didn't you?" I exclaimed to Lash, remembering how he had tried to gnaw at its neck last night. Why hadn't it occurred to me then?

"What on earth's all this?" said Nick, "chalk?" He lifted off the head and blew. Powder flew up into his face, and he sneezed. "Or is it snuff?" He held it out to me. Lash was fussing around it, and I had to stand up so I could get a proper look without him pushing his nose inside.

The camel was full to the brim with an off-white powder, like flour and ashes.

"I don't get it," I said, "this powder can't be valuable either. Let's empty it, and see if there's anything else in here."

"All the powder," put in the dwarf, "might just be there to stop the jewel, or whatever it is, from rattling about and getting scratched." He passed me an old porcelain jar. "Empty it into here," he said.

I stuffed the open neck into the jar and shook the camel. Clouds of powder rose as it all poured through. Lash, his ears erect, was transfixed, and kept giving short excited yelps as the stuff trickled out. We all watched eagerly for something else to fall into the jar — but no, just a steady stream of powder was all there was, until the camel was empty and the jar nearly full.

"Well," said Spintwice, disappointed.

"This doesn't make sense," said Nick. "Are you sure there's nothing else in there? Nothing's stuck?"

I shook it, and pressed my eye to the open neck, but could see nothing.

"Let's have some more tea," Spintwice said, getting up.

But I was sitting with my nose in the neck of the jar. I sniffed.

"What are you doing?" Nick asked.

"I don't know," I said, "I think I've smelt this before." I breathed in again.

Suddenly I felt very, very peculiar.

The jar was growing, swelling, like something about to give birth. I held it until it was too big for my hands and then I let it fall, which it did very slowly, as if it were falling through endless space. When I looked up, Nick and Mr. Spintwice had receded, the room suddenly expanding until it was the size of a cornfield: there they were, in their armchairs, miles away, moving their arms like insects, completely silent. Lash's wet nose, shining in the glow of the fire, had become a disembodied ball of light, like a star. All I could hear was the ticking of the clocks, which became louder and louder until it was more like a rush of crashing echoes; the room began to spin and I clutched the arms of the chair in desperation as, lashing like a snake, the world flipped right over and threw me into a blaze of meaningless color, like the pinkest, bluest, blackest sunset that ever smeared its way across the smoky London sky.

8

ENCHANTED MUSIC

As we left Spintwice's I still felt rather strange; though at least the world was no longer expanding and contracting like a concertina. Nick and the dwarf had picked me up and sat me firmly in a chair, where they'd given me tea to drink, and then, as a further measure, brandy. Again I'd declined the offer of a bed for the night, partly out of a desire to protect Spintwice and partly because I had an aching feeling that, the more time I spent in his extraordinary and beguiling house, the less I'd ever want to go back to Cramplock's at all, to work or to sleep. Bravely, Nick had agreed to come with me.

"Are you feeling better?" he asked as we walked up the street in the dark.

"I think so," I said, hesitantly. "Nick, we *can* trust Spintwice, can't we?"

"'Course we can," he said quickly. "I tell him everything, Mog. I always have. He won't say anything to anyone."

The dwarf had been tremendously excited by the whole affair, and thought it was fun to join in our adventure; but I was worried. The tiny man wouldn't present much of an obstacle if a murderous criminal should pay him a visit, determined to get at the camel or its contents. The more I thought about it, the less sure I was that we had done the right thing. I just hoped we'd hidden them well enough, and had been careful enough not to let anyone see us as we came and went.

"We'd better not hang around," I said as we came to the corner where our routes home diverged.

Nick looked up at the dark sky. "I hope Pa's still out," he said, "and Ma Muggerage, too, for that matter. Then I can get back in without being clobbered. Look, I might come back here tomorrow and make sure Spintwice is all right."

"Well, I shan't come," I said, "if you-know-who's watching me, the further away I stay the better." And as I hurried between the unfriendly walls towards home, every face which melted into the shadows at my approach made me stop in my tracks; every cough from a doorway, every murmur from a lighted window, even the rustle as Lash chased a rat into the shadows near my ankles, sent shivers up my spine; and by the time we got back I was running so fast I was completely out of breath.

"Busy today, Mog," Cramplock told me next morning, "invitation cards for Lord Malmsey's daughter's wedding. I want you to cut the card while I engrave this coat of arms." He was peering through his half-glasses at the design he'd been given to work from: a big shield-like coat of arms, featuring banners unfurled, and a motto in Latin I couldn't understand. The emblems on the shield were three white flowers and a lion with a particularly blank expression on its face, as though its brain had been removed.

"A lion and three roses," I said to Cramplock. "Does he like lions, then, this Lord Malmsey?"

"He doesn't have to *like* lions," Cramplock replied, "it's a sign of courage." He went to a cupboard and took out lots of little carving tools. "And the flowers are poppies, I think, not roses."

A little bell rang.

"Customers, customers," said Cramplock, laying down the pencil he'd just picked up. "Mustn't discourage them, I suppose, but really I sometimes think I'd get on a great deal faster without them."

"You'd be a great deal poorer, too," I said, as he finished tapping a fat heap of stiff cards on their edges against the workbench to make them into a neat square pile. I couldn't help being slightly suspicious of Cramplock this morning. Nick's words of caution kept ringing in my ears. He *did* know more than he was saying, that much was certain; otherwise, what had that mysterious note been about? Cramplock put the cards down and went towards the door; but, as he saw who was waiting in the shop, his face changed.

"Mr. Glibstaff," he said, slowly.

I felt a sudden sick misgiving. Glibstaff was a well-known local character: a small, smug, thoroughly unpleasant man who worked for the City Magistrates, and who saw it as his job to uphold justice and public order — which in practice meant he usually pokes his nose into everyone's affairs to tell them what they should and shouldn't be doing. I'd never met anyone with a good word to say about him: as far as I could tell he was completely untrustworthy, and used to threaten people with what he pompously referred to as "the Mysterious Might of the Law," as though he were some kind of divine agent. People who didn't do as he told them — or, more usually, didn't pay him whatever money he fancied charging in return for leaving them alone — tended to find themselves summoned before the Magistrates and accused of some dreamt-up offense, for which they usually ended up paying out even more money in fines. Whatever course of action they chose, a visit from Mr. Glibstaff was usually expensive — and people greeted him in much the same way as they might greet someone who'd come to tell them their house had been condemned, or that all their investments had collapsed.

But my immediate thought was that someone had tipped Glibstaff off about my recent adventures. I hovered by the door, trying to eavesdrop on the conversation. I could see Glibstaff standing, rigid and officious, saying something to Cramplock, who had his back toward me. We have reason to believe, he'd be saying, one of your employees is a thief. I'd like to ask him some questions regarding a camel!

I chewed at my nails. The two men seemed to be deep in conversation. Could it have been Cramplock himself who had called Glibstaff in? Was the game up once and for all? The more I thought about it, the more panic-stricken I became. There would surely be some officers waiting at the back door too, and if I tried to run, I'd run straight into a trap. They were smoking me out like a badger! For an insane moment, I eyed the curved blade of the paper guillotine and began calculating whether my neck would fit underneath it.

Then I heard the shop door rattle shut. There was silence. He'd gone!

I couldn't believe it.

Cramplock came back in. "Another job," he said, reading something.

"A what?" I asked, as if I'd gone deaf with fear.

He looked up. "A murder notice," he said. "We've

got fifty to do by tomorrow. What's the matter, Mog? You look rather — strange."

"It's all right, Mr. Cramplock," I said, breathing more easily, "when I saw it was Glibstaff I, er — that is, I —"

He gave a short chuckle. "Well, for once his visit was for legitimate business reasons," he said, handing me the sheet of paper Glibstaff had given him.

A REWARD
is Offered to PERSONS supplying
Information required by THE CROWN,
concerning a most BRUTAL late

MURDER

in the City of LONDON, being that of
one Wm Jiggs, Esq. Ships Chandler, of
Foulds Walk by Eastcheap on the Night of
20th May

Everything else melted away as I read this. For all I know, I might have been standing there for twenty-four hours.

"Mog? You look — even stranger than before," Cramplock finally said.

"Oh," I said, waking up, "er — it's nothing, Mr. Cramplock."

"I'm glad to hear it. Well, come on then, there's work to be done."

◈

Nick's face, when I told him, turned whiter than any of the paper we had in the shop. It was as though a little tap opened under his chin and all the blood surged away.

"When?" he hissed.

"Last night," I said. "They found him in an abandoned hackney coach — no horse, no driver, just the cab and a dead Jiggs. Near the river, just under the north end of the bridge, it was."

"How did he die?"

"It doesn't say." I reached inside my shirt for the poster I'd taken.

We were sitting in the Doll's Head again; after I finished work I'd gone there with Lash and found Nick already sitting in the corner. As soon as he saw me, he'd known something was up. Now he sat reading the big poster, his eyes leaping up and down the page as though, like me, he couldn't quite believe what he was seeing.

"I s'pose," he said, slowly, "Coben could've done it.

Maybe Jiggs was threatening to blow his cover, or something." But it was clear he was thinking the same as I'd immediately thought. The single most likely murderer was the man who'd recently had an anonymous note, and who'd gone storming off in a rage the night before, believing Coben and Jiggs had taken his most precious possession.

The bosun. And it was all our fault.

"It was our note," I said in a frantic whisper, "if we hadn't written that rubbish with an eye drawn on it, thinking we were being so clever . . ."

"You can't blame it on that," Nick said, "he'd've suspected it was them anyway. They were the people that wanted it most, 'cos they were the people he took it off in the first place."

There was silence. Our minds were rattling with the possibilities.

"Coben will think *I* told someone," I said. "Who else could've split? They were already after me for escaping from the chest."

"But he thinks you're me," said Nick. "He'll just think I've been doing Pa's dirty work as usual, and that *I* told him where they were hiding."

"Okay, so he'll want to kill us both," I hissed, agitated. "What are we going to do, Nick?"

"Look, don't panic," he said, doing a passable

imitation of someone not panicking.

"Have you seen your Pa today?" I asked.

"No. I heard him go out early this morning."

"Did you hear him come in last night?"

"Yep. He was with Ma Muggerage. They were drunk. They fell asleep straight away, far as I could tell."

"Mrs. Muggerage must know, then," I said. "D'you think they both did it? Together?" I pictured the awful pair advancing on the skinny and terrified Jiggs, backing him up against a wall in a dark alley near the river . . . the bosun's arm flexed, with Mrs. Muggerage's cleaver in his hand . . .

A man at a table nearby reached into his bag and pulled out a newspaper. I nudged Nick. We both watched him as he read, and tried to see what stories were on the front page. At one point he saw us straining to read the headlines.

"What do you two want?" he asked haughtily. "It ain't polite, to read somebody else's paper."

"Sorry," said Nick. "Look, Mog," he continued in a loud voice, "that first one's a D, and then there's a A . . . I'm not sure what the next one is." His eyes met those of the man again. "Been learnin' to read, I have," he told the man, with a proud face on.

"Sounds like you're doing very well," said the

man, unsmilingly, and went back to his reading.

"What did you tell him that for?" I whispered.

"Make him think we can't really read," Nick said out of the corner of his mouth. "He might get suspicious otherwise. Do you know who he is?"

"No," I whispered, "I've never seen him before."

"There you are then," Nick said, "he might be anybody! If he thinks we can't read, he might not be so — careful."

Eventually the man folded up his newspaper again, stuck it in his pocket, and rose to leave. He sidled past our table on his way out. "Good evening," he said.

"Oh — evenin'," Nick said, grinning stupidly.

"Evenin'," I added. When I was sure he'd gone, I got up and went to the bar to ask Tassie if she knew who the man was.

"Can't say I know, Maaster Mog," she said, her brow furrowed. "But I seen him once or twice before. Has business in Leadenhall Street, I've heard 'em say."

"What makes you say that?" I asked, intrigued.

"Well, 's funny you should ask about him, 'cos so did another customer a few days back. Just like you, Maaster Mog, started asking questions about 'im the minute he'd gone. A regular conversation started in 'ere, and I heard one man tell how he'd climbed into a cab outside and how he'd distinctly heard him give the instruction 'Leadenhall Street' to the driver. 'S only a guess, though, Maaster Mog."

Tassie was miraculous; nosy, but miraculous.

"That might be important," I said to Nick quietly as I sat down, "did you hear what she said? Other people have been asking after him."

"Leadenhall Street's a long way off," said Nick. "It's near Spintwice's. And he's too smart-looking to live round here. So what's he been doing in here in the first place?"

It was anybody's guess, and I realized that Nick had been completely right to make sure we didn't give too much away. I was anxiously trying to work out how much of our conversation he might have heard before we'd realized he was there.

"Well, anyway," Nick said, "we can read that newspaper in peace now."

"No," I said, puzzled, "he took it with him. I saw him put it in his pocket before he went out."

Nick placed a neatly folded newspaper on the table.

"Shocking, the number of thieves round here," he said.

❖

The item we were interested in took quite a lot of finding. It had a couple of column inches on page two.

CABMEN QUESTIONED

Corpse Found in Abandoned Hackney Carriage

Carriage drivers in the City of London were questioned today over the discovery last night of a man's body in a hackney carriage near Swan Stairs. The deceased has been identified from certain belongings about his person as Mr. William Jiggs of Foulds Walk by Eastcheap. Mr. Jiggs was an unmarried chandler. The authorities are pleading for testimony from witnesses who may have seen or spoken with Mr. Jiggs on the night of May 20th. A gentleman with a bandaged head, described by eyewitnesses as having been with the deceased early in the evening, is urgently sought. Mr. Jiggs is known to have been at the Three Friends Inn, Whitechapel, which he left on foot. The cause of his death is still uncertain as no marks of obvious violence have been found on the body.

"No marks of obvious violence?" I said, surprised. "They didn't cut him up with a meat cleaver then."

"Yeh, that's the surprising bit," Nick agreed. "You don't think he was poisoned, do you? I wouldn't have reckoned that was much in my Pa's line."

I read the column again, fascinated, trying to imagine the events which had led to Jiggs being left for dead in the carriage. "I suppose they followed him home from the Three Friends," I said.

"He wasn't going home," Nick said, "not if he was found down by the river. I'll tell you what I think. I think the murderers were disturbed. I'll bet they did him in somewhere else, and were taking his body to the river to dump it. But for some reason they had to scarper and Jiggs was left in the cab."

"How could they take a dead man in a cab without the driver getting suspicious?"

Nick laughed shortly. "You think most drivers wouldn't just do what they were told, if someone like my Pa turned up in the middle of the night with a dead body over his shoulder and stuck a knife in their face?" he said.

"I wonder where Coben was," I said. "I bet he's lying low, knowing that stuff about a man with a bandage is all around town."

"He'll have taken it off," said Nick. "And I shouldn't be surprised if he's halfway to France."

There was a sudden clatter at the taproom door which made us both jump; and two of the regular customers, men I knew from another of the shops in the square, came bowling in good-naturedly. We greeted them as they strode over to talk to Tassie; and they stopped in their tracks.

"What have we here?" one of them asked. "Two peas in a pod! Well one of you is Mog Winter, but as sure as I'm standing here I can't tell which." And they laughed and pointed and generally drew attention to us for the whole of the next five minutes.

"I think we'd better stop going around together," I said to Nick in a low voice. "Too many people have seen us already. It's not safe to come here anymore. Tomorrow evening, if you can, meet me at the fountain." This was close to Nick's house, and sufficiently busy to make it a likely place for two lads to be seen without arousing suspicion. I got up to leave. "And keep your eye on the jeweller's shop," I said, "if anyone's watching it, watch them!"

"I've done this before," said Nick, "I'm all right. What are you going to do?"

"Keep my head down, I think." I hitched up my pants and tugged at Lash's lead to make him stand up. "See you tomorrow."

"Mog," he said.

I stopped in the doorway. He was sitting looking

very small, with the enormous newspaper spread out in his lap.

"Be careful," he said.

As I left the Doll's Head I looked very carefully in every direction before deciding which way to go. Turning into the little narrow lane which was the quickest route home, I became aware, out of the corner of my eye, of something moving, a little way behind me. Constantly, during the last few days, I'd been convinced that eyes were watching me from every available window and from behind every corner. It crossed my mind, not for the first time, that someone might even have been watching me from the windows of the Doll's Head itself. I'd toyed with the idea of asking Tassie exactly who she was letting rooms to at the moment — but I was wary of arousing even her suspicion. The fewer people who knew what we were mixed up in, the better.

When I turned my head, I could have sworn I saw someone disappearing behind a wall. I was *definitely* being followed. In that case, I thought, I'll confuse them. Grasping Lash's lead and drawing him close to my heels, I made up my mind to follow the most convoluted route home I could possibly devise; and I headed first down a path between red brick walls, leading in completely the wrong direction. On one side, the most ramshackle buildings in the whole parish leaked their effluent not only into the nearby Fleet ditch, but over the cobbles in the lane. In these ruins, with the white spire of St. James's Church rising behind them, were hordes of people for whom London hadn't found a use. This was where they nested, in a dense huddle, sleeping ten or twenty to a room — children alongside grown-ups, healthy people alongside ill people — in disgusting houses which had been here for centuries and which had fallen into such disrepair that they should really have been knocked down years ago. Every now and again, one of them would fall down: with no more warning than a sudden crescendo of creaking, it would just collapse, sending a cascade of dust and bricks and wooden beams out into the lane and leaving a hole between two houses like a gap in a mouth where a tooth had fallen out. Anyone unfortunate enough to be inside at the time would probably be killed among the collapsing rubble. Those who'd ventured out would return to find themselves with no where to live; and the process would start again, of finding another unsafe and squalid building into which to move themselves and their blinking, consumptive family. If their minds were agile enough, they might plot clever and violent crimes; and if their bodies had enough energy they might give a squalid existence to newly wailing little children beside whom the pinkest and baldest of rat-kittens stood a better chance of survival. There was no shortage of stories of people who'd gone down these lanes in the dark and never been seen again; and, in spite of my anxiety to get away from whoever it was who was following me, my heart was in my mouth at every street corner and I stopped each time, plucking up the courage to venture round the corner for fear of what I might find.

But what really frightened me was that I knew I was really no different from the people who lived here, and that if I'd been spilled out from my mother's body onto dirty straw or old newspapers in one of these damp and stinking houses, I'd now be just the same. A cloth-wrapped bone-creature who made other children scared; a thin, jaundiced thing with sunken eyes and no understanding of anything but survival; a scarecrow.

It would be getting dark very soon, and by now I was pretty sure I'd shaken off my pursuer. I'd turned north and west and south and west again and doubled back on myself so many times I'd lost track of where I was. When we rounded the next corner we were suddenly in a familiar, much wider street into which the evening sunshine poured reassuringly, and I could see the unmistakable open space of Clerkenwell Green at the far end. Lash knew where he was now. We weren't far from the back of Cramplock's, and he struck out purposefully for home, practically dragging me behind him.

As we neared the square, I could hear something from one of the houses nearby. At first I thought it was a person singing, but after a couple of seconds' listening I changed my mind. It was certainly music, of some kind, on an instrument which might have been a flute, or a bagpipe, but somehow didn't quite sound like either.

Then I remembered the Irish tramp — who had talked in his own musical way about sounds like snakes. So he hadn't been mad after all: as I stood listening to this convoluted, dizzying music I realized I was hearing exactly what he'd described. Extraordinary, rising and falling, twisting itself up in knots, it was somehow as different from normal music as the strange symbols on the man from Calcutta's note were different from normal writing. Something about it reminded me of those unfathomable squiggles dangling from their line like knife-slashed washing. And I'd heard it somewhere before! Hadn't I heard it, when I thought I was imagining things, locked up in Coben and Jiggs's stolen chest?

Running now, along the lane toward the source of the music, I suddenly knew what I was going to find. And, sure enough, peering through the gates into the dingy backyards, I could tell it was coming from the mysterious empty house next door to Cramplock's.

Lash was straining on his lead to get away.

"This way," I said to him, tugging at the lead to try and rein him in. "Here, boy."

He wouldn't come anywhere near. No amount of trying would make him stay with me, and in the end I just let him go. "Home!" I said as he stood looking at me, at a distance of five or six paces, his head on one side. "Go home!"

He knew what that meant. Turning back to the high iron gate as he scampered off, I stood peering through for a few moments; and, taking a deep breath, I pushed it open.

I found myself venturing into a tiny and hopelessly overgrown little jungle of a garden, surrounded by high brick walls. The strange music now seemed to fill the hot evening air. A twisted old yew tree had clambered, over the years, all the way up the wall, forcing its branches in between the bricks. Ivy and creepers and swathes of big broad leaves clung to every surface. There was a constant drowsy hum of insects, and the heat of the evening and the encroaching vegetation made me feel as though I were suddenly somewhere else entirely, in a foreign country, and that London had somehow melted away completely. I felt very peculiar, as though I was no longer inhabiting my body but seeing myself standing there from the outside — much as I had done while locked in the chest at Coben's, and last night at Spintwice's after we'd opened up the camel. I remember thinking, dimly, how strange it was that I'd never even realized this garden existed: never even imagined there might be such a garden here.

Now the music faded away; and I came to my senses and ventured between the clinging plants to the little back door, listening for signs of activity inside. I couldn't hear anything. I still felt dizzy as I pushed open the door, which swung away slowly and heavily on silent hinges.

It was quite dark, and I stood for a while allowing my eyes to adjust. But I didn't see what I expected to see. I was in a low stairwell, with a set of wooden stairs leading upward ahead of me. The paneled walls seemed to lean at different angles, which made the whole place look a bit like an optical illusion. Dust floated passively in the late evening sunlight. The boards creaked as I ventured in; and as I peered into the little rooms, all of them apparently empty, I became more and more mystified.

I had been in here once before, and it hadn't been like this. Defying Cramplock's warnings, I'd ventured in here, a long time ago, and there had been nothing: no floors, no stairs, no paneling; simply a big, dark, burnt-out shell, with walls of bare blackened brick, and gnarled charred beams reaching across the empty space above my head where an upper floor had once been. I remembered it vividly.

Yet now there wasn't a trace of fire damage to be seen. Someone must have been in here, rebuilding it — although there was no furniture, or any obvious sign of anyone actually living here.

Without even realizing how scared the rest of me was, my feet began to take me slowly upstairs. There were three rooms leading off the landing, all of them as bare and empty as those downstairs: except that the walls of one of them were lined all around with solid oak panels from floor to ceiling. And right in the middle of the room, standing in a shaft of sunlight, there was a kind of pedestal: and, sitting upon it, at my eye level, a little statue.

I went over to it. It was made of brass, and seemed to be of a figure sitting cross-legged with his hands resting, palms upward, on his knees. As I looked at it more closely in the fading light, I noticed the face wasn't that of a man, but of an elephant, with a trunk descending firmly down into its lap and two fine little tusks curving out on either side. In size, and in color, this little statue was very similar to the camel. I ran my fingers over the brass: over the little feet, over the folded robes. In the center of the forehead was a tiny, bright red jewel, shaped like a little teardrop.

The ruby, if that's what it was, was picking up the light of the sinking sun through the window, and glowing with a rich, ethereal light. It looked like a single eye in the center of the elephant's forehead. As I gazed into it, it seemed to glow more brightly, almost fiercely. I couldn't stop looking at it.

I have you, it seemed to say. *I am in control.*

Momentarily, I felt dizzy again; then the light faded, as though the sun had gone behind a cloud or finally sunk below the horizon. My fingers played over the big flat forehead and the little bump the jewel made; and as I ran a forefinger down the smooth, tapering trunk I realized it was hinged, and could move.

Slipping my finger behind the trunk like the trigger of a gun, I pulled; and it sprang up with a sudden click to point upward so that the little elephant-man now seemed to be throwing up his trunk and trumpeting, silently enraged. To my alarm I heard a clatter some-where behind the wall. I froze: I immediately assumed it must be someone coming in, but as I looked around the room I realized what the noise had been. I must have triggered a mechanism which opened a little trap-door over by the far corner, in the oak paneling of the wall. I pushed the elephant's trunk carefully back into place with my thumb, and went over to have a look.

When closed, the panel just looked like any other; but now it was hanging slightly open, at shoulder height, like a flap. Well, how could I resist lifting it to find out what was behind it? With the slightest of squeaks the little door swung up to reveal a secret compartment, about the height of a small adult and not much wider. A hiding place — not a very comfortable one, but big enough for a person to stand in. At first I thought it was empty; but, once my eyes had grown used to the darkness, I realized there was a big, urn-shaped wicker basket standing inside. Intrigued, I reached in and grasped the basket with both hands. It was lighter than I expected: but as I lifted off its lid, I could tell there was something in it.

I peered in. Whatever it was lay in the bottom, dark in color; not, at first sight, very big. What might it be? A piece of cloth? Something edible?

Then, slowly, with a long sinister rustle against the wickerwork, whatever it was moved.

It was something alive! There was just enough light to see it squirming in the bottom of the basket, disturbed by the sudden movement, waking up, rearing up a slender and lethal black head. In mingled panic and revulsion I shoved the wicker lid back on.

A snake. *The* snake! How could I have expected anything else? I had to get out of here.

But as I slipped back out of the secret compartment, I heard the unmistakable sound of a door handle being rattled below; and then slow footsteps, as someone stepped into the hallway and stopped at the bottom of the stairs. I was trapped.

As I looked around the room in a panic, I could hear the footsteps echoing relentlessly up the stairs towards me. There was only one possible place to hide.

Tears welled in my eyes as I crawled back into the secret hiding place. I shoved the snake basket as far forward as it would go, right up against the trapdoor, and pressed myself into the back of the cavity. I didn't know which I was more terrified of: the man from Calcutta, or his snake, which I could even now hear slithering drily around inside the basket.

I held my breath in the darkness. Within seconds the footsteps coming through into the room, and I could do nothing but squeeze farther and farther back against the wall, praying he wouldn't spot me. The grey light of dusk penetrated the hiding place as the flap was lifted open, and a pair of hands reached in and closed around the basket.

I braced myself and stood as rigidly still as I could, my heart pounding, praying I couldn't be seen. A voice began speaking softly, in a foreign language, cooing as if the words were addressed to the snake. The basket was lifted carefully out through the flap; and as the voice continued to sing softly and I pressed myself tightly against the back of the compartment, the trapdoor swung shut, and clicked.

I opened my eyes. Complete darkness. The footsteps were receding, muffled now, thumping down the stairs. My blood was still pounding in my ears. I hadn't been discovered, and the snake had gone — but now I was locked in. For at least a minute I didn't move, my head reeling with the events of the past few minutes. When I did move, it was because I felt the wall of the compartment suddenly shifting behind me.

I tried to stand up, but I'd been leaning with my full weight back against the wall and it was collapsing. Before I had time to do anything about it, I had fallen through in a cascade of bricks, and was lying, grazed and dizzy, on my back in the dark.

9

HIS LORDSHIP

Just as I was telling myself the noise I'd made falling through the wall must surely bring the man from Calcutta back up the stairs to investigate, I felt something wet in my face. In a surge of panic I thought it must be the snake again; but there was something too affectionate, too altogether familiar, about the sensation.

"Lash?" I whispered in astonishment.

He responded to his name by intensifying his licking, his whiskers tickling my face so much I eventually had to push him away in spite of my relief. Pulling myself into a sitting position, I suddenly realized where I was. I was in my own room above Cramplock's shop. I'd fallen through the wall from the house next door into the cupboard of my own bedroom!

Things began to make sense. As I wrapped my arms around Lash's neck, I realized exactly how the snake had been able to get in and out of my room the previous night. The bricks of the dividing wall between my room and the hiding place next door were obviously so loose, the man from Calcutta must just have been able to lift one out and let the snake slide through. At any time of the day or night, he could send it into my room, or come sneaking in himself, just by moving a few bricks! Holding onto Lash's neck to steady myself, I got to my feet and began to brush the dust off myself.

Somehow I had to tell Mr. Cramplock about the wall, so he could get it cemented up as a matter of urgency. Otherwise, I realized with a shiver of fear, I was in real danger of being killed while I lay asleep.

There was no sound in the house, and the place was in darkness — Cramplock had obviously gone home — but there were bricks everywhere, and I'd have to put them back, or the man from Calcutta would immediately discover the hole when he returned.

When I'd finished it looked a bit lopsided, but at least there were no gaping holes, and I told myself it would have to do. It had been a long day, and I suddenly felt an overwhelming urge to lie down. But questions were still darting around my tired head like fireflies. Where might the man from Calcutta have been going with his snake? Wherever he was by now, I was sure he was up to no good.

Lash had disappeared out of the room and I whistled to summon him up from the printing shop downstairs, where he was no doubt sniffing around doing his nightly checks, satisfying himself before bedtime that everything was where it should be, and smelled as it should smell. With a scrabble of feet on the steps he was back, and, as I bent to make a fuss of him, I saw he had something in his mouth.

"Where did you get that?" I asked him.

It was a piece of paper. At first he hung onto it, treating it as a game as I tried to free it from his jaws. But it was going to get torn.

"Lash!" I said sharply, "Drop it!"

I picked it up, and unfolded it.

"Where did you find this?" I asked him again.

It was chewed, and a bit soggy, but I could still easily read the few words it bore, in the same scratchy handwriting as the note Cramplock had found nailed to the door the other night.

BOY,
MUST SPEAK. BAD MEN
FIND YOU. MUST WATCH
3 FRIENDS.

The stilted message made me shiver involuntarily. These were the rushed, misshapen letters of the man from Calcutta again, and very obviously intended for me. But something was different from the threatening note he'd nailed to the door the night before last. I read it four or five times over.

This didn't seem like a threat. It was a warning. As though the man from Calcutta wanted to stop me from getting hurt.

I went to sit down on the bed, and as I did so I kicked something which gave a dull metallic clunk. I felt around on the floor in the half-light, and just underneath the edge of my bed my fingers made contact with my cookie tin of treasures. It had fallen from the shelf and rolled across the floor when I plunged through the back of the cupboard.

I pulled off the lid and reached inside. Among the pieces of paper I found the man from Calcutta's earlier note, with its tatty little nail mark. There was no mistaking the threat there, I decided.

SO CLEAVER FIND HIS CAMEL.
I SHOW HIM DEATH SOON.

But as I stared at it, I began to think about it more carefully. Who was the "him" supposed to mean? I'd assumed it meant me, and if so it was obviously a threat — but "him" could have been anybody. And then, I realized with mounting excitement, "his camel" might not mean my camel at all — but the *bosun's* camel. Maybe it meant *I* was so clever to find *his* camel.

And if "him" was the bosun . . .

"Lash," I said to him, holding his ears up so he'd listen properly, "I think this might be important. Do you understand?"

He licked my nose. My heart was beating fast. I'd been tired a minute ago, but now I couldn't have been more awake. I was bursting to talk to somebody, but at this time of night, in an empty house, there was no one except Lash to talk to.

So I did what I always did when I had something on my mind which couldn't wait until morning. I reached inside the treasure box again, and pulled out Mog's Book.

I'd had so many adventures since my last entry, it was hard to know where to begin.

Something amazing has happened, I wrote. This seemed to be the way I was beginning every page these days.

The man from Calcutta is hiding out next door, I continued. *I have found out where he keeps his snake. The house is full of peculiar music, like an enchanted house, and inside it is all as if the fire had never happened. Now it seems like a dream, but I know it is all real because he has left me another note. I think*

I was stuck.

"What do I think, Lash?" I asked him.

He sneezed, then looked astonished, and his tongue came out to lick his nose.

"A great help you are," I said.

I might have been wrong about him all along. Maybe he wants to help me. Instead I think it may be the bosun he is really after. I have to watch him. He is so scary, yet it is as though I am being pulled toward him, wherever he goes.

My eyes were hurting. I closed the book, pushed everything back into the tin, and put it back in the cupboard. Then I climbed into bed.

But I didn't stay there long. There was so much going on inside my head I could no more sleep than flap my arms and fly. "Must watch the Three Friends," the note had said. So why wasn't I?

I made Lash stay in his basket and, as silently as a black cat, let myself out of the printing shop. It was completely dark now, and some of the poorly lit parts of the city were frightening at this time of night. Almost immediately, I wished I'd brought Lash with me, and very nearly went back to get him. Whispering voices met my ear every now and again, from doorways or from basements beneath my feet. The faces of thieves and bosuns and men with baskets lurked in every shadow, even when no one was really there. I hurried on.

I was still thinking hard about the man from Calcutta. He was obviously a very dangerous man; but was he in danger too? I pictured his tall, alert frame striding through the dark streets with his snake basket, his eyes darting at every sound, the brim of his hat bent secretively over his face.

MUST SPEAK.

How was he intending to talk to me? Climb through the wall in the middle of the night? It was all making me feel very uncomfortable indeed: but although I knew I was still profoundly afraid of him, part of me wanted to talk to him, too.

When I set off I had felt confident of where I was going: but in the darkness the narrow streets of this part of London all seemed very much alike, and I very soon began to wish Nick were here to lead me confidently through the maze as though it were broad daylight. There was a strong smell, and a general air of damp and disease. I'd also lost all sense of direction, so I couldn't tell whether I was going toward the river or away from it, toward the City or away from it. I was quite startled, therefore, when I suddenly emerged from a particularly dilapidated old tenement to find myself on the corner by the Three Friends Inn.

I sneaked across the street to get a better view. The inn stood at the end of a crooked row of tall houses, which leaned toward it as though they were trying to elbow it down the hill and into the river. Opposite the inn was a soaring old church with a small cemetery, and it was in through the cemetery gate I crept as I tried to find a hiding place. At one point the cemetery wall was particularly low, and hidden in shadow. Gravestones stood palely in a mean little cluster, like children refusing to talk to one another. Every now and again a rat would scatter loose earth or scrabble with its sharp feet against a box beneath the soil. Turning my back on all this, I crouched to watch the inn.

Over the road people were loitering, sailors and workmen in their shapeless clothes. The occasional murmur drifted across the road, which became a busy roar whenever the door was opened and smoky light fell over the cobbles. There were still hundreds of people in there: people who probably wouldn't go to bed until dawn broke, or until they fell into a drunken sleep wherever they were sitting. A short distance away down a dark lane, the lights of ships glinted on the dirty water of the Thames. Every now and again I cast a nervous glance behind me. Who might be lurking behind the tombstones? As I listened, I thought I heard something resonate high above me — a faint, stifled *clang*.

But there was a sudden barrage of noise from the opposite direction as a group of men tumbled through the door of the Three Friends to continue a drunken brawl and pushing match for which there hadn't been room inside. One of the men appeared to be being forcibly ejected by the others. He was so hopelessly drunk that he kept falling against the wall as he tried to stagger off along the street. An upstairs window rattled open as the crowd of men were pushing him away, and a woman's voice screamed, "Serve you right, you filthy pig! Come back when you can conductcherself! Pig!" More customers seemed to be gathering in the doorway to see him off, roaring in amusement and looking up at the window above their heads as the woman slammed it shut. I was too far away to pick out the faces of the men as they stood with the light from the inn falling across them, but as I watched I became more and more certain I recognized one. He was currently laughing and pointing, but the last time I'd seen him he'd been slumped stupidly and silently in one of Flethick's chairs.

As the clamor died down, I thought I heard something moving behind me again, in the graveyard; but all I could see when I turned was the silent little cemetery with the blank wall of the church behind. I surveyed the churchyard for a few moments, watching it for movement, straining my eyes in the dark. And now something *did* move, over by the gate where I'd come in.

I watched a big uneasy figure lope out of the shadows into the road, and cross to the inn. My hands tightened around the bricks of the low wall. He was glancing nervously to left and right, and rather than go inside the inn he retreated into the shadow by the wall, to wait.

Coben.

The man I'd seen at Flethick's had spotted Coben too, and after a couple of seconds I saw him venture over to the wall to speak to him. I strained to hear what was being said; but it was drowned out by the clomping of hooves as, at that moment, a carriage came gliding around the corner, made its way up the street, and stopped directly in front of the inn, blocking my view of the villains. The sleek black horse snorted shortly, and shook its head with a jangle of brass. It seemed to be looking down its nose at the poorly dressed people to-ing and fro-ing around the inn; and I noticed it had a long, shiny scar along its flank.

The driver was leaning down and asking one of the men something. There was a murmur, and then a shout went up.

"His Lordship wants you!" someone called. "His Lordship wants to talk."

The carriage stood there, black and silent. Nobody got out. But Coben emerged from behind it — looking very scared, I realized. He stood at the carriage window and began talking in a low voice to whoever was inside. Normally a large, brutal man, he suddenly seemed shrunken: diminished by his fear, and by the gleaming red-painted carriage wheel which was very nearly as high as he was. He wasn't a man accustomed to showing respect to anybody; but, to judge from his body language, this was as close as he got. He kept casting nervous glances up and down the street and over at the cemetery where I was hiding. I shrank back, convinced I'd been seen; but he'd turned again, and was talking to the man in the carriage.

"I don't know!" I suddenly heard him say, in a loud voice. "I told you all I know!"

There was a pause while the man in the carriage said something. Coben's reply, as so often, came in dense slang I couldn't understand.

"Spoked a spavy nose," was what it sounded like; "the bosun's ginch."

Another comment I couldn't hear, from the carriage window.

"Yeah, well it'll serve Damyata right," growled Coben, and banged once on the side of the carriage with the flat of his hand. The driver gave a click and the haughty-looking horse moved off, leaving Coben standing in the road looking after the cab with an expression which, even in the near darkness, I could tell was indescribably nasty.

I watched him stroll up the street a little way, rather aimlessly, as if wondering what to do next. He glanced

at the cemetery gate, and after a few seconds' deliber-
ation he moved off in completely the opposite direction, around the dark corner behind the Three
Friends. From the inn I could hear a great deal of
laughter and song which kept bursting out at odd
moments; yet the noise seemed joyless, even pained,
and the harder I listened the more the laughter began
to sound like wailing, as if the inn were crammed full
of souls in torment. I watched the drab, flickering light
of its windows and suddenly felt cold.

Coben had completely disappeared. It seemed
unlikely there'd be anything else much to see tonight. I
gazed up at the high decorated spire of the church,
which had obviously been white when it was built, but
in whose crevices years of soot had accumulated, rather
as shadows accumulate in the corners of people's eyes
when they haven't had enough sleep. The words of a
song seemed to shimmer on the night air, coming from
the Three Friends: voices raised in a slow, melancholy,
bell-like tune, raucous and wavering.

Ding, dong, ding, dong,
Here's a sweet song:
Ding, dong, ding, dong
Ere long, life's gone.

I felt my eyelids closing and I told myself that my bed
at Cramplock's would be much more comfortable than

the rough wall against which I was leaning. Watching carefully for observers, I crawled towards the cemetery gate and made my way home, while behind me the tinny voices of the drunken singers seemed to echo down the street to the river, across the black rooftops, through the smoky night air of the humming city and into the silent fields and marshes beyond.

❖

I don't have any idea what time it was when I arrived home that night. I had dragged myself back through the streets in an exhausted trance, barely conscious; and when I unlocked the heavy door of the printing shop and crept inside in the darkness, Lash greeted me with all the fervor of a dog who had convinced himself his owner was never coming back. I turned up a lamp and took it upstairs, relieved to be home.

But I was still awake enough to be fretting about something which, before I went to bed, I just had to check. Tonight I'd heard the name "Damyata." It will serve Damyata right, Coben had growled. But I'd heard it before. I'd seen it on the document in the captain's cabin aboard the *Sun of Calcutta*. And I'd also seen it, I was certain, on one of the papers I'd taken from Jiggs's cellar.

For the second time that night I reached for my little biscuit tin of treasures on its shelf in the cupboard. Sitting down on the bed, I pried off the lid.

It was empty.

I must have forgotten to put the things back when I'd taken them out earlier. Had I put them on a different shelf in the cupboard? No. Had they fallen under the bed? I hunted around the room, feeling increasingly sick as I realized my things were nowhere to be found. The notes from the villains had all been taken. Mog's Book had gone too, with my latest thoughts and secrets in it; my peg doll was gone; and most importantly of all, my *bangle*.

I was trembling. I sat down on the bed, with Lash between my knees looking up at me, and tried to think. I was so tired I couldn't actually remember putting anything back in the tin; but there was no trace of the contents anywhere else in the room, and I knew I hadn't taken them with me. So where *were* they? There was only one possible explanation, I realized with a sick feeling. While I was out, for those short hours of darkness, someone must have been in here and taken them.

Could Cramplock have been back while I was out? Had he let himself in late at night, found the place empty, been nosing around my room and found the tin? Or perhaps he had come up to find me, been surprised to find Lash here alone, discovered the tin quite by accident, and taken the contents out of curiosity?

It seemed unlikely. But there was another possibility, I thought, as I stared at the open cupboard before me. The man from Calcutta could have been in here. Knowing I was out, he could have come in through the wall. He'd have seized straight away upon the pieces of paper with the notes and lists of names: they'd be *exactly* what he was after. It was bad enough to lose those, but the bangle . . . my most precious thing, gone! He'd have seen it, and known it was valuable, and possibly even recognized the engraved patterns, as I had.

Blinking back tears, I clung to Lash's neck and whispered my thoughts aloud to him. After every few words he turned his head and licked the salt from below my eyes.

"The man from Calcutta's got them," I told him. "He's got all the papers, Lash, and all the names of who's in the plot!"

The more I thought about the list of names, the more important it seemed. I'd brought the papers away in the full knowledge that they contained vital information; but in all the excitement I simply hadn't had time to sit down and look through them. I'd supposed there'd be plenty of opportunity. Now, it seemed, it was too late.

"And he's got my mother's *bangle*," I said, remembering; and now I really did burst into tears of frustration. The last thing I knew, before I fell asleep from sheer exhaustion, was the sensation of Lash trying to lick my face as I nestled my forehead into the wiry hair of his neck, and sobbed.

❖

The next morning, in the printing shop, I felt dazed. Dawn had seemed to come almost as soon as I'd laid down to sleep, and I'd probably only managed a couple of hours before I'd been woken by the sound of Cramplock letting himself in downstairs. My dreams had been vivid again, and the faces in the fog of the dream more anguished than ever. For the second time in just a few short nights my mother had appeared, and she'd been holding her arm up and pointing to her wrist. "I've lost it, Ma!" I'd sobbed back at her, as she circled her wristbone with the fingers of the other hand to signify the bangle. "I've lost it! I'm sorry! I'm so sorry!" And her lips repeatedly mouthed silent words which looked like "Find it," or "Find him," her face agonized and imploring, drifting away from me.

Now, even though I was awake, everything still seemed a bit unreal. Cautiously, at the beginning of the day, I'd asked Cramplock about the biscuit tin. He'd denied all knowledge of it, as I feared he would; but I didn't dare say any more in case he started asking awkward questions about what was in it, and why it mattered. I kept my lips tight shut and got on with my tasks.

I was waiting for Mr. Glibstaff to come back for his murder announcements, fifty of them stacked neatly on the counter. If I could get away with it, I was hoping to worm some information out of him about the murder investigation. At around half past ten he came in, strutting officiously, leaning on a knobbly and misshapen stick which he carried everywhere and used to wave in people's faces by way of a threat. It was a hot day again and his horrible, bristly little black mustache, which looked like the kind of brush you use for cleaning mud out of the nooks and crannies of boots, was shining with sweat. It was a struggle to be polite to him.

"Hello, Mr. Glibstaff," I said, as brightly as I could, "here are your posters, sir." I glanced back into the workshop, where Cramplock was now busy with a noisy press. I leaned forward over the counter. "Fascinating case this, innit, sir?" I said, putting on my enthusiastic-little-boy voice. "I been readin' about it in the newspapers, sir. No injuries! Curious, innit?"

Glibstaff was looking at me askance.

"Do they know what the gentleman died of, sir?" I asked.

"Yes, as it happens, they do," he said, closing his eyes and lifting his chin as though to stop me looking inside his head for information.

"Poison, I shouldn't wonder," I rabbited, watching his expression. "Strange business, innit? We get all kinds of murders round 'ere, Mr. Glibstaff sir, you wouldn't believe it. Why, only last weekend a murderer escaped from the New Prison! Don't know if they've caughtim yet, but *what* a villain 'e looked!"

My tactics were working. Glibstaff just couldn't resist letting people know he knew more than they did. It made him feel important. "That case and this are connected," he said, pompously. "It's believed the deceased in this case was well known to the escaped jailbird."

I feigned astonishment. "Is that so?" I said, wide-eyed.

"So if you see anything suspicious," he continued, "we'd be grateful for the information."

Oh, the number of suspicious things I could tell him! I had so many pieces of information in my head I felt as though I were beginning to burst. It occurred to me that I could have some fun by feeding him some misleading morsel — but I looked down at his heavy stick and thought better of it. The first thing he'd want to know would be how I had found out, and that would be very hard to explain. I'd probably end up in deeper trouble than anyone else.

Just to reinforce his self-importance he leaned forward and lowered his voice, his little mustache twitching close to my ear. "Nothing you can tell me, is there? Nothing you're — *concealing*, boy, is there?"

"I only know what I've read, sir," I said innocently. "Have they caught the jailbird yet, then, sir?" I persisted.

"No they haven't," he replied. "Still at large. Hiding out somewhere, no doubt . . . but we'll get him. Bow Street are vigilant, and he'll not be able to leave London, by road or by sea."

"I should think not," I said, handing him the stack of posters. Just as he was leaving, I added, "Oh — so was it poison, then?"

"Beg pardon?" he said, stopping in the doorway.

"Was it poison, sir? What the gentleman in the hackney carriage died of?"

"In a manner of speaking it was," Glibstaff said. "If you must know, they have cause to believe it was a snakebite. Good day to you."

I think I must have whistled, because after Glibstaff had gone Cramplock peeped through the door and said, "Something wrong?"

"No," I said, "he liked them."

My blood was buzzing in my veins with the thrill and horror of what I'd just learned. Suddenly I felt extremely wide awake. I was bursting to tell someone about the snakebite. Specifically, of course, I was bursting to tell Nick, and I knew telling Cramplock just wouldn't have the same impact. But I simply couldn't keep it inside.

"He, er — he had an interesting story about the murder," I said, brightly.

"Oh yes," he grunted, squinting distractedly at his type and barely seeming to care whether I told him the story or not.

"The murdered man," I gabbled, "the one in the carriage, you know, Mr. Cramplock, the one described in the murder notice, well, according to Glibstaff, it sounds incredible, but he said —"

"Mog, I need to concentrate for a few minutes," Cramplock said, not unkindly, looking up briefly before returning to his type. He didn't need to say any more. I knew enough to shut up and get on with my work. My eagerness to talk was going to have to wait.

But the events of yesterday and this new piece of information were going round and round in my head all morning. With Coben and Jiggs's list of names now in the hands of the man from Calcutta, I reflected, it was probably only a matter of days before the whole criminal underworld of London was bitten to death. As Cramplock finished his typesetting job and relaxed a little, I remembered there was something else I had been plucking up the courage to ask him, and hadn't yet had the chance.

"Mr. Cramplock," I said, "do you know about watermarks?"

"What about watermarks?"

"Well," I said carefully, "I saw a — an interesting watermark the other day. I've, um — lost the piece of paper I saw it on. But I can sort of remember it. It was like a dog asleep."

"Like a what?" said Cramplock sharply. "A *what*, did you say?"

"A dog," I said, "like this." Taking a pencil, I roughly sketched for him the little watermark I'd seen on the document that had gone missing from my tin. Cramplock eyed the little drawing through his half-glasses, and then eyed me with what looked like suspicion.

"Only one papermaker I know," he said gruffly, "man called Fellman."

"Do you buy paper off him?" I asked.

I seemed to have annoyed him. "Who's been filling your head with questions all of a sudden?" he asked, irritably.

"Nobody," I said, "I'm just interested, that's all." He picked up a huge book, slammed it sharply down on the table in front of him, and opened it, pretending to read. There was silence. My questions had plainly sent him into one of his moods, and I had no doubt that it had something to do with the piece of paper I'd found in the storeroom, with the strange message on it — which of course I'd put in the biscuit tin, and had lost along with everything else. *"I don't appreciate deceit,"* it had begun, the sinister air of a threat lurking behind the polite language. He *was* hiding something. I trod softly around him for a few minutes, doing little inconsequential tidying jobs; and he ignored me, continuing to pore over the huge ledger which I knew very well he wasn't really interested in.

After a while I had another go.

"Have we *got* any of that watermarked paper?" I asked, trying to sound innocent. "From Fellman?"

He sighed. "You don't give up, Mog, do you," he said, resignedly. "I don't buy paper from him anymore, though I used to. I had a bit of a— a *disagreement* with the man, if you must know. Bad temper, he's got. Put a lot of people off his business a few years ago, when his name got linked with, ah — with criminal types."

This was exactly what I wanted to hear.

"But he hasn't stopped making it, has he? I mean, I've seen — " I bit my lip. Perhaps I shouldn't say too much. "Who buys his paper now, then?"

"Oh, I don't think he finds much business anymore. A few of the poorer printing shops, and a newssheet or two, I suppose."

"But not — official things?" I asked. "Not — the Customs House, or anyone like that?"

"Certainly not," Cramplock said, "they only use His Majesty's Stationer, and a royal watermark reserved for official documents." He saw me looking at him intently. "So are you going to tell me what all this is about?"

"Oh — nothing special, Mr. Cramplock," I said.

10

THE MAN FROM CALCUTTA MOVES FAST

I was more worried than ever about Nick. If the bosun was in so much danger, then Nick was too — and now the man from Calcutta really *had* killed somebody.

I'd arranged to meet him after work at the fountain, but very late in the afternoon Cramplock insisted that we clean a whole lot of type particularly thoroughly and, after messing about with spirit and cloths and waste paper, I was at least an hour later in getting away than I'd intended. My cuffs stank of spirit, and I couldn't get rid of the oily sensation on my hands, no matter how much I rubbed them, or how much Lash licked them. I kept having to stop him because I was sure it wouldn't do him any good.

When we arrived, a clock was already chiming eight. It was still hot, but the shadows were growing long and the number of people was diminishing. I lurked on the street corner, watching, trying to catch a glimpse of Nick and yet stay out of sight until I could be sure there was nobody with him.

But there was no sign of him. Maybe he'd gotten tired of waiting, and gone home. Or maybe he hadn't turned up at all. I waited for a while, and then decided to ask someone. There was an old woman sitting by the fountain, surrounded by black skirts, with a shock of red hair billowing up from her head which made her look rather like a volcano. She was selling flowers, and I'd watched her sitting chatting to passersby, and smelling her flowers when there was no one to talk to.

"Excuse me," I said, "have you seen a young lad who looks a bit like me? In the last hour or so?"

"I see all sorts," she told me, "from sittin' 'ere. Soldiers, I seen. Cattle, I seen. Men with pitchforks, men with bottles, men with carts. Boys I seen too." She reached down for a flower and put it to her nose. I waited for her to speak again; but she seemed so engrossed in the flower, I eventually decided she wasn't going to, without prompting.

"So?" I said, "did you see a lad or not? A bit taller than me, sort of skinny, with a big bruise up here."

She was smiling at me from behind her flower. "Boys," she said, "all shapes and sizes, some little, some fat, some blond, some black. Warious," she mused, "as warious as flars. A man I seen with no legs today, swingin' himself about on his fists. A grand man I seen with a wig as long as a horse tail. A man I seen with a big basket. A man I seen kickin' a child, today," she said, tailing off sadly and putting her nose back into the flower.

"Just a minute," I said, "Lash, come *here!* Did you say a man with a big basket?"

Her eyes were twinkling, but she said nothing. I tied Lash's lead to his collar, wary now.

"Where was he going? This man with a basket? Did he have brown skin? Or a mustache, or anything at all?"

Still her eyes twinkled.

"You buy a flar off me," she said, suddenly and sweetly, "and maybe I tell you, mmmm?"

"Oh lor," I said, "just a minute." I fished in my pocket and found a halfpenny. "How many flowers do I get for this?" And how much information, I wondered.

"Roses," she said, "tulips and roses. And lupins." She looked up at me. "And white poppies," she added, "Norfolk white poppies. You give me your ha'pney, and here's half a dozen. Lovely Norfolk white poppies!"

I gave her the money. "Now," I said, "this man with a basket."

"Running," she remembered, "not half an hour

ago, as I sat here, running thataway. Yes — a foreign gentleman all right. 'Andsome, and tall, and his coat black and beautiful. But a nervous gentleman, clutchin' his basket, oh so precious! What was in it? Don't ask me, but precious! Must a been! Thataway," she said again, nodding over to her left, "running."

"And the boy I was asking after?" I said. She shook her head, and went back to the flowers.

So the man from Calcutta's trail had grown warm again suddenly. My mother's face came into my head again, imploring as she had done in my dream this morning, clutching at her wrist. I had to go after him. The way the flower woman had indicated the man had gone was the same direction as Nick's. I might as well head for Lion's Mane Court.

When I got there I left Lash tied to the same post as before, promising him I wouldn't be long. He licked my face trustingly, and I stood up. There was no sound from the bosun's house as I crept through the passage-way into the little courtyard, already bristling with shadow as the dusk closed in. There were no lights burning in the windows; but I thought I'd better watch for a few minutes to make sure the coast was clear — so, as before, I crept into the stable which belonged to the inn next door, and which afforded such a good view of the yard.

The dark corner where I wanted to sit was already

occupied. By a familiar, pale object more than half my height, tapering inward toward the ground. The snake basket.

I stood frozen behind the stall, fervently hoping the horse wasn't going to kick me. There didn't seem to be anyone else here — just the basket, standing there like a silent oriental sculpture. The sun had now gone down completely and there wasn't enough light here in the stable to see inside the basket, even if I had dared to lift the lid. But if I knew the man from Calcutta, he wouldn't have left his precious snake in the basket unattended. The snake must be somewhere else.

And even as I stood there, in the damp corner of the stable, I began to detect from the darkness outside the sound of a low, sinuous voice . . . singing.

Sure enough, a peep through the hole in the stable wall revealed the dark, hunched figure of the man from Calcutta, over in the shadows, bending over the cellar grating.

He must have sent the snake inside.

I SHOW HIM DEATH SOON.

I was gripped by panic. *Nick!* I pictured him backed

against the wall, terrified, as the snake reared its head, coiled at his feet or on his bed, its tongue flicking in the dank air. Agitated, in the dark, I lost my footing in the straw and reached out to grab something to steady myself. My hands clutched at the basket; but it couldn't stop my falling weight and suddenly I was sprawling on the muddy straw. With a terrific clatter the box toppled over against the wooden wall, making the sick horse stir in its stall and give a kind of groan, which seemed to linger and resonate in the timbers of the stable until it was inconceivable that the man from Calcutta hadn't heard it. Cursing myself for my clumsiness, I leaped back up to press my eye to the hole. I could see him looking over at the stable in alarm. He stood up, and began to approach.

I was trapped. He was coming back to the stable door, and there was no other way out! My only chance was to try and hide in the horse's stall, at the back, in the deepest of shadows, and hope I wouldn't be seen. I shuffled alongside the horse, patting the poor creature's mangy flank and whispering, "Easy boy."

The stable door rattled. The man from Calcutta was standing, listening now, just a few feet away, just inside. I couldn't see him; I couldn't hear him; but I could *sense* him, his dark silent presence, between me and freedom. I prayed the horse's wheezing breath would drown mine out, as I sank to my knees in an attempt to get as far out of sight as possible. Now I was kneeling underneath the horse: as I peered out between its trembling black legs, its grimy tail formed a kind of curtain between me and discovery.

I didn't dare move. It was almost too dark to see anything at all, but now I could hear movement in the stable, and the man's low murmuring in his own language. I realized my knees were getting wet, and a foul smell was rising to my nostrils as I crouched there. It was all I could do to stop myself from coughing.

He stayed for about two minutes, I suppose — but it seemed like hours. Then there was the tiniest creak as he left the stable, and all of a sudden the *sense* of him was no longer there. Although I could tell he'd gone, I gave him plenty of time to get away. Just as I'd decided to risk crawling gingerly out of my hiding place, the horse gave a sudden shudder and a jet of something wet began to spray across my back.

I scrambled out and, as I stood up, I banged my head on a beam and doubled up again in pain. What a mess, I thought, clutching my head and feeling the stinking liquid dribbling down my shirt and pants. Why on earth had I let myself get mixed up in all this?

The basket had gone. The courtyard was empty, and the coast was clear. I scuttled across to the cellar window. A few times I hissed, "Nick!" — but there was no reply. Nothing stirred. There was no light.

I had to find out if Nick was safe. I'd have to risk going down into the cellar, through the scullery. I froze as the pink-painted door scraped across the floor when I pushed it ajar; but all seemed silent and still inside; and as I ventured in I saw no one on guard, and nothing blocking the trapdoor down to Nick's little cellar room. Picking a lantern off a hook just inside the door, I ventured over to the trapdoor, pulled it up, and peered into the hole.

"Nick!" I whispered.

Nothing. Of course, I knew he wasn't in there. They would never have left him unguarded with the cellar open like this. But I had to be sure. I took a couple of tentative steps down the ladder.

"Nick!" I squeaked. "It's me!"

Still no sound. As the lantern sent its dim glow around the cellar, it was quite clear there was no one there.

So where was he?

I slid down the last two steps until I was standing on the grubby floor. I'd brought the most revolting smell into the cellar with me, and as I looked down I noticed I'd left little pools around my feet and some strands of yellow straw scattered loosely around the floor. I was very wary in case the man from Calcutta had left his snake down here, and for the first few minutes I just paced, slowly, around the little room, watching and listening for any sign of movement. There was nothing: it was soon clear that the man must have retrieved his snake before he left, having found no one here for it to bite.

Nor were there any clues as to where Nick might have gone: no notes, no sign of a disturbance. There was a low bed in a corner, and a small bare table in the middle of the room, with a flickering stub of candle on it in a waxy old dish. The only thing I discovered was a crumpled handkerchief, sitting on the old bedsheet, spotted with dark blood. What was the story behind *this*, I wondered with a sudden misgiving.

But all further thought was halted as I heard voices up in the courtyard, one of them unmistakably Mrs. Muggerage's.

I was trapped! I suddenly realized I'd left the scullery door open, and I wouldn't even have time to pull the trapdoor shut above my head. It was a dead giveaway. Thinking quickly, I threw a few things into disarray: ruffled up the bedsheet, tipped up the candle, flung open the cupboard, overturned a couple of bottles; then snuffed out the light and dived under the rickety old bed.

There was an almighty clattering from up above; and, almost as soon as I'd hidden myself, a shaft of light broke into the room and Mrs. Muggerage's voice blared, "All right, come out, oo'ever you are! We've caughtcha!"

There was silence for a couple of seconds.

"Get down there and see who it is," she said. And Nick's voice piped up.

"But what if they — "

"Shut up and get down there!" There was a sudden series of thuds as someone half fell, half ran down the steps.

"There's nobody here."

"What?" Mrs. Muggerage sounded contemptuous, as usual.

"It's empty," said Nick's voice, "there's nobody here."

I held my breath as Nick's feet came close to the bed.

"Someone's been here, looking for something. But they've gone."

There was a clomping sound as Mrs. Muggerage came down to see for herself. Eventually I heard her grunt with disappointment.

"Well," she said, "you can stay down 'ere now. I'm going to put the keg back and if I hears one peep out o' you . . ." Her threat remained unspoken.

The trapdoor was slammed and I heard Nick sigh. There was a creak as he sat on the bed; and then came the sound of the heavy keg being scraped back into place on top of the trapdoor. Nick began to sniff.

At first I thought he'd detected the smell of the horse manure I was covered in; but I soon realized he was crying. I lay there listening to him, not daring to move.

Eventually I whispered, "Nick!"

There was a creak as he sat up, startled.

"Nick, it's Mog," I hissed, "I'm under the bed. Ssssh!" Trying to be as quiet as possible, I shuffled out, and sat up on the floor, blinking.

"Mog! What are you doing here? Why did you —"

"Listen," I said, "the man from Calcutta's been here. I watched him letting his snake into this cellar. He was after you, Nick, or somebody in this house any-way." I got up and sat on the bed, so I didn't have to whisper so loud. "He's only just left," I said, "two min-utes earlier and you'd have disturbed him."

"Mog," Nick said, still sniffing, "you stink. *Again!*"

"I know, I had to hide under a horse. Where've you been?"

"It's a long story." Nick wiped his nose on his sleeve, and then his eyes. "How are you going to get out of here now?"

I hadn't thought of this, I'd been so relieved to find Nick was all right; but I was more impatient to hear his story than to worry about how we might escape.

"Can Mrs. Muggerage hear us?" I asked.

"Not if we whisper."

I decided I'd better try and start from the beginning. I told him about the snakebite; about the house next door to Cramplock's; about the elephant statue and the cubbyhole; about the man from Calcutta's latest note.

"He's got it in for your Pa," I said. "I've been thinking about that other note he left. And I'm pretty sure when he wrote 'I show him death soon,' he really meant the bosun."

A sudden noise from above made us both jump; I stopped talking abruptly and we listened; but it seemed it was only Mrs. Muggerage slamming a door somewhere.

"I thought it was my Pa coming in," said Nick. "He was so angry when he came home last night — mainly about you. He thinks you're a spy for Coben. He kept asking me about you and I told him you were a saddlemaker's boy called Jake. He beat me black and blue, Mog, I thought he was going to kill me." He wiped his eyes again. "He didn't believe a word I said. Oh, I hate my Pa, Mog! I hate him *so* much!"

Nick sounded as though he was about to cry again. I remembered what he'd said the other day, when I'd first met him, about my being better off than he was, despite not having parents at all. At first I'd thought he'd be anxious to learn his Pa was in so much danger; but now I was beginning to realize just what it might be like having someone like the bosun for a father.

He was silent for a few moments, swallowing his tears.

"So, where've you been?" I asked eventually.

"Ma Muggerage told him how I kept sneaking out," he continued, wiping his nose, "and this evening he came bursting in and said if I was so good at crawling through windows I could come and help him. He took me to this little house where he said Coben had been living. I suppose it must have been Jiggs's house, you know, where they took you and locked you up the other day. And he made me crawl in through a broken window to look for the Camel. I had to smash the glass some more to squeeze in, but I cut my leg. And he wanted me to look for a load of papers. He said he had to have them and I had to find them. Well, they weren't there, Mog. I knew they wouldn't be, but I couldn't tell him that, could I?"

"How did you know they wouldn't be there?"

"What? Well — because — because *you* took them, didn't you?"

"Yes," I said, suddenly realizing, "yes, I suppose I did. But Nick — they've gone!"

"Who have?"

"Not who — the papers, I mean." I was embarrassed. After all Nick's worries about the safety of

Cramplock's shop, I now had to admit the most important evidence in the whole affair had been taken from there, under my very nose. "They've been stolen," I said rather sheepishly. "And so have — " I bit my lower lip, wondering suddenly whether I should mention my treasure tin. Nick might think it silly and sentimental. "Some other stuff's disappeared from my room with them," I said vaguely. "The man from Calcutta must have taken them. He's probably been in through the wall."

There was too much information to swap at once and neither of us was really understanding what the other said at this stage. Mrs. Muggerage hadn't left him a lamp, but she had at least lit the candle; and in the flickering light I watched his face, the remains of his tears still glinting on his cheeks.

"Well," he said at length, "Coben's not living there any more, of course, he's probably in France by now. But my Pa still hit me when I couldn't find anything, as if it was *my* fault Coben had gone. He's so *stupid*, Mog."

"I saw Coben," I said slowly, "at the Three Friends last night."

Nick's jaw dropped. "You went *there* as well?"

I told him about the cab, and the conversation Coben had had with the man they called His Lordship.

"He was nervous, Nick, you could tell. This Lordship must be someone pretty frightening. And

Coben was talking to him about — "

I was about to say, about Damyata. But something made me stop. Up to now I'd told Nick everything I'd found out. I *had* to trust him — I had to trust *somebody* — it was the only way I could prevent myself going mad. Except that something, deep inside me, was nagging at me to keep it to myself. Just this name. Just for the time being.

Nick was too interested to notice I'd stopped halfway through a sentence. "So where did Coben go after that?" he urged me.

"I don't know," I continued rather lamely. I'd run out of story now. "Into the darkness somewhere. I couldn't follow him."

Nick was looking at me. "You've had even more adventures than me," he said, and sniffed deeply again. He looked at me. "Your hair's all wet," he said, "and your clothes . . . what on earth happened to you?"

"I told you," I said, "I had to hide under that old horse in the stable over the way."

"I still don't —" he began, and then stopped. A look of horror crossed his face as he realized what had happened, and then he began to laugh.

I couldn't help laughing too; but then I remembered Mrs. Muggerage upstairs. "Ssssssshhh!" I hissed.

Nick reached over and threw me a ragged old towel, with which I thankfully dried myself as best I could. "Here, stick these on," he whispered, rooting out a pair of pants and an old brown shirt.

Making a face, I pulled my stinking wet shirt over my head. But as I was doing so there was a sudden clatter from above and Mrs. Muggerage's face appeared at the trapdoor. I rolled off the bed onto the floor and Nick stood up.

"What is it, Ma?" he called, just a little too quickly.

"Who's down there with you? I can 'ear whisperin', and . . . and *laughin*'," she added bitterly, as though the latter were the worst crime she could imagine.

"No, Ma. Honest."

A foot appeared on the top step. I held my breath. "I been listenin', Nick boy, and you been talkin' to someone. It's that nasty little boy Jake again, innit? 'Ow did 'e get in?" She came stamping down the stairs.

"There's no one here, Ma," Nick protested, his voice quavering with fear. I hadn't had time to scramble completely under the bed, and I was desperately hoping I couldn't be seen.

"Don't you lie to me," the huge woman snapped.

"I ain't lyin', Ma, honest. You don't have to come down. Honest."

"You've 'ad enough warnin', Master Nicholas," she growled. Her voice was deep with menace, in a way I'd never heard a woman's voice sound before. "You've told enough lies lately, yer little rat. One more lie, Nick boy." She advanced into the room. "Come on. One more lie!"

Something very peculiar happened to Mrs. Muggerage when she got really irate. She seemed to grow, for one thing, until she completely blocked out every other object in sight, as though someone were inflating her from behind. And her muscles seemed to tense, and her neck grew stiff, and her head shook slightly, and her eyes went glassy. It was as if, at some sudden prompting, every last trace of humanity drained out of her and she became an animal, or even a machine, perfectly adapted for violence.

"Don't!" moaned Nick. He sounded utterly terrified. All at once I understood what he'd been suffering all his life. In his voice I could hear the pure sick fear his guardians' violence could reduce him to. Groping on the floor around me, the first thing I found was my sopping old shirt. Silently, I pulled it towards me.

"You lie to me, Nick," the woman cajoled, "come on. You open your mouth." As the giant shadow fell over me, I saw my chance. I launched myself up onto the bed and, before she could really react, I flung the vile-smelling shirt over her head and pulled the corners sharply.

She struggled, her face buried in the wet cotton, her neck pulled back unexpectedly.

"Gragh!" she coughed as the revolting stuff filled her eyes and mouth.

"Run, Nick!" I screamed; giving the shirt a final twist and ducking a huge swipe from her trunklike arms, I followed Nick up the stairs.

We virtually fell out of the trapdoor into the scullery; and I slammed the door down, fumbling in panic to pull the heavy keg across the top.

"It might not hold her for long," I said as there came a huge thump from beneath. "But it might be long enough." I was gasping for breath. "Come on," I urged, and reached out to grab Nick's arm. He met me in a bear hug, sudden and tight. In two seconds in the dark scullery his fear and his relief shuddered through me, like a trapped fish escaping into open water. Two seconds: then he let go.

And we ran.

❖

We broke our run only to untie Lash from his post; and we finally stopped at a street corner nearly a mile away, where we clung to a cornerstone and gasped for breath like hounds.

"She . . . hasn't followed us," Nick said, holding his sides. "I thought she . . . was going to kill us . . . both."

We stood panting for a while in the dark.

"I think," I said, "we'd better go and check on Mr. Spintwice."

As we moved through the streets, keeping Lash on a tight lead, I told Nick more about my expedition the previous night. We were careful to keep our voices down in case unwanted ears were close at hand. At one point we felt stones raining down on us, and when we turned we saw a couple of ragged boys haring off into a dim passageway. Even the most harmless of kids, we knew, could for a couple of pennies give up information to someone with really malicious intent. These apparently innocent children were the eyes and ears of the underworld.

Nick, of course, could tell at a glance who was who. "Swell," he'd murmur, and pull us back into the shadows as a well-dressed young man with a face scarred by smallpox sauntered by, casting a shrewd eye about him as he went. Dodging thieves such as this, we eventually reached the little silversmith's shop.

Lash was straining at the lead.

"What is it?" I asked him. He'd picked up a scent, and was pulling us not towards the front door but to a high gate at the side of the house, stained green with mold.

"Is that a way through to the back?" I asked. "Only,

Lash seems to want us to go that way."

We felt our way down the lane, so narrow we could touch both sides without even stretching our arms. The ground was covered in mounds of smelly garbage left outside the backs of the houses; stumbling over these, we found Spintwice's tiny back door. Lash stood there expectantly, looking up at us.

Nick knocked, and we waited. He knocked again.

"He sleeps in this back room," he whispered, "he ought to hear us." He knocked harder.

There was no reply. The more we knocked, the more undeniable the responding silence. Lash started scrabbling at the door with his front paws. We tried knocking on the grimy little window.

"Mr. Spintwice!" Nick called softly.

Lash was whimpering now and I was getting worried. "You don't think something's happened to him, do you?" I asked anxiously. Nick said nothing. He was feeling around the window sash, and in a couple of seconds he'd slid it open.

"Mr. Spintwice!" he called in.

Putting our heads inside, we could hear a muffled banging sound as though someone was trying to attract our attention.

"Come on," said Nick, "he's in trouble." I helped push him up through the little window. Lash bounded up after him; and I followed, Nick pulling me through into the little back room where the banging sounded quite distinctly now.

"Mr. Spintwice!" Nick called.

We tried to avoid the tiny furniture as we dashed through the house. The noise turned out to be coming from a tea chest on the floor of the shop. Its lid was firmly nailed down. "Mr. Spintwice!" Nick called through the side of the chest, "is that you?"

"Mmmmmmppphhhggg!" came a strangled voice from inside, followed by a long and furious storm of kicks. Nick found a claw hammer, and soon the long brown nails were pried out of the chest lid and Mr. Spintwice was revealed, trussed up like a turkey, with a silk handkerchief around his mouth.

"Thank heavens you've come," he said as soon as we pulled the gag off his face. "I thought I was going to suffocate."

"Who did this to you?" asked Nick.

For the first time since I'd met him, Spintwice wasn't grinning. There was a dark crease of fear across his face. If we hadn't come to check up on him, it might have been days before anyone came by, I realized. He really *had* believed he was going to die; and again I felt ashamed at having involved him in all this in the first place.

"A man with a pointy mustache," piped up Spintwice when he'd got his breath, "your snake-man from

Calcutta, I suppose. No sign of his snake tonight, at least." He was very shaken, and we helped him into a chair. "I came in here to check the locks before going to bed," he explained, "and what did I find but this fellow standing here in a cloak and looking at me with his big eyes. Didn't expect to find anyone here, I suppose. Thought he could sneak about to his heart's content! Well I soon saw to *that.*"

"But how did you end up in the chest?" asked Nick.

"Well, he was bigger than me," said the dwarf grudgingly. "I threatened him, and told him to get out, and — well, he *laughed.* As if I was some sort of . . . of circus act," he spluttered. "Next thing I know I'm being bundled in there and he's banging nails in!"

I'm afraid neither Nick nor I could suppress a smile at the thought of Spintwice trying to put up a fight. We were relieved we'd arrived in time to rescue him. But there was a lump of dread in the pit of my stomach as we tried to establish what the man from Calcutta had gotten away with. A few seconds' feeling inside a nearby cupboard was enough to make it clear he'd taken the camel; but what about the jar with the powdery contents in?

"That should be on the mantelpiece in there," Spintwice said, indicating the little sitting room across the corridor. And, indeed, that's where it still was.

I gave a guffaw of joy.

"But won't he realize the camel's empty?" Nick asked, looking worried. "He might come back for the rest."

"Shouldn't do," Spintwice said. "After you'd gone I had a thought, and I filled the camel up with flour. It'll keep him happy till he gets back to Calcutta, I should think. And then his wife can use it to make bread with, and stop his mouth from complaining."

"Mr. Spintwice," said Nick, "you're worth your weight in gold."

"As little as that?" said Spintwice, pretending to be offended. "That doesn't amount to much." He was getting his sense of humor back.

"So . . . what's he going to do with it now?" wondered Nick.

"That's his business," Spintwice butted in. "Sit down and let me make you cocoa. I think we're all better off without having camels in the house, if the consequences involve being hammered into tea chests by strange men."

I looked at Nick. He had a resigned expression on his face. He knew I wouldn't be content to sit here having cocoa with a dwarf while the villains were still running around all over London.

"I don't think we should waste much time," I said.

"How long had you been in there, Mr. Spintwice?" I asked him.

"Quite long enough, thank you," he snapped. Then he realized I really wanted him to tell me, and he thought for a moment. "It was a minute or two after nine when I came in here and found him," he recalled. He had every reason to be precise: there were enough clocks in here, after all.

"It's nearly half past ten now," I said. "You were in there more than an hour." I chewed my lip. "He's had ages. He could be anywhere by now."

"Well, precisely," said Nick. "The important thing is, he's gone, and Mr. Spintwice is safe. That's all that matters. Why don't you sit *down?*"

I was agitated. There was something that didn't make sense.

"Something's wrong, Nick. He wouldn't have had *time* to get here by nine o'clock, after I saw him at Lion's Mane Court. It must already have been very nearly nine by then."

"Well, obviously he just moves fast," said Nick.

"It must have taken us nearly half an hour to get here, Nick," I persisted. "He'd have had to do more than move fast. He'd have had to have a — " I looked at Mr. Spintwice, and remembered the book Nick had shown me the first time we'd come "— a magic carpet," I said.

Mr. Spintwice laughed shortly. "Well, if I ever see him again I'll make sure I've a carpet beater handy so I can take a swipe as he comes past."

It was plain that Spintwice needed something hot to drink to revive him, and Nick and I offered to go and make cocoa while he sat and recovered his composure.

"Why don't you calm down?" Nick asked quietly, once we were out of earshot in the little scullery. The hiss from the water heating up in the kettle was quite loud enough to make our conversation inaudible in the next room.

"There's definitely something not quite right," I said. "The more we see of that man, the more magic he seems."

"Well we can't do anything about him just now."

"I'd just love to know where he goes with the camel now he's got it back," I said.

"Mog," Nick said, "you said yourself, he'll be miles away by now. We couldn't begin to find out where he's gone."

"We've got a pretty good idea, Nick. He's probably gone back to that house next door to Cramplock's."

"And what are you going to do? Go in and fight him?" He suddenly looked dreadfully tired.

I stirred, uselessly. "I just think we ought to be doing *something*," I said. "He's got the camel, and he's

got a snake which bites people, and he's got — " *My bangle,* I thought; but I stopped myself from saying it. "I'm afraid more people are going to get killed," I said instead. "Where's your Pa?"

"How should I know?" snapped Nick, irritable now. "I'm not going anywhere where I stand a chance of meeting my Pa. Or anybody else," he added, "murderers or snake charmers or anyone. We can't stop them. We'd just be taking a stupid risk."

He poured the boiling water into three little mugs, and stirred cocoa into them. I carried the tray back through the little door into the parlor, steam pouring off the mugs like factory chimneys. Mr. Spintwice was looking much happier, and had produced a big glistening ginger cake from somewhere. He'd placed it on a low table in front of him, and was making a fuss of Lash, who was sitting between his feet, licking the little man's fingers affectionately. No wonder Nick liked coming here so much. My resistance was being broken down, and I was both exasperated and delighted.

"You're exhausted, Mog," said Nick, coming in to join us. "You spent most of last night running around after criminals, and so did I. We all need a rest. Just forget about the man from Calcutta for a bit."

I eyed the cake, my heart torn. "You're right," I sighed.

Mr. Spintwice beamed even more broadly than usual. "I think I would really be happier," he said quietly, "if you two stayed here. Just tonight."

11

THE PAPERMAKER

When I woke up the sun was in my eyes, and at first I wasn't sure where I was; but after a few seconds it dawned on me. I also realized that it was Sunday, and I didn't have to work; which was rather lucky, since the first sound I heard was the jangling of the parish bells calling people to church, and if it had been a working day I'd have overslept by three hours. We'd both slept at Spintwice's; and as I lifted my head I saw that I was alone in the big spare bed, with nothing more than a crumpling of the sheet beside me to indicate where Nick had slept. I remembered a few tired murmurs we'd exchanged before we went to sleep, but you couldn't call it a conversation. I had dropped off in no time at all, the troubled whirling in my head of the recent events and mysteries pacified, at least for a while, by the dwarf's good nature. For the first time in about a week, I'd had no dreams — or, if I had, I couldn't remember them when I woke up. Now the sun pasted bright cutouts on the plaster wall, and I sat propped up on one elbow watching Lash, curled at the foot of my bed with his tail under his chin a bit like the dog on the watermark. He twitched, whimpered a brief "Good morning," and yawned hugely.

I could hear faint voices from another room. I stretched luxuriously under the sheet, staring up at the ceiling where a large fly was revolving in agitation, caught in a spider's web, buzzing like clockwork. Details and questions began to return, lazily, to my mind.

"Nick," I said later, as Spintwice served up bacon and bread for breakfast, "I'm going to explore today. Will you come?"

"Explore where?"

I chewed contemplatively. "Not sure," I said. "Back to the Three Friends, maybe."

"You'll have to be careful, in broad daylight," said Nick.

"I shan't do anything silly," I said, a bit impatiently. "Are you going to come?

Spintwice looked from one to the other of us. "I'd rather hoped," he said, "that Nick might help me with something this morning. I got a box of books the other day and I haven't had time to look at them or sort them out. I thought you might enjoy giving me a hand."

This was too much for Nick to resist, of course, and

I realized it would be. I promised to come back in the afternoon and tell them what I'd found out; but Lash and I were alone, and swift, as we left the shop and joined the life of the streets. Darting through the narrow lanes of Clerkenwell, we headed towards the City.

After a short time we passed a row of tall, well-kept brick mansion houses with railings outside, the servants' quarters in the basement, and a short flight of steps up to a grand front door with a hanging basket of flowers above. They were the kind of houses where fashionable doctors and merchants lived. A couple of hopeless beggars, old men in broken hats which opened up at the top like round boxes, were wandering along pestering the servants at the doors. Waiting outside one of the houses was a black carriage drawn by a patient, aristocratic-looking horse.

I stopped and grasped one of the spiked railings. I'd seen this horse and carriage before.

Just to make sure, I crossed the street to take a look at the horse from the other side: and sure enough, along its right flank, there was an unmistakable smooth, long scar.

At that very moment a gentleman in black and grey, with shiny shoes, stepped briskly out of the nearest house and down the steps to the carriage. I didn't have time to hide, but just had to try and look as inconspicuous as possible on the other side of the road, picking at the leaves on an overhanging tree and hoping he wouldn't notice me. I watched him carefully. He had a haughty face, his nose held high and his cheeks sucked in, as though there were an off-putting smell beneath his nostrils. There was a low murmur of conversation as he greeted someone who was already in the carriage: the man known as his Lordship, presumably. Someone called an instruction to the driver and, as he lifted the reins, the driver turned his head back towards the carriage window and repeated the address with perfect clarity.

"Fellman's in the City Road, *Milord*. Gee up!"

The carriage moved off. I couldn't believe my luck. Fellman was the name of the crooked papermaker Cramplock had told me about!

My only problem now was keeping track of where they were going. They were moving quickly and smoothly, the carriage black and polished, the red wheels spinning almost silently as it sped along the street. I scampered along the flagstones with Lash beside me, keeping my distance behind the carriage in case I was being watched from the back window; but I soon lost sight of it, and it didn't take me long to realize I had no chance of catching it up. The road was good and it would be at its destination in just a few minutes. I stopped running.

The air began to smell fresher and fresher as we walked on, the houses around us were newer, and soon there was even a glimpse of open fields and distant green hills between some of the buildings. When we reached the City Road I began looking up and down for signs of the well-dressed man, but well-dressed men were not such a novelty around here, and I knew he wouldn't have attracted anyone's attention. I asked a man if he knew where Fellman's was, and he pointed obligingly up the road in the direction of the Angel. There was no sign, he told me, but Fellman's mill was well known.

In spite of the Sunday sunshine the buildings here seemed to admit very little light. Two rows of tall, dark-bricked houses formed a forbidding narrow gorge, in which there was scant sign of human activity. As I turned into the street, Lash lingered and started sniffing around by the corner, as though reluctant to swap the sunlight for this chilly gloom. I told him not to be so silly; but I felt goose bumps of sudden cold as, further up the street, I noticed the unmistakable, imposing black carriage of His Lordship, silent and waiting.

I led Lash up the street, quietly, and before we'd got as far as the carriage the strangest smell met my nostrils. On our right was a high brick arch, with a grubby rectangular plate on which I could just make out the three words "High Stile Passage." Venturing through the arch I found myself in a small, overgrown courtyard, in which the unpleasant smell was stronger still. This was the paper mill all right, though there wasn't much sign of industry here today: the workshop which stretched along one side of the yard had bars across the windows, with no sign of light or movement inside. Lash trotted over to one corner of the cobbled yard where there was a huge tub with something rotting and smelly in it to keep him amused. A couple of large iron bins stood in another corner, and when I lifted a lid I found a soupy, reeking mess of wet, gluey linen which made me turn up my nose and drop the lid back on with an overloud *clang*.

To my surprise, when I tried the door of the workshop it yielded with a soft creak.

"Lash!" I whispered sharply.

He came trotting back; and, leaving the door ajar, I tied his lead to a fencepost around the back of the yard, sternly instructing him to stay quiet until I came back outside. He licked his lips and sat down to wait.

The familiar smell of damp paper greeted me as I tiptoed inside. I was in what seemed to be a storeroom, with piles of boxes, shelves full of paper, old sacks, and a big iron bin exactly like the ones outside. I fingered some of the paper on the piles. It was coarse, yellow stuff which looked as though it had been here for years, judging by the thick layer of dust I blew off it. Fellman, it seemed, might be having trouble selling his papers these days. "It's all done by machine now," Cramplock never tired of telling me whenever he started a newly opened ream. Lifting a sheet up against the light, I wasn't surprised to find the familiar sleeping dog shape boldly watermarked.

To my right, through an open door, I could see the workshop with vats and benches and drying frames, and to my left another small door — behind which, as I listened closer, I could hear men's muffled voices. I couldn't make out a word that was being said, though there seemed to be more than two people talking in there. As I tiptoed back towards the door, I spotted some unmistakable words, in bold black type, on a scrap of filthy paper beneath my feet.

the Most REMARKABLE CURIOSITY that Ever was Seen!

CAMILLA
the PRESCIENT ASS

This was what I'd printed myself only the other day! I picked it up — it was definitely one of my posters. How had it come to be here?

Actually, it was *half* of one of my posters. It had been torn quite cleanly in two, and folded. When I turned it over I found there was writing on the back. And I recognized that as well.

They are closing in. I have lied.

But they already know too much and they are watching the shop.

I'm only warning you.

WHC

I struggled through the crabbed handwriting with difficulty. There was no mistaking it. This had been written by Mr. Cramplock.

But almost as soon as I'd read it, voices and clatters from behind the door suddenly made me jump. Someone was coming! Stuffing the piece of paper into my pocket, I cast about for somewhere to hide. The only place seemed to be the big iron trash can. Jumping inside, I found it had some smelly pieces of old torn sheets in the bottom; but I sank down into them and pulled the lid over me, just in the nick of time.

Through the chink under the lid I could see some men emerging through the door. There were three: the high-nosed gentleman whose carriage I'd followed; then a fat man I'd never seen before, dressed in nasty old clothes; and then — with a sudden tingle of excitement I recognized the man Nick and I had encountered in the Doll's Head, and whose newspaper we'd stolen!

It looked as though the two of them were preparing to leave; but they were lingering, only a couple of feet away from the bin where I was hiding. I tried my hardest not to breathe.

"This letter explains it all," the haughty man was saying, in a voice so pompous and drawling that it was difficult to understand.

There was a guttural cough, almost a laugh. "I don't doubt that it does," came the reply, "but you knows very well I can't read it. I just makes the paper, and I leaves it to other people to put whatever they wants onto it, and take whatever they wants off of it."

"I can't help worrying it might be a trap," the third man said. "Word reaches me that little devil's been seen where he shouldn't be."

I felt my skin crawl.

"You mean that whippet of the bosun's," came the papermaker's coarse voice. "He's everywhere, so they say. But there'll be plenty of us." To my horror, he now came right over and leaned on the lid of the bin, his voice resonating just an inch or two from the top of my head. "Boys and bosuns," he snarled, "is easily disposed of."

I swallowed hard.

"Don't worry about the bosun," said the well-dressed man sharply, "it's not his sort you need to fear the most."

"Anyway," said the third man, "let's go and pass the

message on, and we'll see you by the Old Tup at nine."

The Old Tup! It was an inn about halfway between Cramplock's shop and the prison, even more notorious than the rest of the inns thereabouts for the dishonesty of the customers it attracted.

The haughty man's voice drawled out again. "I wish you luck, gentlemen. His Lordship and I shall expect to be informed of developments at the earliest opportunity. Good day." And he left them, presumably to return to the silently waiting carriage, and to His mysterious Lordship sitting patiently inside.

"Are you going to Flethick's now?" grunted Fellman to the other man.

"I may as well," came the reply, "it's just about on my route."

At this point there was a rhythmic *clanging* on the side of the can which sent a resonating sizzle through my head. When the man by the can next spoke, his voice was indistinct, as though he'd been tapping out his pipe and had now put it to his mouth to light.

"Just . . . make sure," he said through half-closed lips, "you ain't . . . followed."

"Do you take me for a fool, Mr. Fellman?"

"I takes people for fools till I finds 'em to be otherwise, Mr. Follyfeather." This caused a slightly tense silence. "Now," Fellman continued, "if you'll excuse me, I 'ave some rags to boil."

Through the chink in the can lid I saw the other man take his leave; and Fellman watched him from the window for fully two or three minutes, until he was quite sure he'd gone, before going back through the door into the next room.

So! That man we'd met in the Doll's Head was Mr. Follyfeather from the Customs House. I remembered the name instantly, from the customs document I'd found at Coben and Jiggs's hideout. But Nick and I plainly hadn't been as inconspicuous as we'd hoped. I cursed myself, realizing that our every move had probably been watched — even if they'd made the mistake of believing we were actually the same person. These people were a very different kettle of fish from Coben and Jiggs, or from the bosun. Fellman had a streak of coarseness about him, but the other two were obviously wealthy, educated, important people — though no less criminal, it seemed, and somehow even more frightening.

Gingerly, I lifted the can lid and put my head out. Was it safe to sneak away?

No, it wasn't. Almost immediately Fellman came back through the door and I sank back into the can. He was heavily built, with skin like dough and patches of sweat darkening his clothes in several places, almost bald except for a few wisps of hair above both ears. Since he'd been speaking to his well-dressed visitors he'd donned a big greasy apron — and he was carrying a bucket. As he approached the can, I scrabbled to push the tatty bits of old sheet over my head to try and cover myself as best I could. I had a horrible feeling I knew what he was about to do. I shut my eyes and held my breath, and just hoped, as I heard him open the can lid above me, that I was hidden well enough.

The next thing I knew, a mass of cold, gooey water came tumbling into the can like flour paste, soaking through my clothes and filling my mouth and eyes. I gasped for breath. Fellman hadn't seen me: but he'd gone back into the next room for more water, and he was back almost immediately with another bucketful. There was nothing I could do except lie there and let him pour horrible porridgey water all over me again. I could hear him whistling; and as he came back with a third bucket, I began to worry that I might drown.

❖

Nick and Mr. Spintwice, in the meantime, had been rummaging through the old books the dwarf had bought from a barrow for sixpence. Sitting cross-legged on the threadbare carpet, Nick had unwrapped the newspaper parcel they'd been tied up in, blown the dust off each one, and sorted them into two piles, one to keep and the other to throw out.

He and Spintwice had just taken a break for lunch, and begun attacking a plump cheese, when I arrived.

"Don't laugh," I told them, as I stalked in. But I was wasting my time. They took one look at me and started to giggle. The gluey stuff I'd got covered in had begun to dry and stiffen in the sun on my way back, and I must have looked rather like a walking statue. Only when the bin had been nearly full of gooey liquid and old rags, and Fellman had yanked it outside into the yard to stand with the others, had I been able to crawl out, retrieve Lash, and escape. I couldn't bend my legs, and I couldn't really move my mouth to speak. Lash began yapping, as though he were joining in their laughter.

"You've turned to cardboard," said Nick. "Did you meet a witch?"

"Don't tell me," said Spintwice, "a man thought you were a fence, and whitewashed you."

"It's all very well laughing," I said, "I nearly drowned." As I stood there gradually solidifying, I told them all about Fellman's mill and the gentlemen visitors, and how I'd had to hide, and what I'd overheard. I was actually feeling quite shaken; but it was difficult to be taken seriously in this state.

"You mean to say you've walked through the streets like that?" giggled Nick.

"I didn't have much choice," I grumbled.

"Don't sit down anywhere," said Spintwice; "I'll fill a bath."

He went into the back room and I heard him lighting the stove; a few moments later he returned, dragging a large tin bathtub into the little sitting room.

I began to feel very nervous.

"You really don't have to bother, Mr. Spintwice," I said.

"Nonsense," he said breezily, "what are you going to do, sit there like a statue for the rest of the day? This hot water will see to that sticky plaster in no time, especially if I help scrape it off you once you're in. We'll soon have you clean, Mog, you'll see."

Nick showed me some of the books they'd been sorting out. I tried my best to seem interested; but my mind was racing, and I couldn't take my eyes off Spintwice, as he trotted backward and forward for about ten minutes, filling the bath with jugs and pans of hot water.

"Should be just about ready now, Mog," he said, pouring the last jug of water into the tub.

"I really don't —" I began; but I didn't know how to continue. I just stood there, awkwardly. Nick and Spintwice looked up at me expectantly from their armchairs; it was plain they hadn't the slightest intention of moving.

I looked from one to another of them, helplessly. There really wasn't a sensible excuse which would get me out of this. I had trusted them both with a lot of secrets by now, I told myself. They were my friends. They deserved to know.

I sat down, took a deep breath, and told them the biggest secret of all.

❖

I could see Nick just didn't believe me at first.

"No you're *not*," he said, scornfully, as though it were perfectly obvious it wasn't true.

"I am, Nick," I said. "I'm a girl. I might look like a boy, and dress like a boy, and talk like a boy, but I'm not one. So now you know, all right? And I'd rather you didn't spread it around. It sort of suits me that people think I'm a boy. In fact," I said after a short pause, "I don't know where I'd be if they didn't."

I often thought about this. For one thing, I wouldn't be working for Cramplock, because girls couldn't be printers' devils, and they couldn't really be apprentices of any sort, come to that. It was only because I looked so much like a boy, and had found it working to my advantage when I was still in the orphanage, that I'd been able to break out of there and make my own way in the world at all. For years now I'd been doing all the things girls weren't meant to do, like run and whistle and swear — at first because it helped me to keep up the pretense, but after a while just because that was *me*, and it came naturally.

Being like a girl would be all but impossible, after all this time, probably.

Spintwice's dumbstruck astonishment had softened, and he was looking at me with something like admiration by now; but Nick was still skeptical. "So Mog's a girl's name, is it?" he said.

"Well, it's —" I began, and then stopped. I couldn't bring myself to tell him quite *everything*, not just yet.

I was named Imogen, after my mother, but I genuinely couldn't remember ever having been called that. Even in the orphanage I was Mog. I suppose it must have started as a kind of pet name; but as far as I was concerned the two spare bits of my name had just fallen off at either end and been forgotten. "It's both, isn't it," I said in the end. "and it's, kind of neither, too."

I watched him considering this. But he was still having trouble with it.

"But you're not — *like* a girl," was all he could say.

"So what are girls like?" I asked him, smiling.

"Well — they're — well, they're not much like you," he muttered eventually, defeated.

"So do you still want to be friends?" I asked him.

"I s'pose."

"It's got to be a secret," I said. "You're the only people I've ever told. Please promise me you'll keep it."

Spintwice gabbled his assent, eagerly, and began to apologize; but Nick was still quiet.

"Nick?" said Spintwice, in a tone of reproach.

"I might forget," said Nick, a bit sullenly.

"Try and remember," I said.

He looked at me, a smile tugging at the corners of his mouth despite himself.

"It's just a shock," he said at last. "Of course I will, Mog."

I felt a sudden strange elation, as though I'd scored some kind of victory, in a way I can't really explain. My fingers were working with nervous energy, scratching and kneading Lash's ears as he sat at my feet, and he was growling with pleasure. *He* knew, of course, without being told; but I'd never confided in another human being about this. I'd become so used to behaving like a boy that I suppose I half believed I *was* one, for much of the time. The truth I'd carried around with me for years only mattered when I was alone. Now, at last, I'd found someone I felt I could trust sufficiently to tell; and only now did I realize how much effort it had really taken not to give myself away. It was like having a great burden lifted from my back.

Perhaps — in Nick's company, and Mr. Spintwice's — I might be able to feel comfortable *behaving* like a girl. As it sank in, and I saw the way they both looked at me, and the way their reaction to me had suddenly changed, I couldn't stop grinning. It made me feel almost as dizzy as the smell of the powder in the camel.

The clothes the dwarf had dug out for me were an appalling fit; and, after I'd had my bath and gotten dressed, with Nick and Mr. Spintwice keeping out of the way in the back parlor, I looked like something out of a traveling circus. But I had to make do with them as I went through to join them for tea and cheese — and at least I was feeling better with all that paste washed off.

They were being *incredibly* nice to me all of a sudden, all their earlier teasing quite banished.

"How did you two do then?" I asked between mouthfuls, looking around at the piles of books.

"Some of them turned out to be good," Nick replied.

Chewing, I hitched up my awful pants and crouched in front of the piles of books to look at the spines. *"Crimes of the Last Century,"* I read, "Being a Catalogue of Misdeeds, featuring most unsavory Murders, Poisonings, Robberies and Waylayings."

"Thought we might keep that one," Nick said, almost embarrassed.

I picked up another. *"A Booke of Devils.* True Hiftories of Wickednesse and Witch-Craft." Flicking through its fragile pages, I found lots of engravings of sad-faced men being pulled apart by grinning creatures with hooves and pitchforks. "Some of these books are ancient," I said.

"I know. They're falling to pieces mostly. There are even one or two in Latin," said Nick.

But my eye had fallen across something else — and it was more interesting than the books. "Just a minute," I said. "Nick, have you seen this?" I lifted one of the discarded sheets of newspaper which had been used to wrap the books. "Listen," I said, excited.

PRECIOUS LANTERN STOLEN

Indian Jewel removed from
Ship at Dead of Night

Authorities Baffled

The SUN OF CALCUTTA, a gold lantern worth several thousands of pounds, has been reported stolen from the East Indiaman which bears its name. It had been widely rumored that the ship, lately docked, was bearing items of great value, and the popular intelligence has now been exploited, as was confirmed today by Capt. George Shakeshere. Customs authorities guarding the ship all night expressed incredulity at the loss of the object, which was first found to be missing after a routine search of the ship at dawn. For the East India Company, Mr. Follyfeather spoke of his astonishment and anger. Few eyewitnesses have come forward but a foreign gentleman in a black cloak, seen in the vicinity late last night, is urgently sought.

"I can't believe I'm seeing this," I said.

"What is it?" asked Spintwice, holding out his hand for the crumpled sheet of paper. Nick and I just stared at one another while he read it. "I suppose this is the lantern you saw when you went snooping around the ship that time, Mog?" I nodded. "And there's your man from Calcutta again," he added as he read further. "I'm getting rather sick of hearing about him."

"Follyfeather's got some nerve," said Nick, "going on about how shocked he is, when he's really after it himself."

I was thinking hard. "I bet this is what they were talking about this morning," I said. "They were making plans to meet tonight at the Old Tup. You know where that is? Near the prison. Just around the corner from the man from Calcutta's hideout. I bet they're planning to go round there and look for the lantern."

"It seems to me," said Spintwice, "they were asking for trouble leaving a gold lantern on board like that. I mean, you didn't have any trouble getting aboard, did you, Mog?"

"No," I said, "but I nearly didn't get off again."

"Still," said the dwarf, "it sounds almost as though it was *too* easy to steal. As if — someone *wanted* them to take it."

"You mean, it might have been left there to trap them?" said Nick, grasping for the dwarf's logic.

"Perhaps. Of course, it could be that the very people who were meant to be guarding it are the ones who've taken it."

"That makes sense," I said, "that means Folly-feather."

Nick suddenly said, "I can think of someone else who could get onboard that ship any time of the day or night." I looked at him. "My Pa," he said. "Nobody would challenge him."

"We've got to go to the Old Tup tonight," I said; "they're all going to be there. You'll come with me, won't you, Nick?"

"Oh dear," said Spintwice.

"Oh, *Mog,*" sighed Nick.

12

DARKNESS FALLS

The Old Tup was a squat, ugly little inn crouching stubbornly between much newer brick houses, having dug its heels in centuries ago and resisted the demolition men's sledgehammers ever since. It was notorious. Its regular clientele consisted of thieves and habitual drunkards, and it seemed a very appropriate spot for Fellman, Flethick and Follyfeather, and their assorted alliterative crew, to be gathering.

It was even hotter tonight, if possible, than at any point during the last week. The Old Tup was built virtually right on top of the Fleet, and the stench was so strong tonight that the air almost hummed. The sunset blazed pink behind the city roofs, and the bricks of the nearby houses had absorbed so much of the sun's heat today that they were warm to the touch as we pressed ourselves against them to watch from a convenient corner. "This place is popular tonight," Nick whispered. "We're not the only ones watching it. Word's got about. Look!"

It took a little while, but as I scanned the street in the gathering darkness, I began to be aware of numerous peeping, dodging little faces in corners and hidey-holes, gathering information about what the criminal world was up to, their eyes shining in the dark like fireflies. And it was clearer than ever, after the conversation at Fellman's, that we, too, were being watched.

Slowly, in twos and threes, the villains gathered. They greeted one another in low monosyllables, but they said almost nothing else as they stood in the shadows, waiting. I recognized Flethick and one of the men I'd seen in his smoking den. Then Follyfeather turned up, impeccable and confident, with a man I'd never seen before. Finally, a stocky threesome strode into view, led by Fellman the papermaker. With him was a much larger man, built like a wrestler, whose face was so similar to Fellman's that they might have been brothers; and another especially violent-looking character with a stick and a severe limp, and a withered arm held tight against his side in a short black velvet coat.

They were a very unpleasant-looking crew indeed. I couldn't help remembering, with a tingle of fear, the words Fellman had growled while I was hiding at the mill this morning: "Boys and bosuns is easily disposed of." Almost as soon as the last of them had arrived, they'd melted into the darkness: but they were off up the street which led to Cramplock's shop, and to the strange house next door where I'd found the man from Calcutta's hideout.

"Come on," I said, "let's go round the other way."

Trying to be as quiet as possible unlocking the heavy front door, I let Nick into Cramplock's and followed him inside. I was really frightened now, and I wasn't entirely sure what we were going to do: but it seemed like we'd come too far to stop now. With Lash scampering ahead of us, we went up the stairs and into my little room. Nick's face was solemn in the low lamplight as I showed him the cupboard with no back, and the bricks which lifted out to reveal the secret crawl hole.

"Are we going in?" he whispered.

"Not if the snake's in there," I said.

We stood there for a while, not moving. Eventually Nick said, "Well? Let's find out!"

I looked at him. "I can't move, Nick," I said, "I'm scared."

Nick tutted, and knelt to feel around in the hole. "This was your idea in the first place," he said, pushing his head inside.

"Keep your voice down," I whispered.

"Give me that lamp," he said, holding out his arm.

Slowly, Nick crawled into the hole. All I could see were his feet disappearing inside.

"Can you see the basket?" I whispered, anxiously. I

was holding onto Lash's collar, waiting for him to start growling or barking as he sensed the snake's presence. He sneezed a couple of times as the dust from the dislodged bricks met his nostrils, but otherwise he didn't seem bothered. Maybe the snake wasn't there.

Nick's voice was muffled, sounding a terribly long way off. "There's nothing in here."

"Can you get out of the trapdoor?"

There was a muffled clatter, and a few moments' silence. Then Nick came shuffling back out, backward.

"There's nothing there," he said, "I mean — nothing. No snake. No trapdoor. Just a big, empty house, all dust."

What was he talking about?

"Did you hear any voices or anything?"

"Not a whisper," he said.

I gathered my courage. The snake evidently wasn't there, and we could take Lash in with us, if he'd come.

"After you," I said.

Nick went first again, clutching the lamp; but as I crawled through after him, he stopped.

"Go on," I whispered, trying to push his backside with my head.

"Hang on," said his muffled voice, sounding irritated. There was a scraping sound as he climbed gingerly out the other side.

"Whoa," I heard him say softly.

Something was wrong. The trapdoor was missing. The little hidey-hole wasn't even here. All I could feel was rough, damp bricks scraping on my knees as I crawled through. Now that Nick was through the hole he wasn't moving. He was standing, holding up the lamp, looking around. As I poked my head out, a slow creeping horror spread through me.

Nick spoke first. He was as bewildered as I was.

"This can't be —" he began.

I knelt in the rough brick hole, staring dumbly at the scene the lamp was illuminating before us.

Everything was gone. The walls, the floorboards, the trapdoor, the snake basket, the pedestal with its elephant statue. The stairs. The house was an empty, burnt-out shell. Blackened beams stretched out into the gloom ahead of us. Dust floated thickly in the yellow lamplight. Nick was standing gingerly on a thick plank which had once supported the floorboards of the rooms upstairs; now there were great yawning gaps through which we would fall twenty feet to the ground below if he took one false step. Above us, the ceilings had gone too. Nick lifted the lamp to light up a huge empty roof space, the wooden supports again apparently charred by fire. Everything was rotten and abandoned, just as it had been when I'd been in here that time years ago.

"This isn't what I expected," Nick was saying.

"I can't believe my eyes," I said, my voice trembling.

He handed the lamp back to me and shuffled slowly along the plank, his arms held out to steady himself. What if the beam was rotten?

"Nick, don't," I said.

Halfway across the beam, he stopped, hovering, like an apparition, in midair, in the middle of the giant empty space.

"Come back," I urged him.

He was agile, but the lamp was tipping him off balance a bit, and he wobbled alarmingly as he stepped back along the plank toward me.

"I thought you said —" he began.

"Nick, I can't understand this. This isn't how it was. I don't think this can be the right house."

"What do you mean, not the right house? Where else could we have ended up, climbing through the cupboard wall?"

"I don't know," I said, terrified, "but this isn't what it was like, Nick. It was properly paneled, with strong new floors, all polished. Like there was someone really living here. And there was a statue of an elephant with — Nick, it's all gone! Like it was never here at all."

My head was swimming with confusion. Had I dreamt everything the other night? I remembered the details of the house with the utmost clarity. How could

I have gotten it wrong? Had I been in a completely different house? But there could be no mistake. Hiding from the snake-man that night, I'd fallen through the same hole in the wall we'd just climbed through.

There was a sudden dry clatter from the back of the house, like a gate banging. In the shock of the last few moments I'd forgotten about the villains.

"It's them," I said, in a panic, grabbing Nick's sleeve.

"Watch it!" he hissed. "You'll push me off!"

We listened. There seemed to be no further sounds. They were biding their time, lurking at the back of the house, discussing their strategy, perhaps.

"But what have they come looking for?" Nick asked in a whisper. "I don't understand. The house is completely bare."

"I know," I said, "everything is gone. But it was here, the other day. I can't quite believe it, but I think the man from Calcutta must have just scarpered, and taken everything with him. It's the only explanation."

I knew it didn't make sense. He couldn't possibly have stripped out all those floorboards, that staircase, those panels, not to mention the heavy and conspicuous elephant statue, in the two short days since I'd last stood there. So had the house been burnt up in another fire since then? And, if it had, how could I not have known about it?

I sat in the hole in the bricks, with my legs dangling through, watching Nick as he moved. Quickly and acrobatically, he dropped to the floor below, with a barely audible thud. There was a sudden scrabbling and rustling as the floor around him cleared of rats. Then, for a few moments, he was gone into the shadows, and I couldn't see him; until the lamplight picked up his movement again, over by the opposite wall. He'd done this a thousand times before: sizing up an unfamiliar house in the dark, looking for possible escape routes. I could see him looking out through a filthy old window onto the garden.

"Can you see anything?" I whispered down to him.

"Not really. It's too dark. But they'll see your lamp, Mog. Put it out, and come down."

"I can't climb down there," I whispered.

"Yes you can. I'll catch you. But leave the lamp."

"What about Lash?"

"He'll stay where he is, won't he? Tell him to stay."

I couldn't think of any more excuses. Resignedly, I leaned back into the hole and reached out for Lash, waiting patiently on the other side of the wall. His muzzle met my fingers in no time and started licking them.

"Stay," I told him, "I won't be long, old boy. Stay there. Lie down. Good dog."

As I stood up, I clutched one of the bricks to steady myself, and it came away in my hand with a sharp scraping sound, making me teeter and flail in thin air for a few seconds before I stuck out a foot to stop myself falling. By a miracle, my foot made contact with the beam; but the brick plummeted ten feet to the floor, landing with a clatter near Nick's feet; and as I tried to steady myself, I also lost my grip on the lamp. I think I screamed as it fell with a loud smash, missing Nick by inches; and then I screamed again, much more loudly, as it immediately burst into flames, sending a sheet of bright fire licking up the walls, lighting up the entire cavernous interior of the house.

Things happened too quickly now for me to remember them very clearly. I remember being terrified, gripping the beam, trying to lower myself toward Nick's outstretched hands without getting burnt. I remember looking down into his grim face as he grabbed my ankles, and a jarring pain in my knee as we both collapsed awkwardly to the floor.

And I remember a sudden burst of activity at the back door, as whoever was out there heard the noise, and saw the light of the fire, and started trying to break the door down to get inside. Any moment now it was going to give way, and we'd be caught. I was too frightened to say or do anything.

Nick's face was frightened and black with filth, his eyes darting around for a means of escape. There was another door, leading out onto the street; but to get there we'd have to run through the rising flames. Some of the dry timbers and bundles of old paper which littered the floor had begun to catch fire, and the house was filling with smoke. For long, agonizing seconds, we both stood looking at one another's black serious eyes, not moving a muscle.

"Chimney," whispered Nick suddenly, and ducked past me to investigate the huge dark fireplace, which I hadn't even noticed.

"Nick, we've got to get *out*," I said, panic-stricken, as I watched him leaning into the grate to peer up the chimney. "We'll be suffocated — burnt up. Can't we make it to the front door?"

"We haven't' got time," he shouted. "Over here! Quick!"

I scrambled over the uneven floor, away from the rising flames, to join him by the fireplace. The hearth was broken, and the stone surround burnt and disfigured, but as he stuck his head up into the cavity Nick could see it was easily broad enough for a child to climb into.

"Follow me," he said. "I think there's room up here. We'll have to stay still."

"Don't worry," I muttered, pushing him from below as he heaved himself up the chimney. I knew the flimsy wooden door wasn't going to prove to be an obstacle for long.

And it didn't. I'd only just scrabbled my way up into

the pitch black hole, grazing my elbow on the sooty bricks as Nick pulled me up by the forearm, when I heard the door fly open and determined footsteps enter the house. I didn't have a very good foothold, and my feet were sending quiet showers of soot cascading down into the fireplace. Looking up, I could see nothing — not even Nick. The chimney was narrow, and seemed to get narrower as it got higher. I could feel years of filth filling my hair and trickling in a gritty stream down my neck.

There was more than one man in the house now. I could hear clattering sounds and voices from below, though I couldn't really make out what they were saying. I was convinced we were going to suffocate up here; if the fire took hold beneath us we were completely trapped, because the only way out was up. As though he'd read my mind, Nick began moving his feet, looking for footholds so he could wriggle further up into the chimney. He was standing on my fingers. *What are you doing, you idiot,* I wanted to scream . . . but I didn't dare make a sound.

Below us there were several sets of footsteps clomping on the echoing floor; trying to stamp out the fire, maybe. But there were also shouts, and now there came gasps of what sounded like pain. It came like a rhythm: a thud, immediately below me, no more than a few feet away from the fireplace — followed by a groan of anguish. Another thud — another groan. Someone was being beaten up.

Soot was still trickling down on top of me, dislodged by Nick's movements, and it was filling my mouth now, too, coating my tongue like foul sand. I was feeling so dizzy I was sure I couldn't hold on much longer.

The thuds seemed to stop. Nick had stopped moving and we hung there, in the airless darkness, clinging on for dear life. Had the men gone? I was no longer really aware of anything except my own discomfort and inability to breathe. I was going to die. We were both going to suffocate. I reached up in a panic for Nick's ankle.

But I couldn't find it, and my fingers couldn't find their handhold again, and anyway I no longer had the strength to hold on. I slid painfully down the filthy bricks, falling rapidly, plunging out into the fireplace amid a rainstorm of black dirt.

I had to hold my fists against my eyes because they were hurting, grit-filled, impossible to open without pain. After a few seconds I realized I could feel something soft and wet around my face; and as I reached up to investigate I found the unmistakable shape of Lash's head and the cold dampness of his nose. He was whimpering slightly with pleasure and relief at having found me.

"Lash!" I whispered, thrilled. "How did you get down here?"

I could hardly believe it, but there seemed to be no one else there to greet me; no gleeful villains closing in to wring my neck. And there was, I realized, no fire. The men must have put it out before it took proper hold.

In a second Nick had slithered down too, and was whispering into my ear in the darkness. "Are you all right? What happened?"

I coughed, as quietly as I could.

"Don't worry," I said, wiping my eyes, "I don't think I'm hurt."

"I thought someone had pulled you from underneath," said Nick. Then, with sudden surprise, as he felt a damp muzzle in his palm: "Lash?"

"He was here waiting for us," I said. "He must have escaped. Did you chase the nasty men away, Lash old boy? Good dog!"

Nick stood up. There was silence in the house. Dust and soot were billowing around us. It was pitch dark now, the crazy shadows and leaping yellow light of the oil-fire killed.

"They've gone."

We stood, listening, for a long time, just to be sure. As our eyes got used to the darkness we could make out the back door, wide open; moonlight coming in between the thick foliage of the trees outside and through the panes of the grimy windows.

"It sounded as though they were killing each other," I whispered, still blinking to clear the soot from my eyes.

Nick crouched down to examine something by his feet. He reached out a hand and dabbed it on the ground.

"Look," he said.

His hand had come up wet. He showed it to me, doing his best to keep it away from Lash's sniffing nose; but there really wasn't enough light to see, and it was only by the smell that I, too, could identify what he'd found.

"Blood," I said, scared.

Nick said nothing.

"Do you think they got him?" I asked. "They've killed somebody, haven't they, Nick? Do you think it was Damyata?"

He was still silent. At first I thought he hadn't heard me.

"I said do you think — "

"Did you say Damyata?" he interrupted me, in a quiet voice.

"Yes. Do you think it — "

He leaned forward and took me by the shoulders. "What do you mean, *Damyata?* Where did you get that from?" He was still speaking very quietly, but there was an urgency in his voice which was almost anger, as though I'd said something to hurt him. His breath was in my face. I was confused. I'd obviously never mentioned the name to Nick before, but I couldn't understand why it made him so upset.

"The man from Calcutta," I said.

"What makes you say *Damyata?*" He was insistent, barely restraining himself. I could feel his hands trembling as they held me by the tops of my arms. Something I had said had shocked him, and I didn't know why.

"Because that's his name, I think," I said.

"How do you know?"

"I don't — I don't, really, it's just a guess. I heard — I heard somebody say it."

"I fear," Nick said, after a long sigh, "it will not be possible to reach Damyata now."

Now it was my turn to freeze. Where had I heard that before?

"I can say no more, and I am feeling weak," said Nick. "Please God this letter reaches you."

At first I thought he must have hit his head as he came down the chimney. It was as though someone else were speaking, but using Nick's voice. He was still holding my shoulders, but he'd relaxed his grip; he seemed to have gone into a kind of trance. The hairs stood up on the back of my neck as he continued to talk. I didn't like this. I clutched Lash's neck tighter. "Nick," I pleaded.

"And that you do not think too ill of me to grant some mercy to the gentle, perfect creatures who accompany it," Nick was saying, refusing to be interrupted. He seemed to be talking complete nonsense, and yet there was something familiar about the words. "My dear, Good-bye, and with all the remaining life in my body, I thank you. Your undeserving Imogen."

"Nick!" I said, in a panic, "Stop it! What are you talking about?" I was really frightened now, and the mention of my own name sent a shiver through my entire soul. It was this *house*. He was possessed by the man from Calcutta's magic.

"Nick!" I said again.

There was what seemed an interminable silence before he lifted his head to peer into my face. "You don't know what that is, do you?" he said.

"I — I've heard it before," I stammered. I was trembling. I wanted him to tell me what was happening.

"That's my *mother's letter,*" he said. "The only thing I've got from her. My mother's letter, Mog. I've had it my whole life, and I know pretty much every word of it, but I've never heard anybody else say the word Damyata before."

"What does it mean?" I asked.

"I've never known," he said. "And I still don't. Why

298

did you call the man from Calcutta Damyata?"

My head was swimming. I didn't know. I'd seen the name, heard the name . . . "It will serve Damyata right," I said, dredging my memory. "Coben said it — at the inn the other night. And I've read it. And I've read the words you just said." Many of the things which had happened in the last few days had seemed unreal, but none of them quite as unreal as this. Somehow, this was the strangest, most inexplicable, most awful moment of all.

But now I felt Lash stiffen, and sure enough there came the low sound of voices from the garden again. Nick sprang to his feet. "Mog!" he said in a clenched whisper, "my Pa!"

I joined him at the window, holding tight to Lash to stop him from growling and giving us away. Dark figures were running through the back garden and out into the lane. The branches of the willow flailed as two men wrestled with one another beneath it.

Another fight — or the same one, still going on. We stood transfixed as they rolled into a shaft of moonlight lancing between the neighboring houses. On the grass, the bosun knelt over his opponent and delivered a short series of powerful blows with his fist. There was no more sound from the house or the garden; and after a few seconds the bosun stood up, a silhouette, a purposeful and terrifying bulk.

"We've got to get out of here," I whispered, pulling Nick away from the window. "Let's try the door at the front, come on."

In the darkness we half-fell over the loose bricks and fallen, blackened timbers in our desperation to be out. The front door was heavy, and hard to open because there was so much rubble piled up against it. After we'd kicked the trash out of the way we managed to pull it open just far enough to launch ourselves through: me first, Nick behind.

"Come on!" I remember saying, before hurling myself down the steps and tumbling onto the dirty cobbles below, Lash's grubby shaggy limbs getting mixed up with mine as we sprawled on the ground.

Out here in the street, everything seemed strangely quiet, and completely still, as though oblivious of the violent activity at the back of the mysterious house. My blood was pounding in my ears, and I felt around for Nick's hand to drag him off up the street to safety.

My arms flailed around in thin air. "Nick!" I whispered.

There was only myself and Lash in the street.

I stood up. Above me, at the top of the steps, the door of the house slowly creaked shut. A dreadful silence was coming from inside: a silence of death and shock which seemed to infect the night air all around. Nick hadn't come out. I stared up at the huge dark

300

door and knew I had to go back inside. I began to feel my legs giving way, and I clutched at the railing in front of the house.

It was all too obvious what had happened. Nick had been intercepted, a familiar pair of tough seaman's hands wrapping themselves around his sides like iron clamps as he'd tried to follow me through the gap in the door. He had been *so* close. I went back up the stairs and tried to push the door open; but it was shut tight, the rubble kicked back hard against it to stop anyone coming in. Desperately, I ran, with Lash beside me, down the street and down the back lane towards the back of the house. I no longer cared who we met; I had no thought for my own peril in the face of the bosun. My only concern was to find Nick. Emerging at the end of the lane, I was just in time to see the gate swinging shut at the back of the overgrown garden, and beyond it the bosun bundling Nick into a waiting cab, which moved off with a shudder like the throes of death.

The house and garden were deserted. The little back door gaped open. Beneath the tree a man lay motionless.

My whole life seemed to sink through the soles of my feet and drain away into the earth. To let Nick be caught by the bosun, after all this! It was no use chasing the cab: it was almost out of sight already, and my body felt so weak it refused to move fast enough, or move at all. I sank against the wall, clutching at Lash to bring him close. It was all over. It was all hopeless. All the help Nick had given me in my crazy, fruitless chasings, and how did I repay him? I remembered how I'd had to persuade him, time and again, that the adventure was worth the risk. And now we'd blundered into a chaos of violence — of murder — all against Nick's will. He'd been right all along, and I'd been stupid and childish and reckless, and now the villains had escaped, and he'd been seized by his father, and heaven only knew what his father might do to him now.

The conversation we'd had before I escaped from the house was still ringing in my head. Nick had frightened me; but somehow I suddenly felt closer to him than I ever had. Something had changed: and the mysterious words he'd spoken about Damyata and Imogen haunted me, as though they mattered more than anything we'd yet encountered together. Furthermore, Nick himself seemed to matter. And, for all I knew now, I'd lost him.

Big wet blotches of black soot like paint covered my hands as I cried. I buried my face in Lash's neck; my sobs broke the awful silence, and it was a relief. Somewhere nearby, a window sash rattled. Lash lapped dutifully and cheerfully at my salty, sooty face; but never, in all the years I could remember, had I felt so helpless.

I was about to test my legs to see if they'd let me

stand up, when somebody grabbed me from behind. Instinctively, I lashed out; but an arm folded itself around my face and I was pulled back into an immobilizing wrestler's hold. "Shut it. Don't scream," said a quiet voice in my ear as I was dragged backwards into the garden, "don't make a sound."

13

THE LURK

The bosun didn't say a word to Nick as they rattled through the streets in the hackney cab. Every time the lad tried to raise his head it was pushed roughly back to the floor by the bosun, who was wearing an expression of grim satisfaction on his unshaven face. This time, he obviously thought, he was winning. Nick later confessed that, crushed on the floor of the cab, barely able to breathe, he'd been sure the bosun was taking him to the river to drown him like an unwanted kitten.

But it was on the seedy corner by the Three Friends that he was finally bundled out of the cab into the rancid night air. The bosun took a few quick glances around him in all directions, and pushed Nick roughly over to a low wall where they both crouched, out of sight of the inn. This was where his father opened his mouth for the first time.

"You sees that church there, boy," he snarled softly, twisting Nick's earlobe between sharp fingernails, and turning his head up to look at the blackened old spire. "You talk to me, boy, and tell me you sees it."

"Yes, Pa," gasped Nick, though his eyes were watering far too much for the spire to be anything more than a long dark blur.

Suddenly he felt the barrel of a gun pressing its hard circle against his neck.

"Up there," came the bosun's voice, still deadly quiet, "that's the lurk, Nick. That's 'is lurk. I smelt 'im out."

There was a revolting bubbly sound as the bosun sniffed hard, then spat copiously into the dirt at his feet. Nick said nothing, not daring to move a single muscle while the gun dug deep into the flesh beneath his ear.

"I could shootchoo," the bosun said, as though suddenly realizing, and relishing, the option. "Shootchoo dead, boy, soon as spit." His words seemed to be making so little sound Nick wondered if he was imagining them. "In that lurk, boy, there's a partickler enemy o' mine. The biggest felon what's ever crossed me. I wants 'im dead, Nick. 'E's up there, Nick, up there where the bell is. I smelt 'im. I seen 'im. I knows."

Dripping with sweat, Nick flinched as the gun-barrel bit into him harder still.

"You crawls, boy," the bosun was saying, "you crawls and you wriggles, fit to be a rat. In 'ere, out o' there. Well, now you can crawl for me. Crawl up in that lurk and shake out the worm. Bang 'im out!"

And as the bosun laughed and grunted in quiet enjoyment, Nick found himself led to a tiny doorway in the base of the church spire, in the blackness of the building's shadow, separated from the oily light of the Three Friends by a quiet, reeking graveyard.

"You show me," growled the bosun, "you can do your Pa some duty. Precious little use you been to me all these years, Nick lad. Precious little. Precious little loyalty, precious little duty, not what you'd rightly say a son owes a father. Well now's yer chance, lad. Do me this, and show me why I shouldn't blow you out." Hot breath filled Nick's face and he saw his father's yellow teeth and gums just inches away, shining dimly with strands of spit. "You shoot me that Coben, Nick boy, or I shootchoo." The crazed, inhuman expression on the man's face was meant to be a grin. "Up in the bells, Nick!" He pushed open the door in the church wall and flung Nick inside.

It was a while before he could see anything; but by feeling around, Nick soon found he was in a very narrow space with a stone wall in front of him and some very steep steps, almost like the rungs of a ladder, to one side.

"Up in the bells, Nick!" came his father's voice again; and as he peered back out of the little door Nick found his arm grasped roughly and the butt of a gun pressed into his hand. His fingers closed around it and his father pushed him backward with a gentle grunt.

He was going to be trapped in there, with nowhere to go but up, and a murderer waiting for him in the pitch blackness a hundred feet above his head.

"No!"

He flung himself back at the door, but it was already closed against him, the bosun's muffled snorts condemning him to the musty darkness.

"No, Pa, no!"

He banged on the door, panic-stricken, in the dark. He couldn't even see his hand in front of his face.

"Pa! No! Let me out!"

But there was no sound from outside. Either the bosun had walked away, or he was standing there saying nothing. It was a waste of time shouting.

Clutching at the space around him, Nick made contact with the wooden steps again; and as he felt his way up he could feel an extremely narrow hole in the ceiling into which they disappeared. There was no wonder his father had enlisted his help: the space was far too small for the great bosun to crawl into, even if he'd stopped eating for a month.

In fact, if Coben really was hiding up here, Nick couldn't fathom how he'd managed to get through the hole either.

Tucking the bosun's gun into his trouser belt, he pulled himself slowly upward, hitting his head several times on the jutting beams, making him swear. He had no idea what he was going to do. He couldn't possibly kill Coben, even if he found him. It was far more likely that Coben would kill him before he got the chance. But he'd do anything rather than face his father again.

It was a long, slow climb in the darkness: at each step he reached out above his head to ensure that nothing was lurking there waiting for him. "If I'd been able to think straight," he told me later, "I wouldn't've kept climbing. If I'd really known where I was going, I'd've sat there at the bottom and waited for help."

At length, however, he found himself standing on a little platform with a narrow slit-like window in the stone wall above him, which cast a slender ray of moonlight inside. He was in the hollow tower. For the first time now he could see the bell ropes, as still as if they were woven from solid lead, hanging down through a hole in the platform. Above him, they soared to the top where, in the dim dispersing light, he could make out the great round bottoms of the bells, black and bulbous and silent. There was nothing to suggest Coben might be up there. No sight, no sound, to give him away.

The stairwell continued upward from the platform, in the darkest corner of the tower; and Nick continued to climb gingerly, taking care to make as little noise as possible. Before long he found he'd climbed on a level with the bells, and their shapes filled the cavity like giant, sleeping creatures, the more awesome in slumber because of the enormous noise they could unleash when they were disturbed. Tucked in behind the bells was a tiny little cubbyhole, with an old blanket lying on the floor, its end trailing over the beams to dangle by the bell ropes. This had obviously been used as a hiding place by someone, and recently. A shiver ran through him. But no amount of fear could distract him from the instinct, developed over years of thieving, to size up his surroundings and notice things he might need to know: signs of danger, routes of escape. Crouching to peep in, he saw two other things. A half-empty bottle of rum. And, propped against the wall, a long, curved sword.

Reaching forward, he grasped it by the handle to assess its weight. This must be the sword Mog found in the chest, he said to himself, remembering the story I'd told him about how I'd scared off the man from Calcutta.

He put it back, and sat down on the beam, dangling his legs over the edge. If he'd kicked out, he could have struck the biggest of the bells with his foot. He uncorked the rum bottle and took a small swig, closing his eyes as the burning liquid went down. But it made him feel better. Peering down, he could see the tower like a shaft falling away beneath him, to the platform he'd stood on a few minutes earlier. Just above him were massive beams to which the bells were attached, suspended from thick ropes to enable them to swing and chime. And decorative windows in the very top of the spire afforded him a view, six or seven feet above his head, of clouds pouring like smoke across the three-quarter moon. He leaned back against the wall by the little hidey-hole, adjusted the gun in his belt which was digging uncomfortably into his thigh, and soon found himself so comfortable and so tired that his eyes closed and his head sank, gradually, onto his shoulder.

❖

I had no inkling who was holding me, their arm clamped over my mouth, and it was clear they weren't going to reveal themselves until I stopped kicking. I was quite astonished to find myself not being beaten up: I'd expected worse, in fact. All that seemed to be happening was that a voice, which knew my name, was whispering to me not to shout out and not to panic.

"Mog," it hissed, "you must listen. I'm not going to hurt you."

When I stopped struggling, and he released his grip, I managed at last to turn and find out who the mysterious assailant was. I got quite a shock when, in the shadow, I recognized the extremely thin man I'd met in the Three Friends, who had told me the bosun's address. What on earth was he doing here? I asked him as much.

"It's a long story," he whispered; "it's going to take some time to explain."

Something was fishy.

"You used to have a stammer," I said.

"St-st-stammer c-c-comes and-g-goes," he gulped.

I looked at him. My mouth was still in pain from having his hand clamped so tightly over it. Despite looking as if he were made of pipe cleaners, he was obviously very strong. He loomed beside me in the darkness like a pillar. A few yards away, Lash had his head down and his paws out in front of him, attacking a hunk of raw meat, which the thin man must have thrown him as a distraction.

"Who are you?" I challenged him.

"N-name's C-C-Cricklebone," he spluttered, "B-Bow Street."

Now I understood. He wasn't one of the villains, nothing to do with Flethick or His Lordship or the bosun or even the man from Calcutta. It began to make sense. He was spying on them in much the same way as I had been, and that's why he'd been in the Three Friends the morning I'd dropped in. He was a kind of policeman: a Bow Street Runner.

Or, at least, he said he was.

Warily, I tried to find out more.

"What are you doing here?" I asked.

"I might ask you the s-same k-k-question. How m-much do you m-m . . . know about all this?"

"Not enough," I said, cagily. "Look, we mustn't stay here. We've got to find Nick. And the men might come back. Or the man from Calcutta."

"M-man from C-C —" He began to chuckle, before he'd even finished his phrase. "M-man from . . . listen, M-Mog, I've a f-few surp-prises for you."

"What sort of surprises?"

"Big ones." He could detect my mistrust. "How can I prove to you who I am?" he said, his stammer apparently disappearing again. "We've been watching you and your friend for several days. Once we'd worked out that you were two people, not just one, we realized you might be able to help us. There are a lot of useful things I think you know — and one or two quite important things you don't, as yet. What would you say if I told you there is no man from Calcutta?"

"Well, wherever he comes from! I don't know. But he was hiding in this house, or at least I think he was — and he's got a snake, and he killed Jiggs, and he tried to kill me."

"I can see I've got some explaining to do," said Cricklebone.

"Yes, you have," I retorted. "And my friend Nick's just been carried off in a cab by his Pa, the bosun, and I've got to find them before it's too late."

"I'm pretty sure I know where they'll have gone," Cricklebone said.

"What?" I was on my feet in a flash. "We've got to go after them!"

"I think we'd better go and meet someone first," he

replied, getting to his feet and towering over me like a bean plant.

"Lash," I called. "Lash! *Leave* it and come here!"

We followed Cricklebone out into the lane. "You *haven't* got a stammer, have you?" I accused him.

He turned to me. "D-d-dep-pends," he stuttered, his eyebrows jerking.

"Depends on what?"

He didn't reply. He was striding along ahead of us, his insect-like legs covering so much ground we had to run quite fast to keep up. He seemed to consist mainly of endless limbs, and the spread of his frock coat behind him made him look like a grasshopper standing up on its back legs.

"Where are we going?" I panted.

"You'll see."

"When can we go and find Nick?" I worried at him as I ran beside him. "Where is he? Do you really know? What are you going to do about that house? There was a dead man in the garden. Oh, where are we going?"

Suddenly, as we strode a dark lane leading toward the City, I heard a voice singing from beside a wall. I grabbed Cricklebone's arm.

"Who's that?" he called, stopping in mid-stride.

For all we could see, it might have been any old vagrant or pauper, lying in a gateway senseless with gin. But I knew the voice. I held on to Lash, wanting him to stay quiet.

"Well, bless me soul," it suddenly piped up, and it was the Irish tramp Nick and I had met before, "a pair of fine gentlemen, and a handsome dog if I'm not mistaken."

"He's a drunkard," I whispered to Cricklebone.

"Drunk I may be," sang the tramp, "but not deaf, young sir! And not blind neither. Didn't I just see a commotion and a riot going on in that house where the music plays? Where the music plays like heaven in a reed-flute. Magic music, now. And there they were, wicked men." He shivered audibly. "Wicked men!"

"Did a hackney carriage go past here?" I asked him.

"Did it now? That it did, young sir! Shakin' like a bag o' bones, a carriage did go by, yes my young handsome sir, yes it did. And all towards the town I saw it go." It sounded as if he were reciting a ballad, and for a moment I thought he might really not have seen the bosun's cab at all. "From the house of the heavenly music, it came," he continued in his tuneful way, "and past here, and along there."

"Where did the wicked men go?" I asked.

"Past here, and along there," he lilted again. "Now, to be sure, Nature has not lavished her gifts on me, but I can sing, fine sirs, sing like a lark, they tell me. Like a bird above the lough, sirs, a gift I have, they tell me. For just a penny, I'll sing for you! Now this gentleman's a long gentleman, and he'll like a long song. But this other gentleman's a little gentleman, and it'll be a little ditty for him, to be sure! A penny for my song, fine sirs."

"Come on," Cricklebone said shortly, pulling me away, "he's not making much sense."

"No, wait," I said, "he just wants money before he tells us anything. He's — Mr. Cricklebone, wait, why don't we just give him a penny? He might be able to — "

But Cricklebone was off, having evidently decided the man was as insane as he seemed. I had no choice but to leave him sitting there; and as I hurried after the spidery-legged policeman, with Lash following nonchalantly a few paces behind, I heard the voice behind me break into a song which struck me as uncomfortably familiar.

Ding, dong, ding, dong,
Here's a sweet song,
Ding, dong, ding, dong,
Ere long, life's gone.

"Who do we have to meet?" I asked Cricklebone, breathlessly, as he loped up the hill. But all I got in reply was a chuckle: until we came to a street corner close to the enormous west wall of Newgate prison.

Here he stopped and consulted his fob-watch.

"Should be here by now," he said, tucking the watch back into his waistcoat.

"Who should?"

Again, just a short chuckle by way of reply. What a maddening man! And how soon were we going to find Nick? I began to feel very uneasy, and to worry that this Cricklebone might very well be in league with the villains after all. What if this was a dreadful trap, and the person we were waiting for turned out to be His Lordship, or someone? I grew still more uneasy when he grasped me by the wrist; and when a shadow moved on the opposite side of the street he said, "There he is."

I could hardly believe my eyes. The figure which ran across the street to meet us, cloaked in black, with his head down, and holding a hat to his head as he ran, was the man from Calcutta.

Cricklebone had tightened his grip on my wrist, sensing that the sight of the cloaked and hatted figure approaching us might make me want to break free and run; and I could tell that Lash's hackles were up. But there was something not quite right. About the way he ran; about the shape of his head.

"Evening, Mr. Cricklebone," said the man from Calcutta, coming up to us, "who's this you've got here? A chimney sweep? Looks a bit startled, whoever he is."

My mouth must have fallen open in astonishment.

The man from Calcutta was speaking with a Scottish accent.

"Young man by the name of Mog," Cricklebone said in a low voice. "Found him at the old house in Clerkenwell. The bosun's gone off with his companion in a cab."

"Have you told him anything?"

"He probably knows most of it. Mog, may I introduce Mr. McAuchinleck of Bow Street, sometimes known as Dr. Hamish Lothian, sometimes known as Damyata. I think you'll find he means you less harm than good."

I stared at the newcomer. Under the streetlight I could see his face: he wore a long, pointed mustache, and his eyes shone white in contrast to the dark skin around them. But his features were completely the wrong shape. The curving nose was smaller and narrower than I remembered it; the forehead was undistinguished, with wisps of pale hair blowing across it; and the lower part of his face seemed less brown than the rest. Chasing around in the darkness, I'd been completely convinced by Damyata in his long coat, with his bright white eyes. But, in proper light, it was clear he didn't look as though he came from Calcutta at all.

"I'm sorry about the disguise, Master Mog," McAuchinleck said, "but it certainly fooled enough people, yourself included." As he spoke, one half of his black mustache fell out of place, and he had to reach up to adjust it. When he took his hand away again, he'd left a pale smudge under his nose where the brown makeup had come off on his finger.

I could hardly speak for astonishment. I felt like an idiot. How could I have been taken in by this? It wouldn't have fooled anybody.

"You mean the — the man from Calcutta — you're the — there is no man from Calcutta?" I squeaked.

"I'm afraid not."

"B-but the snake! Was it you who sent that snake after me?"

"There was no snake," said the man in the makeup, with a patronizing chuckle. "Listen, Mog, there'll be plenty of time for explanations later. Let's just say that everything you've fallen for, the villains have fallen for too."

"Mr. McAuchinleck has been quite convincing enough," said Cricklebone. "But now, Mog, we need you to help us. We've got a list — which I'm afraid we stole from you — of the people we're after."

I started. "*You* took it? The papers from my treasure box? And all my other things?"

"Quite. Ah — sorry about that. You'll get them back, Mog, I promise, but we had to make it *look* as though the villains had taken them. But the most important thing, Mog, is the camel. We don't have the camel."

I stared at them.

"The camel," Cricklebone went on, "you know, the camel you took from the bosun, which he took from the *Sun of Calcutta*. The, er — brass camel."

They were both looking at me expectantly.

"We need it," McAuchinleck added, "as evidence."

"But you've got it," I told him, gibbering slightly.

They looked at each other.

"You stole it back from Mr. Spintwice's," I said, "didn't you?"

"We were sure," said McAuchinleck uncertainly, "that *you* still had it."

The man was a fool. "Look," I said, "the camel was hidden at Mr. Spintwice's shop. *You* broke in, nailed the shopkeeper into a tea chest, and ran off with his camel."

"Ah," said McAuchinleck, taken aback.

"You mean you didn't?"

"*I* didn't." He looked at Cricklebone. "Did you?"

Cricklebone gripped my shoulders, and bent to look right into my face. He had to bend virtually double, like a pair of tongs.

"Mog," he said, "when did it disappear?" His voice had taken on a quiet urgency.

"Last night," I told him. "Saturday. Late. Nick and I found Mr. Spintwice in a tea chest, and he said a foreign man with a mustache had nailed him in. And the camel was gone."

"But you didn't see the man? The foreign man?

You've only got Spintwice's word for it?"

"Well yes, I suppose we have," I admitted, "but who else — "

"Mog, come with me," Cricklebone interrupted, taking me by the hand again. He looked very worried. "We have to stop whoever it is from selling the camel or anything that's in it."

"It's only flour," I said.

"No, Mog, it certainly isn't flour," said Cricklebone with a grim, humorless laugh, "oh, it most certainly isn't flour."

"Yes, it is," I said, "we swapped the powder for flour. At least, Mr. Spintwice did. So even if they took the camel, they wouldn't have the stuff."

Cricklebone's jaw dropped open.

"It won't take them long to find out," said McAuchinleck, "and then someone's going to get killed."

Cricklebone stood for a moment, thinking. "Get rid of that disguise," he said to the other policeman. "Burn it. And join me at the Three Friends with as many men as you can, in one hour's time. You'd better come with me, Mog. But you do *exactly* as you're told. And you keep the dog on a leash — the whole time. Do you understand?"

14

DEATH I

Our cab stopped at the entrance to a dark lane around the corner from the Three Friends. Lash lay quietly at my feet. On the way, Cricklebone had given me back the contents of my treasure box. He'd kept a few things, he said, because they hadn't quite finished with them: but most of my precious things were there, including the bangle. Apart from this he'd said little, sitting upright in the cab with his cheeks sucked in so far he barely seemed to have a face at all. There were so many questions I wanted to ask him that I didn't know which question to ask first: it seemed simpler to sit here in silence, clutching my treasures for dear life, the night's events whirling almost meaninglessly in my tired head as we rattled through the grimy streets. When we stopped he peered out of the window.

"This is it," he said, opening the door. His voice dropped to a whisper. "Stay very close, Mog, and very quiet." He jumped out; I clambered down after him, and Lash flopped to the ground beside me. Still covered in soot from the chimney we'd hidden in, I must have been almost invisible as I followed him along the greasy cobbles towards the back of the Three Friends.

First we heard it, and then we smelled it. A hubbub of noise, laughter, and voices raised in anger, getting louder and softer as doors opened and closed. And a stench of old fish, old cabbage, and maggoty scraps of meat which had been thrown out to the dogs in the yard or left to fester in the summer heat. There were lights on in the upper rooms of the tall, ancient inn, and it was clear that a great many people were crammed in, in a state of some excitement.

"Tie the dog up," commanded Cricklebone shortly.

When I'd secured Lash, on a very short rein, to an iron ring in the inn wall, Cricklebone took me by the wrist and launched himself into a low-ceilinged passageway. Coughing slightly, as the odor changed to suggest horses, I followed his bent form until we reached a door on our right. Cricklebone had done his detective work: he probably knew every nook and cranny of this place. He led me inside.

Without actually being seen to arrive, we'd appeared among the crowd in the taproom, as if by magic. It was roasting hot in here. People were drinking, and laughing, in animated little groups between us and the bar, standing so closely packed together that I thought I was going to be smothered. Cricklebone was trying to clear a route through the crush with polite "Excuse me's." He was ducking and nodding like an enormous goose, and he was being completely ignored.

"Oh, for goodness' sake," I muttered, and pushed my way in front of him, squeezing and wriggling between the people who stood in our way.

"Nobody's going to excuse you in a place like this," I said over my shoulder to Cricklebone. "You just have to use your elbows."

When I turned to move forward again, a man was blocking my way, glaring down at me. "Whatchoo mean by comin' in 'ere muckin everybody up?" He held out his shirt sleeve to demonstrate a huge splotch of soot I'd inadvertently left on it. "Stripe me, stow makin' everybody black."

A couple of other men joined in the protest. "Yeh, moke off aht of it."

"Flamin' sweep in 'ere, what next?"

They were gathering round rather threateningly; but I suddenly felt myself being yanked off by the collar, and the men watched helplessly as I disappeared, backward, through the crowd, making apologetic faces at them through my coating of dirt.

"And your elbows will get you into a fight, if you're not careful," Cricklebone said reproachfully, letting go of me as we reached the stairs. "You're *drawing attention to us*," he added in a low voice, through clenched teeth. "Now, come on."

I followed him sheepishly up the narrow staircase, squeezing past men and women standing in huddled pairs. The occasional low laugh sounded in my ear as I edged past, trying not to leave black marks on the women's skirts, which practically filled the stairwell.

As we reached the top we could hear bizarre growls penetrating the hum of voices. The room opened out into a long, crooked space with no furniture and a low, beamed ceiling. The atmosphere up here was distinctly different from downstairs. It was packed full of people, terribly hot, and very dark; and gradually I realized there seemed to be no women up here at all. The voices of the men were full of aggression, and I tried to stay as close as I could to Cricklebone so as not to draw attention to myself. Surrounded by taller people, I couldn't see much of what was going on, and it took me a while to realize that there was a kind of empty space towards the back of the room, and an air of expectation, as though the men were waiting for a boxing match. But some low metal cages by the wall, containing dark muzzled shapes scratching and grunting, soon assured us it was dogs rather than people who were going to fight. I was suddenly thankful we'd left Lash outside.

Cricklebone bent close to my ear.

"If you see someone you recognize," he said, "ignore 'em. Don't stare. Don't give the game away." He'd been eyeing the crowd shrewdly. "Flethick's here," he said into my ear, "and one or two others. Don't look!"

In the corners of the room there were pairs and groups of men, standing whispering and occasionally glancing over their shoulders at the crowd. Men were going through the room collecting money — bets on the dogs — but I also noticed money changing hands which didn't seem to have anything to do with the dogfight.

Cricklebone settled himself, leaning against the wall by a small four-paned window, and drew a pipe out of his coat pocket. He looked quite shabby enough to fit in well with the assembled company: and when a man with broken teeth tottered up to us to shout for stakes, Cricklebone pulled coins out of his pocket and told the man they were bets for himself and his young friend — meaning me. The man winked at me as though we were entering into the subtlest of contracts. His face looked pockmarked and distorted, disfigured as though he himself were a bulldog who'd seen too many fights.

"Gentlemen, gentlemen!" came a sudden loud voice, "we'll start the match, if you please." As people gathered and shuffled aside I noticed that the back part of the room contained a sort of enclosure, an arena boxed off by low wooden planks the height of a man's knee.

"No shoving!" someone shouted, "and clear a way

there! Ho, clear a way!" The cages were brought on: and out of them were hauled two squat, powerful dogs, with wrinkled flat faces and skin like old upholstery, snarling and squinting in the smoky light. I wasn't sure that I wanted to see this. Cupping my hand against the glass, I peered out of the window.

The dogs were held up to cheers from the crowd. When one of them snapped with a loud clack of its teeth at a hovering bluebottle, it received extra-loud roars of enthusiasm.

"'E's in a grand mood!" someone near me enthused, "a fightin' mood!"

Outside, the street seemed quiet. The window was filthy and covered in scratches, and most of its surface was almost opaque; but through a small clear corner I could make out the tapering spire of the church opposite, and at ground level the gates giving onto the cemetery where I'd hidden, the other night when I'd watched Coben. I craned my neck to see if I could spot Lash, and make sure he was all right; but the place where I'd tied him was out of sight of the window. I was about to turn back to the scene in the room when a moving figure outside caught my eye.

I pressed my nose against the glass and tried to block off the room's reflections with my hands. I watched him walk, unconcerned, along the street on the cemetery side, and cross into the light. Tall, heavily built, in coarse dark clothes with no hat, it was unmistakably the bosun.

But he was alone. Where was Nick?

I tugged at Cricklebone's sleeve.

In the pit, the dogs stood poised, restrained by their owners and chivied by the enthusiasm of the crowd which set the air buzzing. One of them scrabbled impatiently on the floorboards, trying to lunge at his adversary.

I watched the bosun walk under my line of vision, as though to stand against the wall of the inn, or maybe to come inside. And now my heart gave a sudden jolt, as somebody else ran into sight. From the opposite direction, and again sticking close to the cemetery wall, a black-cloaked and black-hatted figure moved with graceful wary speed, clutching something to his chest.

"Mr. Cricklebone!" I hissed, bashing his arm.

"What is it?" He bent close and I caught the scent of his tobacco.

"I thought you told your friend to burn his disguise."

"So I did."

"Well then, who's *that?*"

The man from Calcutta stood deliberating, directly opposite the inn. He was looking up and down the street. The object in his grasp flashed briefly and I thought it looked familiar. Suddenly he was off down the hill to the river, and although I couldn't be certain it was the camel he was holding, it was the right size.

Five seconds later the bosun crossed the street again — and began running, awkwardly, down the hill in pursuit. He was gaining on the man from Calcutta very quickly indeed.

"Come on," said Cricklebone, taking my arm, "after them."

As we pushed through the crowd, the dogs leaped forward. Snarling like drills, they went for one another in a blur of hide and teeth, powerful legs lashing out, clawing wildly. Teeth seemed to slide over the smooth cannonball heads, desperate for a grip.

"Excuse me," said Cricklebone, time and time again.

They were well-matched. The supporters roared them on as they stumbled and kicked out in the wooden pit, shaking each other by the neck, yowling and crunching their jaws together. Blood had been drawn and it smeared dark lines across the dogs' foreheads as they jumped and slid together in vicious rage.

We were having trouble getting out. People were so engrossed in the fight, shouting so loudly, they formed a moving wall between us and the door, impervious to our requests or our attempts to push through. Cricklebone gave up saying "Excuse me" and began forcing his lanky way through the throng.

The dogs showed no signs of flagging. Each was determined to wear the other away, leaping back for more after every assault, ignoring the wounds which were opening up, scrabbling among the fur lying loose on the floorboards. Almost comically, amid all the violence, they assessed one another with furrowed brows before lunging again, snapping at one another's throats.

At last we reached the top of the stairs and Cricklebone sent me down first, hanging onto my arm from behind, almost pushing me in his urgency. The roars continued from upstairs as the bulldogs clashed resiliently, tearing open splits in their opponents' faces, biting at eyes and lips.

The heat was bringing cascades of black sweat down my face as I pushed through the crowd downstairs, taking little heed this time of people's clothes, treading on their feet and digging my elbows into their bones as I forced a path between them. The roar of violence upstairs rang in my ears; and just as we reached the front door a huge cheer seemed to go up, as though one of the dogs had finally been defeated and was lying in a silent, bleeding heap, as the grim, spattered victor was held up for applause.

❖

Nick opened his eyes, and at first he didn't believe them.

Bells?

Then in a flash it came back to him. How long had he been up here? How had he managed to fall asleep? He sat up, rubbing his neck, which had acquired a sharp welt from being pressed too closely against a beam corner.

There was a sudden hollow sound from far below. Everything was still utterly dark: but someone was moving. The sound came again. It must have been this which had woken him.

Gingerly he pulled himself to his knees and peered over the planks down into the long shaft of the hollow tower, his line of sight guided by the bell ropes which hung down, down into the darkness. He could see nothing. But there were scufflings echoing up through the fusty air, getting increasingly distinct. And he thought he could hear someone panting.

His father must be coming up to see what he was doing.

Trying to be as quiet as possible, he stood up and pressed himself back into the hollow space. And a gun slipped quietly out of his belt and fell, before he could catch it, over the planks and down, down into the depths.

The scufflings stopped as it landed with a metallic bang somewhere far below. What an idiot he was! He'd completely forgotten he even had the gun, and now . . .

"Oozat?"

A voice boomed up at him from the depths, and he froze, letting the echoes subside. There were a few seconds of silence; then the sound of slow, purposeful footsteps.

Nick swallowed hard. Suddenly he felt sharply and brilliantly awake. He could see the bells glinting very slightly in the moonlight. His mind was racing. The voice wasn't his father's. Below him was Coben, the man he'd been sent to shoot. Coben knew someone was up here. And he was coming up to get him. Nick was suddenly convinced he was going to be killed. There were only two ways down: to use the steps and meet Coben coming up, or to fall down the shaft to the platform forty, fifty feet below. Still the hollow steps echoed up the tower, and the panting, more controlled, was getting nearer and nearer. If only he hadn't dropped the gun!

He couldn't resist a brief glance out over the edge, between the bells, into the chasm. He saw nothing. But there was an almighty *crack*, and the whole tower seemed to tremble, and one of the bells gave out a sharp, buzzing ring. It took Nick a few seconds to realize it had been a bullet. He flung himself back into the hole.

Coben was shooting at him. He'd probably picked up the gun as it fell at his feet. Now he was firing up at the bells, trying to hit Nick.

"Come down or I'll shoot yer down!" The words were confused and jumbled by the echoing stone. But there was no mistaking the second shot, when it came, crashing through the still air and pinging off the bells.

Kicking out at the nearest bell, Nick set it swinging

slowly towards its neighbor. There was no sound. But when it swung back he pushed it again with his foot, and reluctantly it heaved out a deep, shuddering *clang*. He set another bell swinging. If only he could attract attention from outside! The ringing was getting louder as the bells lurched back and forth, and Nick kicked out every time they swung towards him, sending them in a long arc, forcing out their piercing chimes. Beneath them the long ropes snaked crazily, swishing through the hot air of the tower, rippling wildly. His ears buzzed with the noise, but he kept kicking, propelling each bell away, rejoicing at each deafening peal, gasping with effort. The bells were rolling backward and forward: everything else, all thought, was lost in the noise.

As a huge bell swung aside he saw Coben's face almost immediately beneath. He was leaning out into the shaft, clinging to a plank under the bell house, his face moist and his teeth clenched in a determined and murderous grimace. The bell swung back and hid him, then came forward again and there he was, with the gun raised, its barrel aiming right between the bells and up at Nick's face.

Nick pressed himself into the cubbyhole and his fingers closed around something hard and unfamiliar.

The sword! The breath he took when he realized what it was seemed almost to drown out the noise of the bells. Coben kept trying to take aim, waiting for a moment when he could fire between the swinging bells. And he had the advantage. He was too far away for Nick to reach him with the sword; and if he wasn't careful, Nick would end up dropping the sword as well. They watched one another as the bells swung apart again. For a split second the moonlight bouncing off the bells illuminated Coben's face and picked out a dazzling gold tooth, a vicious glint in a murderous grin.

And now Nick raised the sword.

In what seemed like the slowest second of his life, he stepped forward and, with a single clean motion, hacked apart the rope which held the nearest bell. As the chimes echoed through the tower he watched the bell falling, and as it did so he caught sight of Coben, terrified, putting up his arm to shield himself from the plummeting weight.

It was a very long way to fall. And in the dying noise of the bells, Nick couldn't be sure whether he'd heard a long, receding scream, or not.

❖

Outside the inn I gave my soft, silly, uncombative Lash the biggest hug of his life when I untied him. Cricklebone, with his huge strides, was off down the hill and I couldn't possibly keep up. But the relief of breathing fresh air again after the murk and smoke and doghair of the tavern propelled me after him, and in less than half a minute I found him crouching by an unlit doorway.

Something was lying in the hay and dirt at the edge of the road, and it was wearing the man from Calcutta's clothes.

"It's not your —" I began.

"No, it's not McAuchinleck." Cricklebone was subdued and breathless. He stood tall, looking down the road to the river, where only a few low and shabby huts separated us from the creaking, rat-infested ships.

"Has the bosun escaped?" I asked.

"For the time being." He seemed to be talking more to himself than to me, looking up and down, as if waiting for someone.

"Is he . . . dead?" I asked, nervously glancing at the inert shape lying by the wall, pulling Lash back to stop him sniffing at it. There was no reply. Cricklebone was behaving very uneasily indeed, almost twitching. I stared at the lights on the dirty river and took a deep breath.

I'd become aware of a ringing in my ears, and the deeper I breathed, the louder it seemed to get.

Cricklebone suddenly looked at me. "Bells," he said, astonished.

And so it was. I realized that the church, the one up the hill from which we'd just come, was pealing out the most tuneless racket London had ever heard. Like the anguished jangle of someone in awful distress. Its discordant urgency penetrated my bones and I felt my skin crawl in the heavy night air.

"Come on."

Cricklebone led us, at a gallop, back up the hill. People were looking out of the windows of the Three Friends, and figures were milling in the street and across the graveyard. A man met us as we rushed up.

"I've sent a couple of men in, sir."

"Good. Where's McAuchinleck?"

"There, Mr. Cricklebone, sir, by the inn." But McAuchinleck had seen us and he came over, meeting us in the middle of the road. His face was grave, and very different without its oriental disguise. He had a small, gingery mustache.

"You're too late," Cricklebone said shortly. "The bosun's got the camel and he's off. And he's just killed someone."

"Who?"

"I don't know." Cricklebone sounded disturbed. "What did you do with that disguise?"

"I burnt it, like you said."

"Are you sure?"

McAuchinleck stared. "Of course I'm sure."

Still the bells rang. Where was Nick? I watched the policemen running here and there, some of them talking to the crowd which had gathered by the Three Friends, a couple of them going off in the direction of the river. What on earth was going on? As I watched a couple of shadows moving by the church wall, the bells seemed to die, their sound thinning out and eventually stopping altogether. The silence they left in the hot night was heavy, dull, and dreadful. I gazed up at the ornate church spire, a dirty spike against the smoky sky: and for a second or two the place looked so silent, so motionless, and so sinister I wondered with a shiver whether the bells had been ringing on their own.

Against the sky, rising on a thermal current, a single crow swooped, fluttering around the black spire, circling it, before disappearing into the darkness with a hoarse distant squawk.

Cricklebone had gone striding off towards the inn at McAuchinleck's prompting; and, left alone with Lash in the middle of the street, I suddenly felt exposed. Over by the church there was a lot of activity by the little door under the spire; and I could hear a massive commotion. Someone was being brought out of the church, and it was taking a whole horde of policemen to do it. Black shapes struggled in the grey churchyard, and Coben's voice roared obscenely from the melee. They must have arrested him, then! Was it Coben who'd been ringing the bells?

I was about to move toward the inn when I noticed another figure emerging by the cemetery gates, between two policemen. A figure about half their height.

He'd seen me, and five seconds later he had me in

a tight hug, his silent tears of relief making my neck wet, as Lash jumped excitedly around us.

❖

At first I thought something dreadful had happened to Nick; when I spoke to him he didn't seem to hear me. He just stood there looking dazed, wiping the remnants of tears from his cheeks with a dirty sleeve. But he managed to explain his ears were still buzzing from being so close to the bells.

"I can't hear," he said in a loud voice. And then, "Have they found my Pa?"

Cricklebone had disappeared, someone said in the direction of the river; and we set off through the dark little streets in pursuit. A Bow Street Runner had tried to stop us, but by the time he'd asked us who we were, we'd already fled halfway down the hill towards the docks. Nick seemed to think we were going in the right direction. By the time we arrived, breathless, at a dark corner close to the river, his hearing had partly returned. I was able to explain who Cricklebone was.

"My Pa," he panted, "sent me up there to kill Coben. He's desperate. He could do anything."

"He already has," I said, remembering the corpse in the man from Calcutta's clothes.

"What?"

"He's — we found — at least —" I wasn't quite

sure how to put it. Who *had* we found?

"He'll hide in the docks," Nick said. "He knows every corner of them. In the wet cellars, where even dogs won't be able to sniff him out. Onboard the ships. In the rigging. Anywhere. They'll never find him. He'll be out on the next tide."

"Come on, then." I pulled Lash towards the warehouses lining the riverbank, towards the greasy jetties and the groaning ships. I'd never been here in the dark before and it felt very uncomfortable. Eyes seemed to watch from shadows; every now and again a low whistle or a hollow footstep would make me jump. I stayed so close to Nick I was almost treading on his heels as he walked: I was determined not to let him out of my sight now, and I was hoping that any minute we'd spot Cricklebone's angular figure coming out of the shadow. The water was high in the dock and the decks of the smaller boats alongside were just an easy leap away. Nick was right. The bosun could have gotten lost in the maze of masts and rigging in seconds. A dim lamp was raised on a small boat as we went by, and a boy no older than us, with a palsied face, regarded us unsmilingly from under a black cap.

Suddenly Lash lurched off towards the water's edge.

"Heel!" I hissed; but he was whimpering, and tugging me back. What had he found? A cat, no doubt, or a water rat; or something rancid, but to him enticing, which someone had spilt on the dock. As I took a couple of steps toward him my feet struck something solid, and there was a clatter as it skidded towards the water's edge. After starting from the sudden noise, I bent to pick it up.

It was the camel.

I couldn't believe it. "Look!" I said, clutching at Nick. Holding it by its back legs, I unscrewed the head. It was completely empty. The head lay severed and stupid in my palm.

"So where's the man from Calcutta?" Nick asked.

"That might be hard to explain," I muttered, shaking the camel to make sure there was nothing inside. As we stood, silent, I became aware of a conversation going on in a low shed near the water. As we approached we could see a faint lamp glow from the half-open door.

We edged up to the doorway, and I peeped in. It was a tiny, bare shack. Cricklebone was busy lifting up rags and tarpaulins, searching for something. And McAuchinleck was there too, in a bizarre twisted position, with a burly man pinioned between him and the wooden wall. The shadows loomed high and the place stank of rotten wood and urine.

"There's nothing here," Cricklebone was saying.

McAuchinleck seemed to tighten his armlock on the stocky man, and as he moved I noticed for the first time that it was Fellman the papermaker, looking unshaven and very surly.

"Now listen," said Cricklebone, addressing Fellman, "we got a tip-off from Tenderloin. When did you last see him, and what did he give you?"

Fellman suddenly spat with obvious pleasure. "You'll get no tip-off from me," he grunted. "I told you, there was no deal."

"Who is it?" Nick asked in a very loud whisper.

"Ssh!" I returned; but it was too late. Cricklebone flung open the door and held up the lamp to see us standing there, ragged and tired, me with my mouth open about to offer an explanation.

"What are you doing here?" he barked. "Get off back to the inn. It's too dangerous here."

"Mr. Cricklebone," I said, and held up the camel. "I, er — found —"

He came out.

"Where'd you find it?" he asked with urgency, holding the lamp close to my face.

"On the ground, just — back there." I pointed. "Lash found it first. I nearly kicked it into the river."

Cricklebone grabbed it and started unscrewing the head.

"It's empty," I told him, helpfully.

"What?"

I nodded.

He took the head off and shook it. Nothing. He stared out over the black river. "Stay there," he ordered suddenly, and went back into the shed.

I sat down on the dark dockside, pulling Lash close, and dangled my legs over the black water. A warm stench was wafting up between the boards of the jetty. Downriver, the horizon was grey with the first fetid light of another dawn. In a couple of hours the sun would be up again, and hot, and the dockside would have exploded into noisy life. I yawned, hugely.

"It's nearly morning," I said. I felt around in my pockets to make sure the things Cricklebone had given me back from my treasure box were still there. Nick came and sat down on the planks beside me.

"What do you think's happened?" he asked.

"I'm not too sure." That was putting it mildly. I was struggling to make any sense at all, really, of what had happened tonight. Suddenly, sitting here, I'd realized how tired I was. "The man from Calcutta," I said, "was Mr. McAuchinleck in disguise. That policeman in there. All the time. Except . . ."

"Except what?"

"Except your Pa's just killed someone who looked exactly like the man from Calcutta. And took the camel off him."

"And took the stuff from inside it," said Nick.

"I suppose so."

There were some more indistinct shouts from the shed, and then quiet. I was finding it hard to think of what to say next. Several days ago now, Nick had said to me, rather disdainfully: "This ain't a game, you know, Mog." The words echoed in my head, as though they were only really sinking in now. A lot of our adventure *had* seemed like a game at the time. Now, as we sat overcome by exhaustion on the filthy edge of the dock, it seemed serious and terrible.

"What happened in the church tower?" I asked, at length.

Nick's voice was low in replying, and when it came it wavered. "I had to climb up there. My Pa said Coben was hiding out in the bells. But he wasn't there so I waited."

"And then he came back?"

"Mmm." He didn't want to talk about it. He looked down at the clump of paper and the other treasures I was holding in my hand. "What have you got there?"

"Cricklebone gave them back to me," I said, suddenly feeling embarrassed again as I fingered the peg doll and the fat, rough oblong of Mog's Book. "They're the bits of paper I took from Coben's hide-out, and — a few other bits of stuff. You know I told you they'd been stolen? Cricklebone had them all along."

"What's this?"

Nick's eyes had fallen on the bangle — which, for safekeeping, I'd slipped over my wrist. To my surprise, he reached out and pulled it off me.

"That's my —"

"What are you doing with this?" he said.

I tried to think of something to say. He thought the bangle was a silly thing to have. And I suppose it was, a bit — but —

"What are you *doing* with this?" he repeated, suddenly aggressive.

"Nick," I said, "give it back, you'll drop it."

He leaped to his feet. The bangle glinted in his hand, reflecting the torchlight from the shed and the dangling lamps of the nearby ships.

"WHAT — ARE YOU DOING — WITH THIS?" he repeated.

I was bewildered. I didn't really know the answer. I suddenly felt frightened of him, as I had when he'd started questioning me about the name "Damyata," back in the empty old house.

"It — it's mine," I stammered nervously. "I've always had it."

"What do you mean, *always* had it?"

"Well — all my life. It's from my mother."

"You're lying, aren't you?"

"No, of course not. It's —"

"It's *mine,*" he shouted. "*I've* had it all my life, from

my mother! What are you trying to do? Why are you pretending to be me all the time?"

"I'm *not*," I said, "I've never pretended — I didn't know —" I couldn't understand why he was getting so angry, and despite myself I felt tears welling in my eyes. "Give it back," I pleaded, "I don't know what you're talking about."

"Yes you do," he said accusingly. "This is *my* bangle, from *my* mother, Imogen. *I* got it, with her letter, when I was a baby, so long ago I don't even remember. So how can it possibly be yours?"

I felt very peculiar. He'd just accused me of pretending to be him — but now here he was, pretending to be me. What he said couldn't possibly be true; and yet somewhere in the back of my head things began to fit together. The letter he'd quoted, back in the old house. He'd said "Imogen" then — a name no one had called me for years. But it wasn't *my* name he'd been quoting at all . . .

"Nick," I said, "I think I can explain all this."

I couldn't, of course, not yet. But I had the strange sensation that something incredibly important had happened, or was about to happen. Far too important, really, to be true. The implications seeped and spread through my brain, a growing patch of warm excitement, making me feel thrilled and sick at the same time. I *knew*, but I still didn't quite understand.

Beneath my dangling foot something bumped against the oily wooden support which was holding up the jetty. I looked down, but could see nothing in the leaden water. There was another bump. Lash dropped his head over the side, and barked three or four times. I reached over, and with my arm stretched down to its fullest extent I could just feel something soft, touch some coarse cloth, something in the water.

Now my heart went cold.

"Nick," I said, reaching out an arm for him. He was still standing beside me, silent and suspicious. I was about to tell him to come over and look, but then I realized it might be better if he didn't.

"Mr. Cricklebone," I called between clenched teeth, "Mr. Cricklebone!"

He brought the lamp. Its light shimmered over the dirty river and I think I remember screaming as it illuminated the bosun, floating face down, his head knocking gently against the beam.

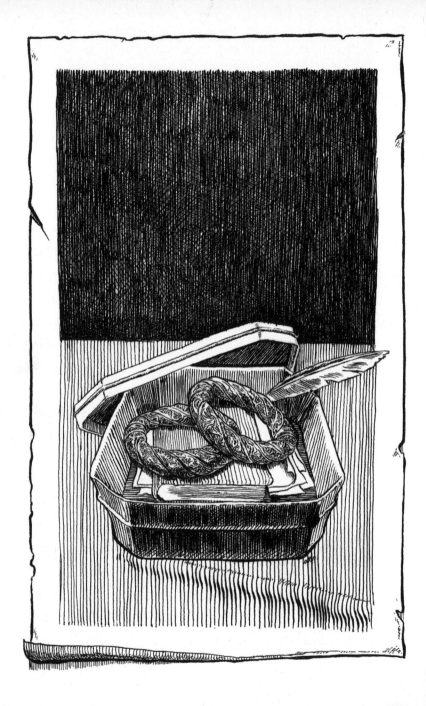

15

DEATH II

Once it was all over, it rained. Big, sooty drops fell through the heavy air, spattering and staining everything in the hot city. It made the worn stones of the streets glisten and sent streams running down their curbs, which swelled out into pools halfway across the road at intervals; it turned the dust of the back lanes into ankle-deep mud; it swelled the black river and submerged the oil-smeared carpet of rags, bottles, and dead animals on the stinking slopes between the water and the embankment walls.

Rumors buzzed around the city like fat black flies. The only certainty was that every story contradicted all the others. Tassie, with her usual air of authority, had assured me that two members of Parliament had been found dead in a basket of snakes, and that the Captain of an East Indiaman had been sentenced to hang from his own mast for the murder of the bosun, who was actually a policeman in disguise.

At work, we were printing any number of news sheets describing the crimes, each of them vying to outsell the others by including more garish and fanciful details; but needless to say none of them seemed to help explain exactly what it was we'd been caught up in, this past couple of weeks. It didn't take long for word to get around that I had been involved in it all: some versions of the story evidently had me as the hero of the entire episode, judging by the people who stopped by the shop and congratulated me in the first few days. To begin with, I tried to protest.

"I really didn't do anything," I told them. "I didn't catch anybody. I don't even really know what was happening." But nobody seemed to believe me, and they pinched my cheek and shook my hand with admiration despite my denials. So in the end I gave up protesting, and just accepted the praise.

"It was a mixture of luck and — well, kind of spying," I started telling people, bashfully, as they gazed at me with new respect. "But I had a bit of help — here and there."

After a few days it was impossible to go anywhere without hearing people talking about the printer's devil who'd foiled a whole gang of villains single-handedly, and I was feeling so important I had almost started to believe it.

"Well I must admit, if I hadn't been there to witness

Coben and Jiggs up to no good at the docks, they'd all have gotten away with it," I boasted. "And they didn't bargain for me spying on Fellman when they were laying their wicked plans. Of course, I can't say too much about it, because Bow Street has sworn me to secrecy on some matters."

All this celebrity meant that I had very little time to myself for the first few days after it all happened, and I hadn't had a spare moment to go and see Nick.

Actually, that's what I told myself; but the real truth was, I was terrified of going. The last time I'd seen him, he'd been furious with me. He'd shouted, and behaved in a way I didn't know how to explain. After we'd found the bosun's dead body in the Thames, Cricklebone had sent me home; and I'd left them on the dockside, Nick looking tiny and shaken, with Cricklebone's arm around his shoulders. I was convinced Nick would simply never want to see me again; that he'd blame me for everything. Despite all my public bravado, I secretly wished that I'd never gotten involved in the first place, that I hadn't been so nosy, and most of all that I hadn't dragged Nick into it. We'd been through so much; and something had happened, during that last awful night, to bring us together in a way neither of us could yet quite explain. But I was too scared to confront it, and I was avoiding him.

It must have been almost a week afterwards, and

Cramplock had sent me out on my usual errand, delivering things for his customers: a canvas bag loaded with pamphlets, letters, bills. I'd finished the deliveries, and was scuttling back toward Cramplock's with the empty bag over my head to keep out the worst of the rain. Just as I was within sight of the shop, and was calling out to Lash, who was jumping into puddles with the delight of a small child, I literally bumped into Nick on the street corner, looking utterly bedraggled.

At first we didn't say anything. I was embarrassed. Suddenly, momentarily, the events of last week seemed like another life. We stood there, getting wet. It was as though we were looking at one another for the first time.

Then Nick said:

"I thought I'd come and find you."

"I'm sorry I haven't been," I managed to say. "We've —" I was about to say we'd been busy in the shop, and then I realized how pathetic it sounded, so I shut up.

Lash came running back when he realized Nick was there, and dug his sopping wet friendly muzzle into Nick's palm.

"Are you all right?" Nick said, half to me and half to Lash.

"We're fine," I said. "Are you?"

He looked up. "I thought you'd abandoned me," he said quietly, his face streaming with rain.

Lion's Mane Court had been overrun by officers, looking for evidence and information, stopping everyone who tried to call, taking things away. One of the things they'd taken away, mercifully, was Mrs. Muggerage, who had been arrested and charged with receiving stolen goods, while investigations continued into how much of a part she'd played in the bosun's various other crimes. Nobody had shown much concern for Nick, and he'd been living at Spintwice's. He was terrified that if Mrs. Muggerage were freed, he'd have to go back and live with her; in the meantime he was trying not to think about it.

Cramplock was obviously taken aback when I appeared at the door with Nick by my side; but his immediate thought was to help us dry off. In a flutter of kindness, he hustled us in front of the fire in the back room, produced a pile of slightly tattered towels from somewhere, and even poured us hot milky drinks from a newly boiled pan. Lash settled down by the grate and busied himself licking the rainwater out of his fur.

I wrapped one of the towels around my shoulders, and Nick took off his sodden, ragged shirt and laid it across the back of a chair near the fire. Only when we'd gone some way to drying our clothes and flat-tened hair, and the fire was making our cheeks glow, did Cramplock give voice to his initial surprise.

"You know, when you turned up at the door just now I could have sworn I was seeing double," he said. "Has anybody ever told you two boys that you're — that you — why, you could be mistaken for one another."

Nick shot me a significant glance and I just said:

"One or two people *have* noticed, Mr. Cramplock, yes."

He left us, and went through into the shop; and Nick and I began to try and piece together the events of the last few days. Even though we'd been a part of it, we were no more certain than anyone else as to exactly what had been happening. We hadn't seen Cricklebone, or anyone else who could tell us what was going on, since that morning on the dockside. The more we tried to explain, the more elements there seemed to be which didn't fit, or didn't make sense.

The chief villain, it was clear, was the man called His Lordship. He had plainly been using his influence over people such as Follyfeather, in the Custom House, to profit from the smuggling of goods into London. He appeared to have a whole network of thieves operating on his behalf, all of them working for his benefit while seemingly working against each other. People like Flethick and his friends were obviously prepared to pay a lot of money for the powder which they burned and smoked at their strange nighttime gatherings. In turn, they made a tidy profit by selling it to other people.

"It was a load of thugs all trying to outdo each other," Nick said. "It's obvious they all wanted to get their hands on the camel, and the powder that was inside it — and the gold lantern."

I wanted to ask him about the bosun's part in it all. And how did Nick really feel, now that he was dead? But I was too nervous even to bring him up, and Nick showed no inclination to talk about him.

As far as I remember, in fact, he never mentioned his Pa ever again.

Nick had managed to rescue a few of his own things from the house. Reaching for his ragged shirt hanging by the fire, he dug his fingers into the pocket and, half-apologetically, he held out a bangle.

"I wanted you to see this," he said.

Even though I knew it wasn't mine, I couldn't help being seized by the same suspicion Nick had shown on the dockside that morning. It was absolutely identical: the same size, weight, and color, with the same markings snaking around its whole surface. I don't think either of us really believed there were two, until I went to fetch my treasure box, took out my bangle, and put his and mine side by side; and it seemed so strange, so unbelievable, that we both just sat there laughing, unable to speak. What did it mean?

I watched him in the firelight, turning the banglesover in his hands, comparing them. Without his shirt, it was clear that he was even browner than I was myself. Where his skin had been continuously exposed to the sunshine, on his forearms and the back of his neck, it shone a rich, deep chocolate color. He was thin, but — as I suddenly realized with a confusing rush of admiration — strong.

I became aware of Mr. Cramplock in the doorway; and it occurred to me he might have been standing there watching us for quite some time. I felt blood rushing to my cheeks, and I shuffled a bit closer to the fire so he might think I was reddening from the heat.

"Would either of you two ruffians like another hot drink?" he asked.

Nick raised his eyebrows. "We both would, Mr. Cramplock," I said, quickly.

Cramplock had been very quiet as the revelations emerged; and to be honest I was a bit wary of talking about it with him. I still wasn't sure how much of a part he'd played in it all; but he'd been noticeably better-tempered, these past few days. As he brought in the drinks and handed them to us there was a softness in his eyes, which I'd rarely seen in all the years I'd known him. Without thinking about it, I said:

"Mr. Cramplock, I don't think I've really been telling you the truth these past few weeks."

He came and sat down, rubbing his cheek intently. "Mog," he said, "I'm afraid that makes two of us." He seemed to be finding it difficult to think of the right words. "When you kept asking me questions about watermarks . . . and when we kept getting threatening notes . . . I wasn't really trying to stand in your way."

"I never thought you were," I said.

"I thought you suspected me of being in the plot," he said.

I considered this. "Not exactly, Mr. Cramplock," I said. "But I knew you knew the men. You knew Fellman the papermaker. And you knew Flethick. And I thought you were maybe — protecting them."

"I was threatened with death," he said in a quiet voice, "more than once. I was very frightened, Mog, and if you'd had more sense you would have been too."

We watched him as he talked, his voice quiet and his face serious in the glow from the fire.

"I got mixed up with that crew years ago," he said, "and I've been trying to get out of their grasp ever since. They wanted me to do printing jobs for them — forgeries and suchlike. Well, once upon a time, I used to. But I knew I could go to prison if I was found out, and it's not hard to trace the source of printed matter, Mog, as you well know. I started to refuse to work for them. They weren't very pleased with me. And then when Cockburn broke out of prison they happened to find out I was doing the wanted poster."

I suddenly realized what had been going on. "You mean you changed the picture deliberately?" I said, my eyes wide.

"I, er — sabotaged it, in a manner of speaking, yes," he said, looking at the table, "and then I, er — blamed you. Mmmm. It was the only way I could see to stop them beating me to death one night after I left the shop. I had to do something that would satisfy them I was helping."

I looked at Nick, dumbfounded. He gave a short laugh, a mixture of disbelief and relief.

"Why didn't you tell someone?" I asked Cramplock.

He looked at me through his little glasses. "You know better than to ask me that," he said. "Why didn't *you* tell someone what you knew? It's not that simple, Mog. You don't know who to trust, do you?"

"So the wanted poster went out with the wrong face on, and Cockburn got away without being recognized," I said.

"For a while, yes. Of course, he couldn't hide from the criminal types who'd known him for years."

"You docked my wages," I reminded him, indignantly.

"Did I? I'm sorry. I must have been getting carried away."

A thought occurred to me. "Did you write a note to Fellman?" I asked.

"After the poster, yes," he said. "I decided it had all gotten too dangerous. I wrote to him to warn him this shop was being watched, and that I'd had threatening notes."

"And you were being threatened by Follyfeather as well," I said. "I saw a letter . . ."

"I was being threatened by everybody," he said. "And then when you started getting threatening notes too, that's when I got frightened. I thought it was best to pretend I didn't really understand. But I really started to be careful then — and when a man from Bow Street came to see me, my main concern was to make sure they were looking after you."

I suddenly had an enormous amount of respect for Cramplock. Here he'd been, stringing along the criminals, trying to persuade them he was on their side, while all along he'd been cooperating with Cricklebone's men, and watching out for my safety too. I was terribly impressed, and felt rather meek.

There was something else I suddenly realized I ought to ask Cramplock about once again: one of the biggest mysteries of all.

"You know the old house next door," I said, "you haven't seen anyone coming and going in the last few weeks, have you?"

"You asked me that before," he said. "I told you then, it's not safe for anyone to come and go. Nobody in their right mind would hide out in there. I'm quite sure nobody's been in there since the fire, all those years ago."

"No," I said, "no, *I* went in there. Last week. I got trapped in there. I meant to tell you, because I fell through the wall and — made a bit of a mess. But he was hiding out there all the time."

Cramplock was looking at me very strangely indeed. I had lost him completely.

"Who was hiding out?" he asked, baffled.

"Well —" I stopped. This was a trickier question than it seemed. Who *was* it who'd been hiding out next door? The person who had found me in the chest at Coben and Jiggs's lair? The person I'd seen in the stable at Lion's Mane Court? The person who had tied up Mr. Spintwice and taken the camel? The person who had later been left in a lifeless heap at the side of the lane leading down to the docks, on that dreadful night? Or Cricklebone's colleague, in that ridiculous disguise? Were all of these people really the same person?

Eventually Nick spoke. "You *must* have dreamt it, Mog," he said simply.

"No," I said, indignantly, "I *know* I didn't dream it."

"Well, then you must have been in a different house," said Nick patiently. "We went in there. You remember what it was like. Anybody could see it hadn't been lived in for years, Mr. Cramplock's quite right."

I bit my lip. He didn't believe me either. My fingers playing with Lash's silky ears, I tried to remember how I'd felt, on that hot evening, standing in that mysterious garden and walking around the disorienting old house. "I don't know," I said, "but it was as though — when I went into the garden, everything outside it just — stopped existing. As though I was in a completely different place, or a completely different *time*."

I was struggling, and they were still looking at me with complete incomprehension. I knew I hadn't dreamt it, and yet it simply didn't make sense. Neither the man from Calcutta, nor the man from Calcutta's house, could possibly be explained. But there was something important about it all; I just had a feeling, because of my dreams, because of the expression I'd seen on his face. . .

"Nick," I said, "I want you to look at something."

Until I got the bangle out, half an hour ago, I hadn't really looked at the treasures in my tin, since that terrible dawn at the docks. I suppose I hadn't been thinking straight; because I hadn't realized that a lot of what I needed to know was folded up inside. But now, with Nick sitting here and the treasure box open beside me, I found my heart was beating faster.

We emptied the tin, and spread its contents out in front of us, pulling Lash out of the way to stop him treading on them or chewing them.

There was Mog's Book. There were the scrawled notes from the man from Calcutta; pages from newspapers; documents I'd stolen from Coben and Jiggs which we couldn't really understand, and which they probably hadn't made head nor tail of either. Only the list of names was missing — kept as evidence, no doubt, by Cricklebone.

And there was the most important document of all: the letter, signed "your undeserving Imogen," which I'd brought from Coben and Jiggs's hideout. The letter which Nick had quoted word-for-word, out of the blue, the other night. I held it out to him, half afraid of it, as though it might be infected with some sort of dangerous magic.

"This is it," I said, quietly.

This *was* it. He took it from me. "I didn't even know it had gone," he said, smoothing the familiar, fragile old paper out carefully. "Coben must have taken it along with the other stuff he stole from our house. He wouldn't have made any sense of it. We're lucky he didn't just burn it or throw it away."

It was the last page of a letter which, along with the bangle, Nick had owned and treasured all his life. In a fine, fading hand, it covered two sides of a fragile quarto sheet of paper. It was written in a very gracious style, with some long words I didn't completely understand, and the first part of the letter was long lost: but the point of it was quite clear from what remained. As I read it aloud, Nick joined in, without even looking at the page. He'd read it so many times he knew it by heart.

It began in mid-sentence.

. . . *apart from some doses of physic of Mr. Varley's which I privately confess have done nothing to improve my condition. Disease is rife whence we have come, and despite individual kindnesses the arrangements onboard since we left have been insanitary and unnourishing. Whatever the truth, the Good Lord attends, and it fits us not to question His motives. The one vital duty of my last days remains to be discharged, and it is in pursuit of this, principally, that I have written to you.*

You will be surprised and, I fear, aghast, at the request I make of you. Yet I beg you to give this letter your fullest attention, and to consider with the utmost care how you might execute my will. As I have explained, I am delivered of two beautiful children, and in being taken from them I leave them utterly alone and helpless. If I am taken, my sole desire in departing is to know that the warm and desperate little souls to whom my transgression gave life will be spared, and will be able to live, and grow, and laugh, and learn. It is my dying wish that they be cared for, together or separately, in the best circumstances which may be afforded, and that every effort be made to bring them up in virtue and health.

I hope I am not mistaken in assuming that you have the means to oversee such an upbringing, and I pray that, with goodwill and modest financial aid, nature may in time be allowed to heal where she has so mercilessly hurt. My dear, I beg you not to —

It continued over the page:

— spurn my entreaty in this matter, much as your first instinct may be to do so. I charge you with this solemn duty not because I wish to burden your remaining years but because I trust you with all my being. Whatever the imminent fate of the soul, it would indeed be too cruel if the still innocent flesh begotten of my misdeed were made to suffer.

I know of nowhere else to turn. I feel so helpless, my dear, and I pray that you will not feel equally so, upon being charged with the care of these precious infants. I would not blame you. Your first instinct may very well be to enlist help, and even to seek out those who are closer to them in blood. Yet I would be in dereliction of my duty if I did not prepare you for the difficulty, perhaps the impossibility, of ever doing so. You would be attempting to conduct your inquiries in a country where letters are rarely answered, and where there are no formal records of people's names, histories, births, deaths, professions, or whereabouts. I fear it will not be possible to reach Damyata now.

I can say no more; and I am feeling weak. Please God this letter reaches you, and that you do not think too ill of me to grant some mercy to the gentle, perfect creatures who accompany it. My dear, Good-bye, and with all the remaining life in my body, I thank you.

Your undeserving,

Imogen

There was a long silence after I'd finished reading it, while the words sank in. The desperate emotion of it, expressed in such measured and refined language: Imogen, it was clear, had been a remarkable woman. I had to blink back tears. Reading these two fragile faded pages had given a personality, a physical presence, to someone who had never existed for me before, except as a name; and I suddenly felt the loss of her like a new bereavement.

I tried to look up at Nick and smile, but my mouth wouldn't make the right shape, and my eyes were blinded with tears.

"My mother," I said.

I was afraid he'd think I was silly and girlish for crying. But his face and voice were full of understanding, and I suddenly knew he'd come to exactly the same realization as I had, at exactly the same time.

"*Our* mother," he said, gently.

✦

She had come, like the *Sun of Calcutta*, on a ship from the East Indies, twelve years before; and so had we, her twin children. It was impossible to know from the letter whether we had been born on land, or at sea; but we were still tiny and helpless when we arrived in London, that much was obvious; and we'd been delivered into the hands of a family friend or relative, whose name was lost, and who had plainly been unable to look after us for long. I understood how I had come to be in the orphanage; but how Nick had ended up being claimed by the bosun and Mrs. Muggerage was less clear.

But, as we talked, I became convinced of one thing. The man from Calcutta would have been able to tell us everything. On that dreadful hot night, a few minutes of terrible violence outside the Three Friends had probably robbed us of our only chance of finding out who we really were. He had come to find us; and we had spent the entire time running away. "Must talk," his note had said. And now it was too late.

I hardly let Nick out of my sight, now. I spent all my free time at Mr. Spintwice's with him, and he spent quite a lot of every day helping me out in the printing shop. Cramplock seemed genuinely pleased that I had discovered a brother I never knew I had; but not, strangely, especially surprised. He was treating us with noticeable kindness, but he still insisted on hard work, and came over to cluck and chivy us on if he found us talking about the camel adventure instead of getting on with the job. I still couldn't bring myself to tell him that I was a girl and not a boy, and I had sworn Nick to secrecy. It was too much of a risk. In spite of all that had happened, I was more or less sure he'd still decide a girl couldn't be a printer's devil.

We thought we might find out more when, about a week later, Mr. Cricklebone came to see us at Spintwice's.

The dwarf had never had anyone so tall in his house before, and Cricklebone had to bend nearly every joint in his body in order to get through the door. Mr. Spintwice was very polite, but he wore a rather frozen expression throughout the visit, as though he believed people really had no business being so tall, and that, if he were in any sort of power, he'd make it illegal.

Cricklebone had ostensibly come to take down statements from us, gathering evidence to be used against the villains. As it turned out, he was the one who found himself interrogated, as Nick and I showered him with questions from the moment he arrived. He was being very cagey, doing little more than avoiding the subject or tapping the side of his sizeable nose. "There's too much idle talk in London already," he said.

"This isn't idle talk," Nick said; "we want to know what *really* happened."

Cricklebone perched on a chair, sipping tea and trying not to let his gangly elbow stray too far out in case it knocked a clock off Spintwice's mantelpiece.

"*Really*," he said absently, "isn't a very easy word." He put down his teacup, and picked up a pencil and a folded sheet of paper, preparing to write down some notes. "Now," he began, his pencil poised, "perhaps you can —"

"I want to know," I interrupted him, "what Mr. McAuchinleck was up to. Was he really the man from Calcutta all the time? Was it him hiding out in the house next door all that time? Did he kill Jiggs? Did he really have a snake?"

Cricklebone sat silently for a long time, with the end of the pencil in his mouth. "Mmmm-mm," he said, at length, and I thought for one ridiculous moment he was going to pretend to have a stammer again. "Mr. McAuchinleck was following the case for a very long time. We discovered that a completely new kind of drug was circulating in London, something more dangerous and more valuable than anything known before. We knew it was coming in from the East Indies, and there was a whole network of criminals involved — but what we didn't know was just how they were doing it, or who was behind it. So McAuchinleck traveled to and from Calcutta on Captain Shakeshere's vessel. In, ah — incognito, as it were. To watch."

"Was this when he was pretending to be Dr. something?" I asked.

"Hamish Lothian, yes."

"But when he got to London he disguised himself as Damyata?"

"I suppose so." Cricklebone was being a bit irritating. I think he was enjoying the mystery he was creating. "McAuchinleck dressed up a time or two, left a few notes. But the villains did a lot of work for us. They hated each other so much, all Mr. McAuchinleck had to do was play them off against one another. He scared you once or twice . . . but then, you shouldn't have been there in the first place."

"And this drug was so valuable that the villains were quite prepared to kill each other to get hold of it," said Spintwice, beginning to understand.

"It's so valuable," said Cricklebone, "that even the amount contained in the camel could make somebody very rich. You see — once people take it, they can't stop taking it. They find they can't live without it. And they're perfectly prepared to kill for it, yes."

"So who killed Jiggs?" I asked again.

"Jiggs — isn't dead," he replied, surprisingly. "He's in Newgate. We arrested him, and then put notices out pretending he'd been found dead, to scare Cockburn and drive him out of hiding. Well, it worked: he got really scared, had to change his hiding place, and had to explain to His Lordship where the camel had gone."

"What about the lantern? The *Sun of Calcutta?*"

"We pretended that had been stolen too," Cricklebone went on. "The villains were just waiting for the moment when they could run off with that. His Lordship wanted Cockburn to get it for him, and we knew either he or the bosun would go for it sooner or later. So we, er — made out that Damyata had got away with it before any of them had a chance."

"And had he?"

Cricklebone looked uncomfortable. "I'm not sure

what you mean," he mumbled.

"I mean, did the real Damyata get there first?" I said.

There was a short pause while Cricklebone contemplated what he was going to say. "Well, we riled them," he continued, and it became evident he'd decided he was just going to ignore the question. "I've been very impressed with Mr. McAuchinleck's skills. He had everyone well and truly fooled."

"But there was someone else, wasn't there," I persisted. "There really *was* a man from Calcutta in London, wasn't there? It wasn't Mr. McAuchinleck *every* time, was it? What about the man we found lying in the lane that night on the way down to the docks?"

Cricklebone twitched, nervously. He made a few helpless little marks on the paper and stared at them, as though they were going to transform themselves magically into the answers to my questions.

"And what about the man who tied me up, and took the camel?" put in Mr. Spintwice. "If that was your friend in disguise, all I can say is he was taking his masquerade a bit too seriously for my liking."

"And the house next door," I said. "That night when I went inside, and it was all brand-new. Did McAuchinleck have it rebuilt?"

"He couldn't have, could he?" Nick put in. "And then torn it all out again two days later? Why would he do that?"

Cricklebone's mouth opened but no sound came out; so I seized on the silence to tell him about the letter from Imogen; about its reference to the name "Damyata"; about the hunch I'd had that the man from Calcutta had been trying to tell me something important — and hiding out next door all the while. Cricklebone was trying to make his face look as though he already knew every detail of what we were telling him; but behind the stiff expression his eyes were betraying occasional surprise, even alarm, at the mounting list of things he realized he still had to investigate.

"Well," he said at length, with a frog in his throat, "Certainly it must seem to you as if your man from Calcutta is a — a bit of a magician. I admit there are one or two details of Mr. McAuchinleck's activities of which I've yet to be, ah — fully apprised." He'd gone a bit pale during my story, and now he was doing his best not to look crestfallen. "I th-think I've said enough for today," he finally muttered.

"What suspense," remarked Mr. Spintwice, who'd been listening with increasing surprise. "Like finding the last few pages of a book torn out."

Cricklebone pricked up his ears at the metaphor. "Books," he said, "as Mog here well knows, tend to have a few blank pages at the end."

"Yes," I said, "because usually the gatherings have got to be —"

"It's because," Cricklebone interrupted, "the end of a book is very rarely the end of the story." He looked rather pleased with this analogy, and stood up too fast, hitting his head very sharply on the low beam. "Well," he said, his eyes watering, "Good day."

We showed him to the door. As he left, he held out his hand rather awkwardly to shake mine, then Nick's.

"Nick," he said, "Mog. I mean, Mog. Nick. Whichever one of you is which, ha ha. You've ah — you've done some good work for us these past few weeks. Remarkable work, though you might not know it. I wouldn't be too surprised if there were some sort of, er — reward, for this."

Four pairs of wide eyes looked up at him from the doorway: Nick, Spintwice, Lash, and myself.

"Keep out of mischief now, mmm?" he muttered, finally; and he turned, and was off, like a stick-puppet, into the noise and bustle of the city. We never saw him, or McAuchinleck, again.

❖

They hanged Cockburn in October.

It was like a fairground. Everyone was wearing a happy face, as if it were a holiday. A juggler was entertaining for coins. You could buy poorly printed pamphlets relating the gory and embellished history of Cockburn's misdemeanors. Mr. Glibstaff was strutting about looking important, tapping people officiously on the backs of their calves when they were standing where he wanted to walk. Above us, every window on either side of the street was flung wide, with four or five cheery people leaning out of each one to enjoy the spectacle.

Nick and I moved among the crowds, with Lash between us. Costermongers had cleared their carts and were charging people a halfpenny to climb up on them for a better view. I saw Bob Smitchin organizing one such grandstand.

He winked at us.

"Grand day for it," he said. He might have been talking about a picnic. "You'd be a proud feller today, Mog."

"Proud?" I said. "Why?"

"Well, 'e's *your* convict," Bob said cheerfully, "people might say you got a particular interest in the case, Mog."

"Mmmm."

"Serve 'im right," he continued, helping another couple of people up onto his already overcrowded and wobbling cart, "way I see it, a feller chooses to be a miscurrant, or not a miscurrant. Should be prepared for the consey-cutives."

"Anyone would think," I said to Nick, "it was the Devil himself being hanged." Pressing our way between the gathering hundreds, Nick and I spotted several people we knew to be thieves, or thugs, and they seemed to be shouting as loud as anyone else, presumably relieved it was someone else going to the gallows this time.

"Some of this lot should be up there with him," said Nick. He nudged my arm and nodded towards a wily-looking urchin a couple of years older than us who was creeping round a circle of long-coated gentlemen. "Plenty of pockets to pick today."

"They'll find nothing on me," I said, tapping my empty pockets. "That the sort of thing you used to do, is it?"

Nick shrugged.

Since the bosun's death he didn't seem to have stolen anything. People used to patronize him and tell him he'd turned over a new leaf, which irritated him. "I haven't turned over anything," he maintained; "if I wanted to nail stuff, I would." But he didn't seem to. I often reflected that, in the past few months, he seemed a lot older; and he laughed a lot more often.

"And I pray our souls be cleansed," someone was declaring close by, "and our hands stayed by the fear of the Wrath of God." It was a shabby-looking man with a few broken teeth, holding out his hands and orating to the pushing crowds around him. "Bless you," he kept saying, and holding out a crumpled felt hat in which a couple of coins lay. "The Lord," he said when he saw us, "is ever merciful to the righteous, my boys, and fearful to the wicked. A penny from a pauper is more dear to God than all the riches of a nobleman. A camel may more easily pass through a needle's eye than a wealthy man enter heaven."

He must have wondered what lay behind the meaningful glance Nick and I exchanged as we squeezed our way past.

All around us, on posts and hoardings, were multiple copies of a new and arresting poster, which had kept Mr. Cramplock and myself busy for the entirety

THIS THURSDAY at 2PM SHARP

One of the most Notorious ROGUES and MURDERERS
of this Century

IS TO BE

HANGED

At the Place of Public Execution at
NEWGATE

of an autumn evening last week.

"You know what Mr. Spintwice says?" said Nick. "There's no such thing as justice."

Spintwice had, I knew, made no secret of his scorn at the eagerness of people to gather in a big crowd and watch a man being hanged. "What's he mean, then?"

"I think he means," said Nick, "nobody can ever be satisfied. You can't set things right once they've gone wrong, not without turning back time and starting again. Like — hanging someone — it doesn't undo the crime. People want blood, but when they've got it they're no better off, are they?"

The roaring was getting louder as the anticipation mounted. People were becoming aware that it was nearly the appointed time.

"Do you want to stay and watch?" I asked.

"Not really."

"Let's go," I said, and we began pushing back the way we'd come. I had to keep tugging at Lash's lead to drag him away from half-chewed apples and discarded bits of pie which people had dropped on the ground.

As we emerged out of the crush, a woman came up to us to try and sell us sweets.

"Sugared oranges," she cooed, "and cherries and ginger. Treats, my dears, come off the boat from the East Indies." We peered into her tray and saw little squares and diamonds of sugared fruit, some of it wrapped in rice paper. A heavy, spicy smell was wafting up from the sugar-caked board. Nick reached in and took a square of ginger.

"I want to get you this," he said, fishing in his pocket for a grubby coin.

The woman moved off, and he handed me the sweet. I unwrapped the thin crinkly paper it was wrapped in and popped the chunk of ginger into my mouth. Just as I was about to throw the paper away, I noticed some blue markings on it.

"Hang on," I said with my mouth full. Folding out the sticky little sheet, I found it had a printed inscription in faint blue. I stared at it. Slowly, the pale characters sank into my brain.

इम्यता

I looked around. "Where's the woman?" I asked. We tried to call her back, but she'd blended into the excited crowd, and the people were milling too densely for us to catch her.

We turned and set off again, staying close together. The throng was too intent on what it had come to see; no one paid a scrap of attention to the pair of children, remarkably alike, one of them hanging onto a long-limbed dog, and each of them glancing back and forward occasionally to make sure the other was still there — as though, it having taken so many years for them to find one another, they were now determined not to let the other go.

Up the street, a gate in the prison wall swung open, and a broadly built figure was led up the wooden steps to the back of the cart. Above our heads, the bells of St. Sepulchre's began the solemn sequence that preceded the striking of two. Gradually, starting from the front, the jeers of the crowd fell silent, and the silence spread all the way along the street, up the hill, as far as the cathedral.

MYSTERY.
MENACE.
MIRE.

A thousand thrilling adventures await you in

THE GOD OF
MISCHIEF

Sequel to The Printer's Devil

Coming February 2007

TURN THE PAGE FOR A SNEAK PEEK!

1

A BURIAL

The chanting grew gradually louder. I was frightened. I was being swung around, by my feet, by two big grim-faced girls who held onto my ankles with a grip far tighter and more cruel than necessary. Their faces, the only still points in a whirl of figures and furniture, broke into sadistic grins as I stared at them. I was already dizzy and was beginning to feel sick, my short filthy hair feeling the breeze as my head just missed the wall or the edge of a desk by a matter of inches. I kept my arms pulled in tight against my chest to stop them from smashing into something and, with clenched fists, I silently begged them to stop. Round and round I went, faster and faster; the girls couldn't possibly keep control of my whirling body for much longer, and I knew if they didn't stop I was going to hurt myself badly. A few times I tried to shout at them to stop, but they were making too much noise for my voice to be heard; and anyway, I knew from experience that crying out only made them whirl you more violently and gleefully.

As suddenly as the game had started, it was all over. The lookout's warning — "Mrs. Muggerage!" — was taken up by the rest of the girls, until it was simply a general loud hissing sound throughout the room; the girls let go of me and dispersed to the four corners, leaving me spinning on my back, my hair grinding into the filth of the floor, my limbs sprawling.

A terrible silence descended. A huge figure was standing in the doorway. Only gradually did I realize who it was, though at the back of my head was the troubling sense that something was wrong; that this couldn't really be happening. I struggled to sit up, the room continued to spin, and I felt the awful, inescapable sensation of my breakfast trying to escape. As the walls and floor whirled around my head, I brought up a great splattering stomachload of acidic, watery porridge.

A choir of angels couldn't have been more innocent than that roomful of children pretended to be right then. Whether Mrs. Muggerage was fooled, I never knew — if she was, I couldn't understand how — but there was only one child in the room who wasn't sitting bolt upright, with her hands by her sides, looking wide-eyed and morally horrified at what she could see in the middle of the floor. And that was me. Just who else had been involved, it was impossible to tell; but plainly I had been at the center of things, because there I was on the tiles, propped up on one arm, retching.

"Mog Winter," said Mrs. Muggerage, in a tone of grim pleasure at the prospect of being able to mete out some punishment. Her black boots echoing on the bare floor, she walked slowly over to me. There were a few seconds' grace as I wiped my mouth and lifted my dizzy head to look up at her. She stood above me, a woman of awesome bulk and power, a grimy cloth in her hand. She was blocking out most of the light, but gazing up at her shadowy outline, I could tell her expression was without compassion, even slightly sneering with revulsion at my sickness. Then she grasped me by the collar and yanked me to my feet with a single, violent motion. I hung there from her fist like a marionette, weakened, close to tears.

"Mog Winter," she said again. "I coulda guessed. Before I walked in, I coulda guessed."

She turned around, slowly, holding me out to exhibit me to the rest of the children. There was complete silence as they stared at me. I registered the faces of my chief tormentors among the group, and they were looking at me with disdain, as though they were genuinely as disgusted with me as Mrs. Muggerage was.

"What have you got to say fer yourself?" she snarled at me.

"This ain't right!" I said, struggling. "You're not meant to be here."

"No good," Mrs. Muggerage was saying, "can ever come to those what misbehaves. Lord knows if we don't try hard enough, girls and boys, to make it plain. Lord knows if I don't teach the same lesson day after day. No good will ever come to those what can't behave. And Lord knows if, day after day, some dreadful boy or girl don't completely ignore the lesson, so's I'm 'bliged to teach it all over again. *Well.*"

That *"well"* was calculated to send a shiver of fear into every young heart in the room. Although only a single word, it was stretched so it lasted as long as a whole sentence, and it contained more misery in its elongated syllable than any complete sentence you could possibly think of.

She dropped me. Because she'd been holding me up with my feet off the ground, I had to put my hands out to break my fall, and as I tumbled to the floor again my palms went straight into the pool of vile porridge I'd left beneath me, smearing it further and sending it splashing up my arms and across my cheek. Without intending it, but unable to prevent myself, I swore — using a word I'd heard the other children use several times a day. The moment I heard myself say it, I knew my fate was sealed.

Their hearts in their mouths, the other children watched me crouching there, and waited to see what Mrs. Muggerage was going to do.

She said nothing for a long time, while my un-guarded oath resonated in our terrified souls. She said nothing, just stared down at me, for what seemed an eternity. The walls towered around us, cold, dirty and cracked, with barred windows in them so high above our heads that all we could ever see through them was the sun, the clouds, or the night sky. They were that high up on purpose, of course, to prevent us from see-ing what was outside and dreaming or devising plans for escape; but quite often, when we were unsupervised, we used to form acrobatic towers by climbing on top of one another. Four children standing on one another's shoul-ders meant that the person on top could grasp the bars and peer out over the wide sill, and we used to take turns being the one on top. Looking down, we could see the flagstones of the dank little orphanage yard far be-low, and part of the high brick gateway that led to the outside world; but of much more interest to us was the rooftop view, at eye level: the vista of chimneys and church spires receding into the distance and, beyond the city's rooftops, a glimpse of hills to the north. We didn't know any names for the places we were looking at: it was just "Out." When we scrabbled our way up to look through the grimy window, we could see Out; we dreamed constantly of being Out, and staying Out, and never coming back.

And, although I thought about it almost every minute

of every day, I had never longed more to be Out than I did at that moment.

Her teeth bared, Mrs. Muggerage leaned slowly down and pressed her incensed face into mine.

"Do my ears deceive me?" she hissed. Some other child in the room echoed her hiss with a sharp, frightened little intake of breath. The huge, terrible woman clenched the foul wet rag she'd been holding in her left hand, which, I now saw, was smeared and dripping with the contents of whatever disgusting corner of the orphanage she'd just been cleaning. It only seemed to occur to her at this moment that the rag was just the object she needed to make her point, and humiliate me at the same time.

"A mouth as filthy as that," she snarled, "wants a good clean."

"*Don't,*" I moaned, "don't . . . *please* don't . . ." But there was no escaping it, and the next thing I knew she had grabbed me by the back of the neck with a clawlike hand to stop me from moving my head, and the vile-smelling thing was thrust into my face, and squeezed hard until it oozed its slime between my lips and into my nostrils and made me choke and gag.

"*Don't!*" I repeated, "*Please* don't . . . *please* don't . . ."

❖

"Mog," said a familiar voice, "Mog, it's me. Mog! Wake up!"

There still seemed to be something tremendously wet in my face, but, as I came to, I realized it was the eager tongue of my dog, Lash; and the voice was that of Nick, my twin brother, sitting on my bed looking down at me with an expression of urgency in the yellow light of a flickering lamp.

"What's the matter?" he asked.

I reached up my hands in relief, and grabbed my dog's furry head on both sides, both to greet him and to pull him away. His long snout continued to sniff excitedly at my face and I had to strain with all my strength to hold him back from licking me. "*Stop* it," I said, "you *ridiculous* dog."

Lash was as ridiculous and lovable a dog as a child ever owned, a gangling golden-haired mongrel with a huge smile and a long tail which was never still, and curly blond eyelashes so prominent they had given me no choice as to what to call him. I ruffled his head as I blinked in the lamplight and exhaled with relief at the discovery that I wasn't in the terrible orphanage after all.

"I was dreaming again," I said to Nick. "Sorry."

"Must have been a bad one," Nick rejoined, "to make you squeal like that. It sounded like you were being murdered. I came in as fast as I could, but you were about to wake up the whole house."

I was still coming to. "I was in the orphanage," I said, the full horror of the dream coming back to me. "I was being whirled around and around . . . and Nick, guess who was there? Mrs. Muggerage!"

"Well, that *was* a nightmare then," said Nick with sympathy.

We may have been twins, Nick and I, but we hadn't known each other all our lives by any means. We had been born at sea, on a voyage back from India, to the most beautiful and virtuous mother who had ever lived. I had always thought of her this way; and, although she had died when we were just two weeks old, I had pictures of her in my head and some small mementos of her which had always been the most precious things I owned. I was named after her: Imogen was my full name, and I had only acquired the abbreviated name of Mog in the loathsome orphanage to which I was taken as a baby. I lived there until I was six or seven, when I had the good fortune to be taken away. The streets of London were no place for a little girl, on her own with no one to support her; but there was no shortage of work for boys, and because I'd always looked like a boy, I got a job as a printer's devil for Mr. Cramplock, in Clerkenwell. It was a happy life and it contained lots of adventures, which is another story altogether. But ever since I left the orphanage, I'd had dreams like the one from which I'd just awoken, and for several years I'd lived in constant terror of being discovered and dragged back there.

Nick, meanwhile, had somehow become separated from me in our tiniest infancy, and had grown up completely separately. For as long as he could remember, he'd lived among the criminals and sailors of London, looked after by a violent ship's bosun who passed himself off as his father, and by Mrs. Muggerage, the dreadful woman in my nightmare. Together they treated him even worse, if possible, than I was treated in the orphanage. We had only met for the first time, completely by accident, last year, when we were both twelve. It turned out we'd been living less than a mile apart, both of us making our way in the crowded streets of London without knowing one another. Neither of us had any inkling we had a brother or sister at all, let alone that we were *twins,* living so close together all this time.

Of course, we'd been together ever since, Nick, myself, and Lash. I'd never known anything you might call a family, in my entire life; dreams and contemplations of my mother had been the most comfort I could hope for. Now, for the first time, I was getting used to the idea that I wasn't alone. It meant more to me than anything else in the world; and, to be honest, I still lived in fear of waking up one morning and finding it had all been an impossible dream.

I held Lash's soft head firmly between my hands and gazed into his face, pretending to be stern with him.

"You know," I said, "I don't think it would matter

how far away Lash's face was; he could still stick out his tongue and lick my nose. How long do you think it is?"

"It probably never ends," said Nick. "He could sort of *launch* it out of his mouth and lick absolutely anything at all, on the other side of the room, or on the other side of the street. It probably curls up inside his mouth and down his throat and goes on forever, like a kind of snake."

"What time is it?" I asked.

"It's the middle of the night," said Nick, and his voice was suddenly low and quiet as though he'd just remembered how late it was, and how dark.

"Did I wake you up?"

"Yes . . ." He hesitated. "I was dreaming too," he admitted. "I was glad to be woken up, actually." We had both been having especially vivid dreams in the past few weeks, and when we described our dreams to one another it seemed we were both dreaming very similar things, again and again: dreams of being pursued, dreams in which people we knew were in danger and we were powerless to help them.

"Can you hear something?" I asked suddenly.

"I can hear the wind," said Nick.

"No, there's something else," I said, straining to listen.

I stopped making a fuss of Lash, and got out of bed, and went over to the window. There was no curtain or blind, and the window didn't quite fit the frame properly, which meant if it was windy it often used to rattle and keep me awake. Nick had tried to fold some paper to the right thickness to make a wedge to hold the window shut, but it had never really worked, and the wind still used to whistle through the gap in an eerie way.

"Can't you hear it?" I asked him. "A sort of — crying sound."

"It's just the wind," said Nick, yawning.

"It's not," I said. The wind certainly was hissing violently through the trees tonight; and this house had turrets, and gables, and roofs which sloped at crazy angles to one another, all of which hooked and snagged the wind and could make it sound like thunder. But what I could hear was distinct from all that, like a sporadic distant sobbing. "There!" I said. "It's someone crying, Nick. A girl, or a woman." We both listened hard, and every now and then I was sure it was there — somewhere amid the wind, beyond the windowpane, or perhaps in another part of the house. But I could see from Nick's face that he didn't believe me.

I climbed onto the window seat to look outside, but the only thing I could see in the darkness was my own reflection.

"Put the lamp out," I said to Nick.

Now, the scene outside emerged. There was a bright three-quarter moon tonight, which only occasionally appeared between scudding clouds. From where we slept we could see the central tower of the castle, with seven tall chimneys in a row jutting out behind it like a lower jaw against the sky. Rooks' nests poked out from between and inside them, and at dusk the rooks would circle and screech for an hour or more in great excitable flocks. This late at night, they were all roosting, oblivious to the wind which stirred their stiff feathers as they huddled among the chimney stacks. At the foot of the tower, if I craned my neck to peer over the sill, I could see the pale gravel of the courtyard. Behind that were the low stable buildings and the coach-house on the far side, and beyond them the darkness of the forest. Everything was disappointingly calm and normal. I couldn't even hear the sobbing anymore.

"There's no sign of —" I began. But as my eyes grew accustomed to the dark outside, I could see the faint glow of lamplight in one of the windows in the tower, immediately opposite.

"Nick, there's a light!" I whispered.

It was Sir Septimus's study. From this bedroom there was a perfect view across the courtyard into the side of his big oriel window, and Nick and I could often see him sitting there at his desk, in profile, sometimes working, sometimes talking, often just appearing to stare into space ahead of him; and, coming and going, the loyal dark figures of his servants, Bonefinger and Melibee. Like a pair of old black ravens, they attended quietly to his wishes, kept the affairs of the house in order, and were rarely far from his side. As I peered out into the night, there was no sign of Sir Septimus in his customary chair, but tall shadows seemed to be moving in the lamp-lit tower room.

"I can't see him," I said, "but there's *someone* in there."

"He's not normally up as late as this," said Nick. He was kneeling on my bed watching me, still yawning. "Maybe he heard you crying out, and he's gotten up to investigate."

"Come and *look*," I said, impatiently. "It might be a robber." And I pressed my face back to the cold pane.